THE
BODY IN THE WALL

ANNA PENROSE

MUDLARK'S PRESS

First published 2022 by Mudlark's Press

This is a work of fiction. Names, characters, places, and incidents either are the product of the author's imagination or are used fictitiously. Any resemblance to actual persons, living or dead, events, or locales is entirely coincidental.

First paperback edition 2022
Cover design by Miblart

ISBN 9781913628093

You asked for it, Steve!
All my love.

Beginnings, of a sort…

The rat scurried along the dark passageways, having made its way up from the harbour tunnels. At low tide, the pickings on the sand were good but fraught with gulls trying to grab at the fishermen's cast-offs. There was always something in the mud worth eating if you could get ahead of the screaming birds. Now, as the tunnel turned into a passageway, the rat negotiated the dark walkways without the need for light. Its whiskers providing navigation, its long tail, balance.

It climbed over old forgotten sacks and piles of bricks from a collapsed wall. Ahead, the passageway narrowed as the rat navigated the bones wrapped in a rotting carpet. Any morsels on that body had long been devoured, and now it was simply another obstacle to overcome. As the rat continued its route, it emerged through a grating and off along the cobbled lanes of Golden, careful to avoid passing feet and tyres. The ancient fishing village of Golden would always have rats and, from time to time, would also have bodies.

Chapter One

Malachite Peck picked up her fountain pen and sighed. How to begin? Oppy already knew the basics about Mal's new life and would be reading between the lines to find any weakness in her letter. Honestly, her big sister treated her like one of her grandchildren. A new development, and one Mal didn't appreciate. She removed the lid, gave her pen a quick shake and began.

Dear Oppy,

Whilst I wait for the sun to rise, I thought I would just drop you a line to let you know all is well. The bookshop requires a complete overhaul and I shall close next week to begin renovations. Whilst the tourists are here, I'm having a clear-out sale. Fingers crossed they help get rid of a lot for me. And I make a few pennies. It's quite a risk closing during the season. Apparently, I need to make all the money I can before winter.

I started unpacking last night and found my swimming costume, so I am about to go for a swim. I have no idea how successful this will be. The sea looks terribly cold.

I am pretty much keeping to myself, which, as you may understand, suits me perfectly. As they say, the natives seem friendly, but I have no wish to engage beyond the confines of the shop itself.

I will write again when I have more news.

Love Yaffle

Mal reread her letter, then scrunched it up, it read like a letter to a junior colleague, not her beloved big sister. At least she had signed it off with her family nickname. Cross with herself, she noticed the sun had risen and she was wasting the quiet hours. Mal had once commandeered any room she walked into. Now she preferred to keep to the edges. Tutting to herself, she grabbed her gown and headed downstairs.

As she walked out onto the quiet cobbled lane, the rain began. Peering up at the dark skies, she quickly pulled the door shut. Her heavily embroidered silk dressing gown was unlikely to survive the short walk to the harbour, and it certainly wouldn't provide any warmth on the way back if it were already soaked. Muttering crossly to herself, she walked back through the bookshop and out to the workspace, where she unhooked a raincoat and set out once more. The muttering increased when she saw her Burberry trench coat only went as far as her knees, leaving the jewelled colours of her kimono dressing gown sticking out the bottom. She hitched up the fabric, but now her ridiculous rubber shoes were exposed.

The woman in the beach shop had tried to assure her that people wore them in saunas, but Mal had spent her life in saunas and had never once seen anyone in these monstrosities. Her unease had been amplified later when she observed a family queueing for fish and chips, and every one of them was in the same style of rubber shoes with holes. She didn't want to judge, but they didn't seem the sauna sort.

Heading back to the front door, she placed a yellow sou'wester on her head and stepped outside again.

A seagull hopped away from a black bin bag left in front of a holiday let on the other side of the lane. So far, the gull had disembowelled the bag to the tune of one banana skin, a tea bag, and a pizza box. Even now, the gull was dragging a slice away in its beak, all the while keeping a hostile yellow eye on Malachite.

Checking there was no one around, she swore with gusto and strode towards the unprotected bin bag.

'Morning!'

Mal swore again, this time internally, and swung around. An old man had emerged from one of the many little passageways that ran off this lane.

'Them some bloody nuisance,' continued the old man, laughing.

Malachite straightened herself up.

'Yes, good morning. I'm sorry about the swearing. I thought I was on my own. I was going to put that bag over here under my tarpaulin.'

In these lanes, residents were told to put their bin bags out under cover. In the smaller lanes, all the bags were huddled at the end to make it easier for the binmen to collect. In the past seven days, Mal had learnt more about the Cornish refuse system than she thought possible.

'Them birds would make our Lord swear. Never you mind. Pretty dress,' he remarked and walked off to the harbour, having said as much as he was going to.

Mal looked at herself. Her kimono had slipped down, the ruby and sapphire silk birds and flowers swirling around her ankles, the fawn gaberdine trench coat buckled tightly against her small frame, a yellow rain hat, a fluorescent swim bag, and a black bin liner. She had been trying for incognito but appeared to have settled on eccentric. Frustrated, she moved the bin bag under her covers and shooed the gull away, then picked up the other bits of rubbish, stuffed them back in the bag, and headed towards the water. In sixty-five years, she had done a lot of unpleasant things, but picking up a stranger's banana skin covered in baked beans seemed like the absolute nadir.

Holding her hand stiffly away from her side, she walked towards the edge of the harbour. The tide was high and the water gently slapped against the capping stones. Kneeling by the water's edge, she rinsed her hands.

'Can't swim there, love,' called a disembodied voice. 'Too many boats.'

Mal remained where she was and counted to ten. She had wanted to sneak out in the early morning, unnoticed, and try her first sea swim. Instead, she had arrived at Piccadilly Circus. Getting up slowly, she turned to politely address the man, but he was already walking away.

Fishermen seemed to be good at pronouncements rather than actual conversations.

Happy her hand was now clean, she headed away from the bobbing boats and over to the far side of the harbour wall. Despite it being early, the harbour was buzzing with activity. It was a pretty sight: smaller boats in bright blues, reds and yellows were heading in and out, taking advantage of the tide, catches were being offloaded into the ice houses, and forklift trucks were nipping about moving the pallets of fish from boat to warehouse and out onto vans.

She was a good distance from the main bustle of the harbour now. The wall continued out toward the harbour light and a cannon, but just here there was a set of steps leading down to the other side of the wall and into the sea itself. The water on both sides was flat, but neither seemed terribly inviting. Slipping off her silly shoes, she sat on the edge and, having tucked up her layers, dangled her feet in the water. She had read that the sea was at its warmest in autumn and, in truth, it wasn't as cold as she had been expecting. That said, she wasn't instantly transported to Bali.

Out to sea, two swimmers were heading towards her. Their long black arms and pale hands creating arcs as they plunged into the water, oblivious to the drizzle. She watched, impressed with their form as they cut through the sea. Had she ever been that good? She certainly wasn't now; it was five years since she had swum and when she had, it had been in a heated pool in her London gym. One time the heater had broken, and she and her girlfriends had all shivered at the edge and unanimously headed out for cocktails at Claridge's instead. That had been a fun swim.

'Are you thinking of going in?'

Mal was startled out of her reverie and snatched the lapels of her coat tight around her neck, bunching the damp fabric in her hands. The speaker pushed her goggles onto her forehead.

'Sorry, didn't mean to make you jump.' The woman laughed as she climbed the stone steps. 'The water's lovely this morning, no swell and no jellies, but I did see the cat, so watch out for him.'

The woman's companion left the water and the pair of them started unpeeling themselves from their suits and rubbed their skin dry. Mal wondered why they were bothering as the rain fell. One of the swimmers must have caught her expression, as she called over.

'Pointless, isn't it? But at least it gets the salt off.'

She and her friend packed their bags, said goodbye and left. Conversations with random strangers were not something that Mal enjoyed and she wasn't sure how to reply. What was the done thing around here? She wasn't interested in small talk, and from experience, saying the wrong thing to the wrong person could cause no end of grief. By the time she decided that a smile and a nod would be sufficient, they'd gone.

Shrugging off her coat and dressing gown, she wrapped the silk robe within the waterproof coat. It was annoying but she could see no other way to protect her gown and felt stupid at her lack of foresight. Balling them up, she shoved them in the rocky alcove where the two swimmers had stored their bags. Her key was also in her coat pocket, so she decided to only swim within sight of her belongings. Next time she came out she would have to be better prepared.

Chapter Two

It felt bizarre to be standing in the open air wearing only a cossie whilst the rain fell on her skin. Shivering, she tied her hair back with a scrunchie from her wrist. Swimming with long hair was another thing she was unused to, and the idea of getting seaweed trapped in her hair filled her with disgust. She placed her hand on the wet metal balustrade and walked into the water. The concrete steps were rough under her feet and she gasped as the chilly water embraced her inch by inch. She stopped at waist height. Her legs were cold but not painful, but whoever defined this as warm had clearly never swum in the turquoise waters of St Kitts. Looking ahead, the rocks formed a wide gulley leading out towards the open sea with no jellyfish in sight.

Making sure her tow float was free, she pushed off from the step and gasped as the water enveloped her. She had been too enthusiastic and plunged her head under the water. Flapping her hands, she brought herself upright, shuddering at the shock of the chilly water, and was pleased to find she wasn't out of her depth. The rocks under her feet were slippery, but she got herself stable and hoped to God no one was standing on the harbour wall laughing at her surprise.

She turned, ready to scowl, but her only spectator was a lone seagull devouring the cake crumbs the previous swimmers had dropped. The red swim tow tied to her waist bobbed alongside, waiting for her to do something.

'Don't mock. You can't feel the cold,' she chided the float, then chided herself for talking to an inanimate object. But the float had a point. She was in the sea, she was here to swim, there were no waves, no jellyfish, no spectators, and she was damn cold. It was time to move.

Mal decided she would swim to the end of the gulley, have a look around the greater sea, then head back to the steps and home. Without goggles, she ditched her preferred freestyle and ambled with her breaststroke instead. That way, she could also take in more of what was around her. With a smaller gasp this time, she pushed off into the water and headed out towards the open sea. The sensation of the little float tugging along behind her was a nuisance, but she understood the rationale behind it. She would not be scared. Swimming was where she felt most comfortable, even if these were unfamiliar surroundings full of potential hazards.

As she swam, pushing her hands through the water, five years of jail time relaxed out of her limbs – her brain – and she found herself once more in her happy place. The rain on the water muffled the noise of the sea and she swam through a strange soundscape of her breath and the percussive patter of the raindrops. The salinity of the water kept her higher on the surface than she was used to, which was just as well as her muscles murmured in recognition and muffled protest. It was irritating to discover she was woefully out of shape. At the mouth of the gulley, she stopped and hung in the water, looking around. Away from the shelter of the rocks, the sea was a little bouncier and, whilst she enjoyed the gentle surge, she would build up more strength before heading out into the open water. As she examined the left-hand side, she could see a break in the cliffs and a stack she should be able to swim through. It was about two hundred metres away and Mal decided that would be her first goal. Nodding to herself, she turned and headed back to the shelter of the gulley and the steps.

Her arms swept out in front of her, pulling her body through the water and, whilst she wasn't exactly warm, she was comfortable. She looked at her hands as they pulled through the water. The wrinkles in the skin were covered as they caught the odd piece of seaweed. Was this what her thalassotherapist had in mind? It was certainly a lot cheaper. Maybe shivering could also help tighten her skin again?

Five years without a beauty regime had allowed nature and time to take back what was theirs, and Mal knew she had a fight on her hands whenever she studied the mirror in despair. Pausing for breath, she looked into the depths below her pale legs. The rain had stopped and now she could see down to the rocks on the floor beneath her. Seaweed slowly fanned itself back and forth and she watched, mesmerised, lost in the hypnotic sway.

Her tow jerked against her waist, and Mal tried to spin around. An act that was both ungainly and ridiculous in the water. Was she snagged on something? Had a shark swum into the gulley and attacked the buoy. Were the jellyfish uprising? Of all the terrifying thoughts that ran through her head, none prepared her for what she saw as she turned and faced her tow float.

A cat was hanging onto the buoy. It didn't appear distressed. If anything, it seemed annoyed that Mal had stopped swimming. Its wet fur didn't appear to be bothering it and the cat simply stared at Mal, then settled down, happy to have found a resting place. Mal looked at the silver tabby in astonishment. She thought the swimmers had been joking when they mentioned a swimming cat.

Uncertain for a moment, Mal decided against getting closer to the animal. Her bare skin felt very exposed to a set of panicking claws. Admittedly, this cat did not appear disturbed, but she had never had a cat, or any pet for that matter, and was uncertain of their level of predictability. Instead, she swam back to the steps and climbed out. As the buoy reached the edge, her passenger jumped off and swam the last few feet. Reaching land, it shook its fur like a dog, then running past Mal, the cat jumped up onto the rocks and ran off out of sight.

Bemused, Mal grabbed her float, which was already deflating. The designers of SupaTough TowFloat clearly hadn't taken cat claws into account. Towelling herself down, she realised she couldn't put her gown back on. She had forgotten about the salt in the water and didn't want to damage the precious fabric. Instead, she rubbed her hair dry, then slipped her raincoat over her swimming costume and headed back home.

The village was busier now, shops were opening up, street signs were being put out and tables wiped down. She must have been longer than she thought. Picking up her pace, she hurried back home, arriving as a builder's van pulled up in front of the shop.

'Morning, lover, been for a swim?'

Dennis Jenkins was a friend of the shop's owner. Mal had explained to Gary Crampton what she wanted to do with the shop and he'd agreed. She'd made the transatlantic call and Mr Jenkins had arrived the following day to arrange the job. A week later, he had got in touch to say a major contract had fallen through and he could start the following week.

'Are you starting today?' asked Mal, in alarm. 'I thought we agreed Monday? I'm not ready for you.'

This was the last thing she needed. Her timetable was all in place, this would throw things off from the outset. She needed everything to run smoothly. If she wanted to settle here, it was imperative to her state of mind that she did so with the minimum amount of fuss or delay.

'No, maid. Don't you fret. I was in the village anyway to check on some gutters. I just thought I'd check in and see if Monday still suits you?'

Mal let out an audible sigh of relief. Then realised she was standing in the middle of the road, naked but for a cossie and a raincoat. Some sort of middle-aged flasher. Was sixty-five still middle-aged? Her sigh led to a chuckle and she apologised if she had sounded sharp.

'Not a bit of it. You go dry yourself. Reckon it's going to be a busy day. All them holidaymakers will want to go somewhere now the sun's not shining.'

The rain had started again and, saying goodbye, Mal unlocked the door and walked through the bookshop and back up to her flat above. She had enough time to shower and get ready for the day ahead, but only if she didn't linger.

Chapter Three

Over in the newsagent's, the queue had died down a bit after the morning rush for milk and newspapers. Now there was only Ange, who was too lazy to get up any earlier and always late for everything, and Betty, who was too smart to come in early, waiting in the queue. Phyllis was serving a pair of young holidaymakers with her usual care and attention, and Betty wondered how people put up with it.

'Well, that's the price it is,' snapped Phyllis. 'We can't manage fancy supermarket prices. If you want bread, that's the price.'

The young woman flinched and mumbled apologetically, whilst the nicely dressed man by her side, stepped back. It was all very well defending your partner from all that life had to throw at you, but Betty warranted he'd never had a Phyllis thrown at him before.

'I'm sorry,' said the young woman. 'Shall I put it back on the shelf for you?'

'As you like,' snapped Phyllis, and immediately turned her attention to Ange, removing a packet of cigarettes from the shelf and a newspaper from under the counter.

'Tell Martin that the price is going up on these next month. And if he wants to complain about it, tell him to take it up with London.'

Betty wondered if Phyllis had smoked, would the government have dared raise the price on a packet of fags?

She suspected not. The sky was getting dark again, and she hoped Ange and Phyllis would not get into a conversation. It was a half-mile walk home and, whilst she had her brolly, the wind was picking up and she'd rather be at home ahead of that than battling through it. At ninety-one, Betty was used to a bit of rain, but she'd slowed down somewhat over the years. She had passed her ninetieth birthday in amazement.

Her early years had been wild. She smiled ruefully. Her middle years had been no less extreme. If she had told her young self she would make it to ninety, she'd have laughed and said she clearly wasn't playing hard enough. Betty had been a muse for several writers and artists, followed the Silk Road across central Asia, had affairs with statesmen and made friends with their wives. Eventually, in a game of cards in Cairo, she won a cottage from a Cornish landowner and came to investigate the prize. She'd taken one look at it and decided to settle down.

'So, what do you know about her?' said Ange.

Betty groaned inwardly. Gossip. She would never get home. Honestly, this pair could bad-mouth tourists all day long.

'Well, she's not local,' said Phyllis disapprovingly, and Betty snorted. Ange turned towards her and grinned, but Phyllis instantly took offence.

'And what do you mean by that, Betty?'

'Hardly local yourself, are you, Phyllis? Where's it you're from? Truro, isn't it?'

Ange laughed. 'She's got you there, Phil, and you've only been here thirty years. Even Betty's been here longer.'

'On and off.' Betty smiled, trying not to get too drawn in.

'True enough.' said Ange, a large grin on her face. 'Never thought you'd stay the distance, yet here you are decades longer.'

'Not even Cornish though, are you?' huffed Phyllis. Betty laughed. She certainly wasn't a local, but she got on well enough. The trick to fitting in was to swim alongside or marry in. Betty chose to swim alongside. What you really needed to avoid was throwing your weight around. Built like a starving sparrow, she had little enough weight to hold herself down, let alone impose her will on others. She just bobbed along and enjoyed her life.

The couple had come back to the counter with a pack of biscuits, and Phyllis glared at them, happy to have someone she could chastise.

'Just that then?'

The younger woman grimaced when Phyllis demanded three pounds for the digestives.

As they were about to leave, Betty took pity on them. 'They do fresh baked loaves up at the farm shop, over by the gardens.'

Smiling, the couple hurried out as Phyllis protested.

‘Oh, give over, Phyllis. Four pounds for a bag of cheap, white sliced? That’s daylight robbery and you know it.’

‘I’ve got a living to make and they’ve got the money.’

‘Not after shopping in here they don’t,’ said Ange with a laugh.

Everyone knew Phyllis’ grumbles that the village should support local enterprises, but she was forced to fleece the tourists because no one else would do their weekly shop in her stores. The fact was that her stock was overpriced, limited and often out of date. It was barely tolerable for essentials, and if it didn’t also house the village post office, Betty was convinced it would have gone out of business years ago. There were plenty of other little shops in the village.

‘Well, I can’t help that, can I? I can’t get the discounts the supermarkets can. And I bet that new woman won’t shop in here either.’

Betty wanted to get home but if the gossip was village related, she might hang on. Village gossip she loved, so long as you never got sucked in or took sides, it was great fun. Keeping up to date with all the ins and outs of village life also meant that you didn’t inadvertently find yourself taking sides in a feud that was decades long. She wasn’t sure if Barry had forgiven her yet for laughing about the right way to place the lobster pots. Then she remembered he died a few years back. One way to be forgiven was to outlive everyone.

'She's already planning on closing the place. Have you seen in the window? She's getting rid of all the stock. It's not on, the village needs a bookshop.'

'Since when did you ever shop in there? You can't even read!' Ange and Betty laughed but, as usual, Phyllis bristled.

'And when do I have time to read? I'm up at five for the papers and I don't close until seven. But the village can't be without its bookshop. What will the old dears do without it? What about you, Betty?'

Betty raised an eyebrow. *Old dear* indeed. Still, that was revenge for the bread comment, so she let it go.

'Us *old dears* will manage right enough. The lady in the shop told me she was clearing out the old stock and updating the place. Nothing to worry about and we have the mobile library in the meantime. Plus, I got a load of bargains in her clearance.'

Betty had the impression that the younger woman didn't really know the first thing about running a bookshop, but she seemed to have a keen business head on her shoulders, so maybe she would make a go of it. They had discussed favourite authors, and the woman was clearly well read, so maybe they'd get some new stuff in, not just beach reads for the holidaymakers. Or maybe she was tidying it up to sell on at a profit. It used to be owned by Gary Crampton, but he'd moved overseas and the assumption was that the new woman had bought the place. The woman was in her late fifties, at a guess, with a plummy voice and Betty figured this was an early retirement venture.

'You've been in then?' asked Phyllis. 'What did you find out about her? She's only been in here the once and said nothing about her family or her plans or where she comes from. Nothing.'

'Shocking,' murmured Ange, her lips twisting.

'Ah well, I dare say we'll find out more as the weeks go on. Now, can I have my paper before the rain starts up again?'

Heading out into the wind, Betty hoped the younger couple found the farm shop. Billy's idea to sell stuff from his shed all those years back had really paid off, and now his kids worked behind the counter in the holidays. It had been a proper success, and she enjoyed shopping there. That was her idea of supporting local. Fingers crossed, the new woman would make a go of the bookshop as well.

Chapter Four

There was a crash from downstairs, making Mal jump. The builders must be tearing down the wall. She pushed back from the kitchen table, put her pen down and flicked on the kettle. She knew nothing about running a bookshop or living in a Cornish fishing village, but she knew builders worked best on frequent pots of tea.

So far, everything was going according to plan. Last week, she had closed the shop ready for the renovations, she'd had one week of trading and sold a lot of stock in the sale. Now, the charity shop had arrived first thing and taken all the stock she considered unviable. They would pass the books onto to overseas agencies in order to give the books a longer lifespan. The rest had been moved upstairs. The builders had arrived on time and immediately set to. Once she was happy that everything was running as expected, she headed upstairs to catch up with her letters.

When the shop reopened, she had great plans for it. She knew success would be making it viable all year round, which meant involving the local community, not just relying on tourists. Mal had already contacted various clubs and societies, recommending her space for various functions. Workshops, readings and talks. The first response had been a quick and positive yes from the mother and toddlers' group for a weekly morning reading group, and she was looking forward to that immensely.

Children were refreshing little beasts and you could always hand them back at the end of the session. Refreshment was best served in moderation.

For now, though, she could catch up on unpacking and correspondence.

Dear Jasmine,
Do you remember the dreadful, naff, patronising

Mal sighed to herself. Play nicely. Scrunching up the sheet of paper, she threw it into the kindling basket by the woodstove, picked up her pen, giving the ink a quick shake to the nib, and started again.

Dear Jasmine,
Do you remember that charming, lovely, inspirational

Another ball of paper sailed towards the basket and landed a foot away. She knew the last shot had been a fluke. Writing to her nephew's wife was always so difficult. Giles was a lovely boy, but she hadn't had the highest expectations for him. In marrying Jasmine, he hadn't even met *those.* The problem was that whilst Jasmine was as much an airhead as Giles, Mal could turn a blind eye to his faults as she had known and loved him all his life. Jasmine had arrived fully formed and vapid.

Stretching her fingers, she started again.

Dear Jasmine,

Do you remember that book you sent me with lots of motivational ideas? Well, I have been trying something out and taking a photo every day of an image that pleases me. I am building up quite a gallery of the sights around me and taking great pleasure in it. In fact, Will has shown me how to add these to an Instagram account, so that I may see them altogether in one place.

She had been uncertain at first, but Will, one of her godsons, had assured her she could keep her account private. He'd explained hashtags but when he said they were to help people find her posts, she wrote back reminding him that defeated the purpose of a private account.

He replied *#rebel*, which made her smile. She knew he was making some sort of joke, but she was uncertain what it was. She continued with her letter to Jasmine.

I am now on my seventh day here and already have hundreds of images. Will says the trick is to narrow those down to a few images that really refine the experience. His actual words were, avoid image dumping, but I believe that was what he meant.

Without your kind gift, I may never have thought of doing this and I just wanted to drop a quick note to say thank you.

With love

M

Blotting the paper, she folded it, popped it into an envelope and added a second class stamp. The stamp annoyed her, but first class stamps were so damned expensive and for the amount of correspondence she had, the bill soon added up. Several of her family had suggested that she could now send texts and e-mails, but she had developed the habit of letter writing whilst inside and wanted to continue it.

She'd also made a pledge to herself that she would pop money into her replies from any letters she received from her great-nieces, nephews, and godchildren. Letter writing was a skill that needed to be treasured but also nurtured. Since she had taken the time to commit her thoughts to paper, she found comfort between the pen and writing sheets. Her ideas grew as she wrote, and something in her both calmed down and woke up. It was a place for her fears and imagination to fall into proper perspectives, and it was a gift she wanted to pass on to the next generation.

Of course, it was a gift that wasn't immediately obvious to her young friends and so she bribed them. She had always believed in carrots over sticks, but then she'd never had children and knew it was easier to be an expert from afar.

'Mrs Peck,' a voice shouted up the stairs. Mal got up and placed the mugs on the tray and headed over to the top of her stairwell, leaning on the door frame and calling down.

'Tea's on its way. Just waiting for the kettle.'

Mr Jenkins called up again, this time Mal heard the concern in his voice. 'It's not that. Can you come down? There's something...' His voice stopped. 'Sorry, there's something you need to see.'

Mal gripped on to the banister. She wasn't used to the narrowness of the tread, and landing in a heap at the builder's feet was not the entrance she wished to make. At the bottom of the staircase, Mr Jenkins nodded at her, then told her to follow him.

'We found something.'

Inwardly, she groaned. This couldn't be good news and the way he was avoiding eye contact made her think they'd found an awfully expensive problem. She walked out onto the floor of the shop. It was so much bigger now that it was clear of stock. All the shelves had been wrapped in sheets and the wooden floors were protected in plastic sheeting. The room was pale and dusty and resembled a derelict sanatorium, sounds bouncing weirdly off the bare walls. She couldn't wait until it would become a warm and welcoming space, and she could properly start her new life. Dennis' team was standing on the far side of the room, all muttering and looking across at the other wall. Each glance was furtive and followed by another mumble of speculation.

Good grief, thought Mal. If it was bothering the builders, just how much was it going to cost?

'Is it structural, Mr Jenkins? Is the place about to fall down?'

Dennis took a deep breath. 'No, nothing like that. It's what we found behind the wall.'

He stepped to one side and now Mal could see the gaping hole in the wall. As she had suspected, there was a large void behind the wall which, when removed, would add another few feet to the width of the shop. When she had first discussed it with Dennis, he'd agreed the wall seemed false but warned her that the brickwork behind it might be in a shocking condition. They had both agreed the only way to find out was to tear it down.

'So, what's the problem, then? Have we knocked into next door by mistake?'

Mal wouldn't have been surprised by that a bit. She'd only been here a week but already discovered that these properties had all been built then split higgledy-piggledy. Her property went up three levels and, so far, she'd discovered boundaries with five neighbours. Left and right obviously, but also behind, one from another street and her top floor shared a party wall with a neighbour two houses away. There was no such thing as a straight up and down house here. They all slotted together like a drunken block of Jenga.

Now, as she studied the hole in the wall, she could see a large roll of discarded carpet, but, to her untrained eye, nothing untoward.

'I don't want to scare you, Mrs Peck, but what we've found is pretty nasty. I want to warn you now so you don't faint or something.'

Mal raised an eyebrow. 'Do I strike you as the fainting sort, Mr Jenkins? Now, what is it? I can't see a problem.'

Dennis walked towards the carpet. As Mal looked closer, she realised it must have been behind the wall, not put there by the builders. The roll was about six foot long but had slumped to the floor; old black duct tape ran in three bands along its length.

'Oh dear, has someone wrapped up some asbestos?' She laughed nervously.

Mal didn't know why she said that. It was all she could think that would worry the builders. Besides the obvious. There were no two ways about it, looking at a six-foot-long bundle that was roughly body shaped couldn't help but make you think it was, indeed, a body.

'It's not asbestos, Mrs Peck. Look.'

Dennis crouched down now and pointed to one end of the bundle. Poking out through the bottom of the carpet were the thin, delicate bones of a human foot.

Chapter Five

Mal stared at the foot as Dennis' voice washed over her.

'I've called the police. They said not to touch anything, and they'd send someone straight over.'

Her brain scrambled to make sense of what was going on. There was a dead body in the wall and all she could think was whether or not its feet were ticklish.

'Mrs Peck. Are you okay? Can you hear me?'

Dennis sounded concerned, but all Mal could hear was the voice of the judge. 'I sentence you to five years in prison.'

The very last thing she wanted now, after her clean start, was to get caught up with the police again. Hell, she'd rather dance with the corpse than jump through the hoops of the criminal justice system. She'd better not step on his toes, though.

'Mrs Peck!'

Finally, his voice broke through to her, as did the expressions on the other men's faces.

'Save your tears, Mrs Peck. Whoever this is, is long dead.'

Mal faced a sea of concerned male faces. They seemed so alien after five years of women. She flapped her hands at them as she tried to get control. Gulping, she steadied her voice. 'I'm okay. I'm laughing, not crying.'

As their expressions became more alarmed, Mal started laughing harder. This was dreadful. Her laughs turned back into sobs and she tried to grab control of herself.

'I'm going to put the kettle on.'

One of the younger men stepped forward. 'I'll come with you.' He looked over at his boss. 'If that's okay, Dennis?'

Mr Jenkins seemed relieved, and Mal wavered between outrage and relief. At least if she had to focus on the younger man, she'd be able to pull herself together quicker. Her new life was already falling apart.

'Do you have biscuits? My nan always has biscuits.'

Mal paused on the stairs and looked over her shoulder, down at his anxious face. 'I am not your nan, or anyone's for that matter. And I don't have biscuits.'

His face fell and Mal cursed inwardly. He was basically a kid, and she was being rude to her very first guest. Even if he had invited himself in some sort of misplaced concern. Maybe his old nan was some frail old bird. She looked down at him again as she reached the door to her flat.

'But I do have some chocolates?' Her brother, or more likely Wendy, had sent her a box of chocolates from Fortnum's as a house-warming gift. She was waiting for an auspicious moment to open them. A dead body wasn't what she'd had in mind, but it would have to do. Sean grinned up at her and she was pleased to have reassured him.

An hour later, Mal glanced up wearily as yet another stranger walked into her home. Was she destined to never have peace again? She was already being guarded, watched over by a female officer. She really had no idea why this woman was sitting in her kitchen. Sean had barely decided which chocolate to have, his eyes darting from choc to choc, when there had been a knock at the door.

The woman had introduced herself as Police Constable Sophie Taphouse and after a few patronising false starts, she fell silent and told Mal that she would simply sit and wait until her boss arrived.

Glancing over at the woman whilst she tried to write some letters, Mal wondered why anyone would want to join the police force. Maybe here in Cornwall it was a more appealing job. The young PC certainly didn't seem much like a police officer. She looked like she would be more at home in a farm kitchen. She positively radiated good cheer. Her dark brown hair was pulled into a side plait that hung over her shoulder and Mal wondered how safe that was. But then how many violent offenders did this woman have to engage? If she did, she'd likely bore them with tales of her precious children.

Mal knew her thoughts were running towards churlishness, but she was nervous and uncomfortable. With all her heart, she wished she was back at home looking over the London skyline, preparing for an evening out with friends. Just thinking about that made her feel even worse. That memory, like this life, wasn't hers either. Or it least it was, but it had turned out to be a fake one. Where were her friends when the shit hit the fan?

Now there was a knock on the door and the officer leapt up to let in her boss. This man was middle-aged and middle weight, with thinning hair and shiny shoes. His shirt, shoes, and suit all seemed to come from M&S, and his face radiated the intellectual batting average of a can of soup. Another police officer, although this time a detective, and on his own, so Mal was clearly not being treated as a suspect or a threat, just a scared little old lady. Much as the stereotype galled her, Mal decided it was also a fair summation of the situation, not old – since when was sixty-five old? – but certainly scared. But Mal wasn't scared of the corpse below. Mal was scared of the coppers in front of her.

'Are you alright, love? It's Mrs Peck, isn't it?'

Gods, Mal hated that flat midlands accent. Unlike last time, she was in a situation not of her own making and now she felt vulnerable and angry. As he spoke, he sat down, spreading his knees wide to accommodate his paunch and sense of entitlement. She hadn't even asked him to sit.

'I'm not married.'

He looked at her, puzzled, and glanced over to the female police officer. She shrugged, and the detective turned his attentions back to Mal.

'What's that, love?'

‘I said I’m not married. It’s not Mrs. And don’t call me love.’

Why did everyone do that? When she worked in the City, no one gave a fig about her marital status. She was simply Malachite Peck, Peck to those threatened by her, or Mal to those she counted as friends.

‘So what should I call you then? Miss, Ms?’

He laughed as if both options were ridiculous, and it was probably that boorish laugh that wound Mal up and brought her fighting spirit to the surface.

‘Lady.’

Now Hemingstone and Taphouse paused and glanced at each other and Mal decided to double down.

‘It’s Lady Malachite Peck. You can call me Lady Peck.’

And there it was, that instant micro-reaction when Mal went from being viewed as a pathetic old woman to someone to treat carefully. He was a detective, he’d find the truth of it soon enough, but for now Mal felt reckless. She wanted all these people out of her house. The corpse as well.

‘My apologies, Lady Peck. If I can take a few minutes of your time to ask some questions and explain what’s going on downstairs?’

Mal nodded, too tired to speak.

‘We have forensics down there at the moment. They’ll be examining the site before we can remove the, um, the evidence.’

'The body?' asked Mal, getting her mental strength back.

'Yes, the body. After that we'll examine the site again. We will probably need to remove the rest of the wall and examine the entire area. This will probably take a day or two.'

Mal thought it through. That would delay her plans a bit but not as much as she feared. If anything, the police would now do the work of the builders. They could soon get back on track. If they were prepared to. If anyone would ever want to step into the shop again after this.

'In the meantime, we'd like you to consider downstairs a crime scene and avoid it completely.'

Mal exhaled and glared at the detective. 'That's my only exit. Unless you would like me to clamber across the roofs? I have a little rooftop terrace, I think I could probably hop over the railings and clamber down onto the clothes shop roof, but their slates look dodgy to me. What do you think?'

He stared at her. 'You don't have a back door?'

'In Golden? In a seventeenth century property where everyone built on and over each other's properties? No, I don't have a back door.'

Again, the detective looked across at the police officer for confirmation.

'She's not wrong, my sister lives in a place in Looe; for decades she had a door that led right into her neighbour's kitchen. Most of the old villages around here are the same. Also made for great rat runs for avoiding the excise man.'

Mal hadn't thought about that but it made perfect sense in these old ports. Not everyone felt the same way the government did about taxes and duties. Money that went up to London for the common good surely never made its way back to the Cornish and their needs.

'Right then,' said the detective. 'I'll let the boys downstairs know and we'll set up a path for you to use through the scene. Although I must stress that it's vital you don't touch anything. Do you understand?'

'Do not touch the evidence. Yes, I think I understand.'

From experience, Mal knew that authority didn't like belligerence but honestly, there was also an element of Mal loving the knowledge that she was wholly innocent of this crime and could do or say what she wanted without fear of imprisonment.

He narrowed his eyes but continued. 'Now, Mrs, Lady Peck. How long have you owned this property?'

Time to put herself in the clear.

'I don't own this property. I'm running it on behalf of someone else. A Mr Crampton. I shall supply you with his contact details.'

She fervently hoped Gary Crampton had nothing to do with the body in the wall but when she'd mentioned her plans to renovate he had enthusiastically agreed. He had suggested a generous budget and told her to get on with it.

'And how do you know Mr Crampton?'

'I don't. I know him through an associate. He said he wanted to retire and wondered if I would be interested in updating and running his shop.'

Which was more or less the truth.

'And how can I get hold of him?'

Detective Inspector Hemingstone made a big pretence of tutting thoughtfully as he made a quick note of Gary's name and address.

'That's a non-extradition country.'

'So? Do you think if he knew anything about the body in the wall he would have given me permission to knock it down?'

The inspector glanced up and gave Mal a patronising look.

'You can never tell with criminals, Lady Peck. They are a different breed. Still, I doubt Mr Crampton has much to worry about, I'm sure this is a historic crime.'

Mal stared in amazement at Sophie, who was busy trying not to sigh in disbelief.

'Historic?' said Mal, addressing the inspector carefully.

'Yes, you know, like a smuggler or a pirate. That body is just bones.'

Mal now stared at him in amazement, then challenged Sophie directly. 'Officer Taphouse, is he really a detective?'

'Yes, ma'am. Detective Inspector Hemingstone.' She looked like she wanted to say more but closed her mouth quickly.

'This isn't a smuggler or pirate from way back when,' scoffed Mal. 'This body died in recent memory.'

'Oh ho, it's Miss Marple, is it? And what makes you think that?'

'Because the carpet was bound in duct tape and sealed behind a plasterboard wall. Or do you think that whoever put the wall in, found an old body and decided to simply wrap it up like rubbish and tidy it away behind the wall?'

Mal was aware her voice was rising, and took a deep breath to steady her nerves. There was a dead body in her bookshop and an idiotic detective in her kitchen and all she wanted was to go for a swim and clear her head.

'Explain the bones then?'

'What?'

'The victim. Where's the flesh if it's not that old?'

The police officer closed her eyes and shook her head in despair. Mal counted to five and tried again.

'If this was an old murder and the body was hermetically sealed, then mummification would have taken place. You would still have your flesh. But the foot was exposed.'

She waited for him to catch up but he continued to stare at her, a polite smile on his flaccid face.

'The rats, Inspector. The rats got in and picked him clean.'

Mal shuddered, it was a revolting image but no doubt what had happened.

'You seem to know a lot about dead bodies. What is it you do again?'

'I sell books. And I read them.'

Hemingstone flipped his pocketbook closed. 'Well, we're done here, Lady Peck. Thank you for your insights but please leave this to the experts. We know what we're doing.'

He stood up. 'Now, would you like WPC Taphouse to stay with you?'

Mal glanced over at the woman and mouthed 'WPC?' She rolled her eyes again and Mal smiled.

'No, I'm fine, thanks. I'd like to continue unpacking.'

'When did you move in?' asked the younger woman, in a friendly voice.

'Last week.'

'Bummer!'

Mal laughed for the first time in a few hours and smiled gratefully at the officer. 'That's quite an understatement.'

'If you two have finished gossiping?' interrupted Hemingstone. 'Taphouse, we have work to do. Make sure the crime scene officers know that Lady Peck here needs an access route to the front door.' He turned to Mal. 'And, Lady Peck, it goes without saying that you are not to tell anyone what has been found in here.'

Now it was Mal's turn to roll her eyes. 'I won't need to. I'm pretty certain that at least half the village already knows. The other half will know by nightfall.'

'They won't. I've given the builders strict instructions not to say a word.'

'Good luck with that. I've only been here a week and if there's one thing I have discovered, it's that gossip like this will run across the roofs faster than the rats in the tunnels.'

Hemingstone looked properly cross now and told Sophie to take the names of anyone who was spreading stories about what was happening downstairs. Mal thought they had no hope of that. Even if the builders kept schtum, which Mal didn't think would happen for a second, the street had been closed off and the lane was full of police vehicles and anonymous black vans. If the villagers hadn't already decided a body was involved, they would sure as hell invent one.

'Of course, there's the other thing to consider, Inspector.'

He looked at her warily.

'Before today, before the wall came down, someone already knew about that body and, from what little I know of this place, they are probably still living here.'

Chapter Six

An hour later Mal had unpacked some of her boxes. She couldn't bring herself to write to anyone and didn't want to go outside and face the gossip. She hadn't packed the boxes and was using it as an exercise in surprise. What had her family decided was important enough to keep? What had been thrown away?

The first box she encountered was full of her shoes: Louboutin and Jimmy Choo's. She held them in front of her examining the various examples of power dressing or frivolous statements. From their straps and buckles to high heels and perfect red soles, they wouldn't last ten seconds on the cobbled streets of Golden. She smiled wondering which would break first, her heel or her neck.

Repacking the box, she opened another, this time full of paperwork, not even the important stuff like passports, birth certificates, or share certificates, but the random minutiae attached to a life she no longer lived. Her previous clients would now all turn in horror from her. Much as her employers had. She put the papers in the kindling basket.

It seemed an irony of the highest order that she'd arrived here to make a fresh start and had almost immediately been thrown off track by the discovery of a body. The shock of having to deal with the police had passed and now she found herself speculating on the corpse itself. Was it a man or a woman? Statistics suggested a woman but it had been a long bundle, a tall woman then. She'd have stood out around Golden where, for once, Mal found she was an average height. Working in the City she had been teased in the early days for her lack of stature, but as the years piled up and her successes rolled in, people stopped teasing her and treated her with respect, and no small amount of caution.

The body though was probably male, given the height, and almost certainly murdered. No one hides an accidental death, or had someone panicked? That seemed unlikely, but she had heard of worse. People under extreme pressure behaved in ways that no one else could explain. Who built the wall? And how did they drag the body in to the shop? Or had they died there? Was it a builder or an owner? Would anyone else have the skill levels and access?

As the ornate carriage clock chimed the hour from the mantlepiece Mal swore aloud. She had wasted the past hour speculating on things the police would soon resolve, and now she was going to be late. As much as she had wanted to spend the day inside away from spying eyes, she had an appointment. Mal considered cancelling, but she would have to pay the cancellation fee, and right now she wasn't sure what state her finances were in. It was possible that the bookshop would fail before it had even begun. Maybe she should cancel, pay the fee and be done with it. But she shuddered, she had been looking forward to this all week. Five years and one week if she was honest. Sod it.

She had spent all morning trying to avoid gossip and now here she was, picking up her handbag and heading off to the lion's den. She didn't know how much longer she had here, anyway. It wouldn't be long now before people discovered who she was and what she had done. She may as well not bother unpacking; she'd be gone again soon.

The bell rang as she pushed the door open and a room full of women, either sitting in chairs or standing behind them, turned to study her. From behind the counter, a young woman stood up and came forward, smiling brightly. Her roots were showing and she was wearing trainers, jeans, and a t-shirt. This was no Vidal Sassoon. Mal was still trying to count how many face piercings she had when the younger woman interrupted her thoughts.

'Hello, Lady Peck. I didn't think we'd see you today. You know, what with everything.'

Good grief, thought Mal, *Lady Peck sure has sprinted along the lanes.* As she looked around the hairdresser's, she could see about eight women all desperately trying to appear as if they weren't listening.

The silence was brutal.

'Please, call me Mal. And I couldn't just cancel, I know how important a lost booking is.'

The hairdressers in the room all nodded in agreement and a teenager offered to take her jacket and get her a drink. There was no option for a skinny latte or Darjeeling, only straightforward tea or coffee. Mal declined as the receptionist guided her to a chair and introduced herself as Collette, her stylist for the day. The other women sniggered and Mal wondered if this was the first time the word stylist had been used in here.

'So, what's it to be? Trim, colour, set?'

A set? Just how old did Collette think she was?

'Just a trim, please.' She asked for her bag and removed a book, ready to hide in the pages of her latest novel, but then remembered the hairdressers' code. This woman had your hair in her hands. It was necessary to build a rapport and trust her professional skills. Mal had little hope that she had much in the way of skills, but beggars couldn't be choosers.

Collette had already fallen quiet when Mal brought the book out and was now combing through her hair, looking at the condition and considering her options.

Placing her book back down, Mal cleared her throat.

'Actually, I've been swimming in the sea these past few days and I wonder is the salt damaging my hair? I had considered cutting it short, so it dries quicker. What would you say?'

Mal had been used to monthly haircuts; she'd had her own colourist and stylist. Her trips to the salon were a moment to relax and hand over power to someone else.

When she arrived in prison, she gave up on her appearance and pretty much everything else in the first few months. By the time she paid attention to herself, she was facing a woman with silver hair and wild wavy curls passing her shoulders. That woman told her to get a grip and pick herself up. For a while, the woman in the mirror frightened Mal, until she realised it was her teenage self, shouting through the wrinkles. From then on she rallied.

Now, looking in the mirror all she could see was Collette smiling at her.

'Let's start with a simple trim today and a deep condition. You're so lucky to have such thick hair but you do need to protect it from the salt.'

They lapsed into silence as the conversation from the other women started up around them. Mal wondered what would become of her and the shop. The detective said to expect a week's delay minimum but even after that what would she do? Could she convince the builders to return? Would the villagers ever step foot over the threshold? She knew she'd be fine with the tourists but it was essential she had some sort of winter trade.

'When will the toddler session start?' The voice was louder than the general conversation and Mal wondered if she was being addressed.

'Christ, Mandz,' replied Collette, 'she's just found a body in her shop, I doubt she's thinking about some playgroup.'

Mal continued to stare straight ahead. The room had fallen quiet again, and she didn't feel able to make eye contact with so many strangers.

'Well, I was looking forward to it, was all,' complained Mandz.

'Yeah, and I reckon Mal here was looking forward to sleeping at night without being scared out of her wits.'

'I'm not scared.'

The women all fell quiet, waiting to see what the newcomer would say next.

'I mean, it's not pleasant, but it's only a dead body. I imagine every one of these houses has had plenty of dead bodies in them over the centuries.'

The women nodded in agreement. Golden was mentioned in historical records going back to the Middle Ages, more people had died in Golden than lived in it today.

'No one's died in my house,' said Mandz, 'although I could swing for Jack now and then.'

'You going to christen your new place with a murder?' scoffed Collette.

'Why not? We've christened it in every other way!'

There was some very bawdy laughter and Collette leant over Mal's shoulder. 'Ignore us. We're only fooling. It's been a while since we've had any affordable housing in the village. Jack works on the boats and Mandz is part-time at Tesco's. Wouldn't have had a chance of buying here without the new houses.'

Running a comb through Mal's hair, she grinned at Mandz. 'You don't fool any of us. Never seen two people more in love.'

'Mind you,' said one of the other hairdressers, 'it sure is quieter in the pubs now that you two aren't out drinking and fighting.'

Mal looked in the mirror and made eye contact with Collette as the hairdresser explained.

'Mandz and Jack are legends in the village. Fighting since they was teenagers. It was clear to everyone how much they fancied the pants off each other. Even after they got hitched they carried on fighting.'

There was some laughter in the room.

'It wasn't a Saturday night if the Rowses weren't out rowing and laughing.'

Mandz had been laughing along with everyone else and now protested loudly. 'We weren't that bad! What will I say to little Abi if you lot keep telling these dreadful lies about her parents?'

'Little Abi is the only reason you calmed down,' said Collette, and Mal grinned up at her. Deciding to move the teasing away from Mandz, Collette returned to the original topic.

'I reckon every building here in the old part of Golden has had at least one death in it.'

'More than that, I reckon. If a building is three hundred years old and no one used to go to hospital to die, that's a lot of dead people.'

'Not even that far back. Mrs Belsom died in her sleep, remember?'

'Not exactly natural causes though, was it?'

'No, but then Mr Belsom confessed straightaway.'

Mal wanted to know more about the Belsoms but the conversation had moved on. Today the ladies had a fresh scandal to talk about and wouldn't waste their time on old bones.

'Sorry,' called out Mandz, her hair now in foils. 'I don't know how I'd sleep. But I'm that desperate to get out of my house with the baby that even a dead body wouldn't put me off.'

Mal looked over at her as Collette continued to snip away at her hair.

'Don't apologise,' said Mal, with a smile. 'Dead bodies don't scare me. I just wasn't sure if anyone would still want to come into the shop after this.'

'Are you kidding?' Mandz laughed. 'There'll be a stampede.'

'Did you actually see it? Sean said he saw bones.'

Mal wondered how much she could say. She didn't want to get drawn into speculation, these ladies were all locals, as far as she could tell, and were likely going to be affected by the revelation of the body's identity. Especially if Mal was right and the body, despite the bones, wasn't that old.

'I was asked not to say anything,' Mal said apologetically, and shrugged her shoulders.

There was a disappointed pause, then everyone agreed she couldn't talk about it. Mal changed the subject and asked Collette about the condition of her hair, and they fell into a happy chat about various conditioners and treatments to combat salt damage.

As Collette blow-dried her hair, Mal looked in the mirror in pleasure. Her long hair was shining in a way she had never seen before. Always dyed and cut short, these long silver tresses were unfamiliar but she liked them.

At the till, she decided to go mad and told the hairdresser to add a bottle of the conditioner she had used. When Collette told her how much it was, she blanched. A treat was one thing, but that was half the cost of the haircut itself and Mal didn't think her budget would run to that. The shop opening was going to be delayed and her savings were all she had to live on. Embarrassed, she changed her mind and said she'd get it another day.

'Tell you what,' said Collette. 'Have the tester bottle on the house. They changed the logo recently and I need to be using the new design.'

Despite Mal's protests, Collette insisted and realising that her protests were simply drawing attention to her financial predicament, Mal acquiesced and left the shop in mortification. She was, however, also smiling. The revelation of her lack of funds was excruciating to someone who used to handle millions for clients on a daily basis and was indeed not short of a fat bank account herself. Now she couldn't even afford conditioner. But over the past five years she had learnt that freedom was more valuable than money, and she had spent an enjoyable hour having her hair done, chatting with strangers who were full of fun and gossip, and receiving a generous gift. If she could whistle, she would.

As she walked along, she was conscious of her hair bobbing and swaying under the volume of her curls and she laughed aloud, surprising a group of tourists peering in the windows of a gift shop.

As she turned the corner into her lane, she saw the police cordons and once again experienced a momentary lurch of fear. She wanted to lean against the wall and vomit up all the adrenaline that was rushing through her body. These were old memories and old reactions. The police weren't here for her.

She walked toward her front door as a uniformed officer eyed her up, preparing to send her away. A few minutes later she was waved through. Inside, a series of raised metal platforms had been laid down. Her shop now looked like what it was – a crime scene – and she took a photo of the metal stepping stones, taking care to avoid photographing the wall.

She passed the team in their white jumpsuits investigating the wall and the body. Averting her eyes, she headed out the back and moved quickly upstairs, closing the lower door behind her. The shop floor was now her liminal zone: out in the village she was exposed but able to roam; up in her flat she was safe but trapped. Between the two, her new life was being challenged as the crime scene officers examined the body in the place she had hoped to start a new life.

Chapter Seven

Walking upstairs, Mal pulled herself up on the thin banister. Good taste and/or poverty had spared the timber from ever having been painted and the narrow Georgian banister was a dark polished length of wood. As she clasped the smooth surface, she wondered how many hands had held onto this same piece.. It was like holding hands with the past itself.

Had fishwives pulled themselves up after a long day gutting pilchards in the factory, pausing for breath as she did now? Had their husbands made their way down in the darkness, calloused fingers ready to throw the nets out again? Had children run up the stairs on all fours, their hands slapping on the treads? At the top, had they grabbed the newel post and leapt back down the narrow staircase? Mal smiled, hearing their mother shout at them not to break their necks. All these lives, all holding her hand through a simple piece of wood.

As she got to the top, she closed the upper door behind her and leant on it. This wasn't her home yet, she knew it and she sensed the house did as well. For now, though, it was her refuge and that would have to do. She headed over to the table, pulled out her writing kit and penned a letter to her sister.

Dear Oppy,

A quick note but I wonder if you could do me a favour and let everyone know I am alright. It would take too long to write to everyone.

I don't want to alarm you but a dead body was found walled up in the shop below. Obviously, the police are involved but I am not. I would be grateful if you could keep this to yourself, unless it makes the news, in which case please could you inform the others that I am okay. Also, if anyone feels inclined to phone, remind them I won't answer and don't want visitors.

I really am fine, in fact, I have taken up sea swimming. It is very invigorating and I have just been to the hairdressers, so all is well.

Much love,

M

She wondered what she could do to repay Collette's kindness with the conditioner. Remembering that the hairdressers had been talking about a party they were all going to, she had the perfect idea. She would pop back to Collette's in a minute, but she had received a letter from one of her great-nephews and wanted to reply to him first, then she could also post both letters at the same time.

Dear Barnie,

Guess what I did this week? I swam with a cat! He is a silver tabby and seems remarkably unafraid of the water. Although he did hitch a ride on my tow float that I wear to make sure boats and fishermen can see me. Imagine if they accidentally caught me in their nets. What a funny mermaid I would make, plus a cat! Can you picture their faces?

I hope school was better today. Getting selected for the reserves is actually fantastic news. It means you can watch the other team and spot their weaknesses, then when you come on, you can put it into practice. Or try to anyway – remember winning isn't everything.

As regards Jamie, ignore him. He's probably thrilled that you are on the reserves because he is insecure. Only weak people bully others. If he continues to bother you, let me know and we will come up with a plan of attack.

All my love,
Yaffle

She put a pound coin in the envelope and added a second into a jam jar with his name written in black marker on the outside. She had a row of jars, some with more coins than others. When they reached eighteen, Mal planned to hand the jars over to them. It wouldn't amount to the sort of eighteenth birthday present she would have once gifted. But she hoped they appreciated she had always been thinking of them. And, of course, the more they wrote the bigger their present, not that they knew about the jars.

Having finished a few more letters, Mal headed out again. She wanted to mend her tow float, drop her gift off to Collette, post her letters, and show the village she wasn't hiding. It wasn't her body in the wall and it wasn't her fault. She had nothing to be ashamed or embarrassed about, and needed to show everyone that, as far as she was concerned, it was business as usual.

She passed through the shop, relieved that the body had now gone and wondered how much longer the forensics team would be.

As she pushed open the door to the chandlery, a ridiculously loud bell chimed above her head. It was unnecessary as the owner was already behind the counter serving the customer. Both men ignored her, presuming she was lost. Despite the float in her hands. She stood patiently waiting to be acknowledged but then the man behind the counter walked out the back. Mal checked her watch, maybe she could come back later, but she really wanted to swim. She didn't strictly need the float, but for safety it seemed wisest.

'If you leave it on the counter, I'll tell Tommy.'

Mal studied the fisherman: that was definitely a French accent, although gently worn away with age. He was tall and well built, maybe her own age, with a silver goatee and tapered moustache. His blue eyes flashed against suntanned and weathered skin. She decided ruggedly handsome best summed him up, but if he thought his good looks excused his dismissive attitude, he had another think coming.

'Tell Tommy what exactly?'

'That you found someone's float. He'll put a notice in the window.'

'It's my float,' said Mal sharply, annoyed that he assumed she didn't swim. 'A cat punctured it and I was going to see if he had a repair kit.'

'That'll be Mac.'

'Mac does repairs?' asked Mal puzzled, maybe Mac ran the shop with Tommy, who still hadn't reappeared from the back.

'Mackerel is the name of the cat. Here.' So far, he hadn't smiled once and now he stretched out his hand towards her in such a confident manner that she simply handed over the float. He took it from her, blew into it, squeezed it searching for the punctures then nodded to himself.

'I'll get this back to you as soon as I can.'

Mal looked at him in confusion. 'Do you work here?'

'No, but it's an easy fix. Tommy's a good man but charges incomers an arm and a leg.'

'Yes but,' Mal didn't mind paying, although she wondered how much an arm and a leg would be, 'I thought there would be a simple kit like a bike puncture repair?'

'Your call.' He shrugged and turned back to the counter.

Mal was taken aback. The man was being helpful but in such a short manner she was uncertain of her footing. She was more used to loquacious transactions, especially amongst strangers. This abrupt man was throwing her off her stride. Tommy now came back with a selection of clasps for the fisherman to choose from.

'This lady needs a repair kit for her tow float,' said the Frenchman, gesturing in her direction.

Tommy smiled at her and came out from behind the counter, taking the float from the other man.

'Let me look now.' He turned it over in his hands and sucked on his teeth a bit. 'Yep, you need a repair kit, right enough. I reckon this should do the job. Patches up RIBs all day long, it will be perfect for you.' He lifted a small box off a shelf and handed it over to her.

Mal recoiled. 'Forty-five pounds? That's more than the float! Do you sell swimming floats?'

Tommy shook his head sadly, pointing out somewhat patronisingly that he was a chandler's not a sports shop. Mal looked at the snorkels and fins hanging behind his head and decided she would not be played for a fool. She turned to the other man.

'Is your offer still good? I'll pay you.'

Tommy cast the Frenchman a bemused look. 'Offering to rescue the maiden, hey, Jacques?'

Mal snorted at the same time that Jacques did.

'Maiden?' She was fast going off Tommy. She didn't care now what Jacques charged, she had made her mind up. Taking the float out of Tommy's hand, she gave it back to Jacques.

He smiled briefly to himself, then nodded at her. 'I'll have it back to you within the next day or two. You are in the bookshop, yes? You'll be able to swim with it immediately. If you want to swim in the meantime, stay close to the shore.'

He then turned his back on her, and as Tommy saw he would get nothing from her, he ignored her as well.

Surprised at the dismissal, Mal paused, then decided there was nothing to do but leave the shop, clanging the bell as she did.

A bell rang again as she entered the hairdresser's and she wondered if every shop in the village operated on bells. It was old-fashioned but Mal liked the way it announced her arrival.

Collette glanced up from the desk and smiled warmly at her. The hairdresser's was much emptier now with a single customer having her hair washed.

'Everything okay?'

Mal nodded, smiling at the feel of the waves on her face. 'Everything is lovely. I love my cut, but I wanted to say thank you for the conditioner. I felt bad not having the money and I heard you chatting to the girls about wanting something special for a night out, so I wondered if you would like these. I bet you have small feet like me.'

Mal held out her box of Louboutin's as Collette stared at her, blinking.

'I think I only wore them once. And I don't have any parties to go to so I thought you might like them.'

Mal rushed on, embarrassed. She hadn't wanted to offend, it was all she could think to offer but now saw it could look like charity and she was mortified.

'Bloody hell, woman, that red on these soles isn't scuffed at all. I reckon you could take them back and get your money back!'

Mal shook her head. 'Not likely. I bought them years ago.'

She watched as Collette picked out the second shoe and smiled at them.

'And in a bag, proper fancy. Size three is perfect and they are pretty.' Her voice sounded questioning, as though she really wanted to say yes but wasn't sure if Mal meant it.

'You'd be doing me a favour. I was unpacking and realised I have no need for these. What is it you youngsters are all going on about, reduce, reuse, recycle?'

Collette laughed. 'Well, if I'm doing it to save the planet, then okay.'

As Mal left the shop, Collette was already trying the shoes on with her jeans rolled up. She looked good in them and Mal felt happy inside as she watched the hairdressers laughing, the red soles flicking up as Collette twirled back and forth.

That night lying in bed, Mal sighed and placed her book to one side. She had read the same page five times and still couldn't remember what she'd read. Dalgliesh had just spotted something clever but for the life of her Mal couldn't fathom the significance of it. She hadn't read a PD James before and had been thoroughly enjoying it until today. She liked the illusion that detectives were intellectuals and gentlemen, but meeting DI Hemingstone earlier had reminded her of the realities of life. She decided it wasn't Dalgliesh's fault she was distracted, a lot had happened today.

Her first cellmate had taught her breathing techniques to help get through the first few nights until eventually, she could block out the shouts and tears from other cells, her own mounting panic, her spiralling fears, and she was able to Zen out. The other women had nicknamed Tamsin, Little Buddha, and Mal was grateful for all the help she offered her, to the point where she could bring herself to say *namaste* without snorting. Now, lying in bed, she practiced those same breathing techniques as she tried to relax.

How far she had travelled from her London penthouse to a stuffy prison cell, and now a little property by the sea. She was currently on the top floor, a single room with French doors that led out onto an enclosed patio among the roof tiles and chimneys of the other properties. From the roof space, she could see the sea but didn't look over anyone else's patios or windows, and by the same token no one looked down on her. It was a perfect little cubby hole, tucked away out of sight with only the sky above and the sea ahead. It was her favourite place in the entire property, and she had instantly decided to sleep in the top bedroom with the doors wide open until the weather said no.

Had the body downstairs ever stood out on that patio, leant against the railings? Mal wondered if they had lived here. That would be the most obvious explanation. Otherwise getting them into the shop would have taken more effort.

A seagull cried out as it flew overhead. Who knew gulls were nocturnal? It was an impressive achievement for birds that were also awake all day. Were they ever silent? Initially, she had tried to sleep with ear buds but was so disturbed by cutting off one of her senses that she was trying to learn to sleep with the noise.

Pulling a sheet over her, she snuggled under the cool breeze and listened to the birds calling to each other, their harsh mournful cries echoing back and forth across the dark skies. The sound suited her mood and gradually she fell asleep dreaming of skeletons and violence.

Chapter Eight

There was a knock at the door and Mal put her book down with a sigh. She and Dalgliesh had been racing towards the final clue but now it would have to wait. Given that the door led down to the shop, the only person knocking was going to be someone from the investigation. The body had been removed yesterday, and Mal hoped she was going to be given the all-clear to continue with the renovations.

The police had already saved the builders the trouble of removing the rest of the wall and sweeping everything away. Now she wanted to get on with her life. This morning the SOCO team suggested they may be finished today; the crime scene was so old they had little hope of finding much. On top of which they only had a tiny space to investigate.

She swung the door open and saw the police officer she had met previously. The woman was standing there in her ill-fitting uniform, a smile on her face and some jam on her stab vest.

'Mind if I come in?'

Mal sighed. The police were worse than bloody vampires, at least if you said no to vampires they'd go away.

'Lady Malachite? Can I come in?'

That bloody name again, she was going to have to nip that in the bud.

'I'm not a Lady, I was simply fed up with everyone trying to give me a title based on my marital status.'

Sophie laughed and nodded her head, then spotted the jam.

'Bugger, can I use your tap?'

Sighing, Mal let her past and directed her to the kitchen sink. As she walked, Mal wondered what she was looking at. What judgements was she making? She'd been here almost a fortnight and yet most of her packing boxes were still sealed.

'Sorry about the jam. It's not how I like to present myself. Although who am I kidding?' She turned from the sink where she was dabbing jam off her chest. 'If I drop or spill anything my wretched boobs catch the lot. They're like some bloody floating shelf. Sometimes I swear you can tell everything I ate that day.'

She dabbed at her black stab vest and carried on. 'Makes me think I should wear a bib. Not that I should have been eating a doughnut, I've been dieting and lost two stone already!' She looked expectantly at Mal waiting for her to say something but when she didn't, she carried on, regardless. 'Mind you, Jennie's doughnuts are the best thing about Golden. Have you tried one yet?'

Mal shook her head, waiting for the policewoman to leave. Despite herself, she was drawn to the friendly woman but still, the sooner she was gone the better.

'I tell you, one more stone and I reckon this uniform will finally feel comfortable. Every new pair of trousers I get is just as bad as the last.'

'I don't think that outfit was designed with a woman's body in mind,' said Mal, cautiously. She hadn't wanted to engage, but she hated seeing how women had to fit into men's roles rather than have things designed for them.

'I know, right? It's like someone explained the concept of a woman and told them to make a pair of trousers to fit that shape. I swear to God, these trousers would only look good on Kate Moss or someone skinnier.'

She laughed at her own joke, then filled the kettle. Mal raised an eyebrow, and the officer smiled apologetically.

'Do you mind? Ruth only had tea, and I hate tea. No matter how many cups I've had. Hate the stuff, but what can you say to someone who's recently bereaved. *Your loved one's dead and I don't much care for your tea.* Not bloody likely, so you drink your tea and wipe their tears and try to remember why you went into policing in the first place. That's why I had a doughnut. To cheer myself up.'

As she talked, she moved around the kitchen, scooping coffee grounds into the cafetiere and getting the milk from the fridge as Mal watched on in bemusement. She wasn't in the slightest perturbed by this woman making herself at home and Mal wondered if that was because it didn't actually feel like her home yet. All the furniture was here when she arrived, the pictures on the wall and the knick-knacks weren't hers either. Why had she even put up with those ghastly figurines for so long? Eventually, the police officer put everything on the table and waved at Mal to join her.

'So that's the reason I've called. To inform you that we have identified the body.'

'That was quick!' It seemed indelicate to point out that the body was no more than bones, but Mal hadn't realised DNA tests were so quick.

'There was a wallet in the trouser pocket.'

Sophie sipped her coffee and sat back with a satisfied sigh.

'No inspector?' said Mal, as Sophie took a second sip.

'Not bloody likely after you scolded him last time. I reckon he's scared of you. What with being a Lady and a smart-arse.'

'Are you like this with the bereaved?' asked Mal, curiously.

'As if! Didn't I tell you I drink the tea? No, you don't strike me as someone that needs pussyfooting around, so I won't insult you by doing that.'

Mal thought about it and agreed. Honestly, she was warming to this woman and relaxed.

'I didn't think I was a smart-arse, just surprised he couldn't see what was obvious.'

'And in his eyes that will make you a smart-arse. This is his first murder investigation, apparently. He got promoted and shunted out of Coventry. I was chatting to a colleague who's stationed up there and she said he was rubbish and they were desperate to get rid of him. Apparently, he was persuaded that applying for a job in Cornwall would be good for his career. It was certainly good for their division. It looks like we lucked out.'

As she chattered on, Mal was trying to work out if Sophie was being indiscreet or trying to ingratiate herself. It wasn't as if she were telling Mal anything she couldn't have guessed herself, but it still struck her as unprofessional, unless the woman was playing with her.

'Wondering if I should be saying this, aren't you? Speaking out of turn and the like? Fact is, he hasn't impressed me much and I'm trying to put you at ease.'

She pushed her cup away and gave a quick burp, apologising as she did so.

'That's better. So, the body. As you feared, it's recent and local. The man's name was Roger Jago, disappeared fifteen years ago. His boat was found adrift at sea and everyone presumed he'd drowned. Of course, now we'll have to revisit that. I've been chatting to his widow, Ruth, she still lives in the village, as does Piran. That's their boy. He came rushing over and the two of them were praying even before we'd left the house. Big supporters of the church those two. Never was a tombola or a fundraiser that Ruth wasn't selling tickets for or baking cakes.'

She let Mal take it in.

'Sounds like you're a local?'

Sophie beamed at her. 'That I am. Grew up here, even went to school with Piran, Connor and Billy.'

'Her other sons?'

'No. They're the Trebetherick twins, them and Piran used to be thick as thieves at school. Their dad was Paul Trebetherick, and he was Roger's partner on the boat.'

'Was?' Mal wondered if there was more tragedy in this story.

'He committed suicide some five years after Roger disappeared. People say he couldn't live with the grief of Roger's drowning.'

She paused significantly.

'Oh dear. Doesn't look so good now, does it?' said Mal.

Sophie tilted her head, and smiled at Mal. 'Quick, aren't you?'

Mal shrugged. 'Seems obvious to me but then I'm an outsider. Does his widow, Roger's widow, that is, know about the body yet?'

'The inspector is there now with a colleague. Now he's looking at a murder, I've been relegated to holding people's hands and drinking tea.'

Mal thought that was a mistake: this woman was a police officer rather than a detective, but she was certainly sharp enough.

'You were never tempted to become a detective?'

'I'd be bored out of my wits. Policing, proper policing, getting to know your community, that's much more my cup of tea, or coffee. Besides, with the children, I want a timetable that suits their lives. If you're a detective, you get jerked about much more than a good old-fashioned bobby. Pay might be better, but that's not everything.'

'So where is the inspector now?'

'Oh, he's still in the village. Sharon still lives here, that's Paul's widow.'

'Neither woman moved away?'

'Why would they?' Sophie looked puzzled. 'This is their home?'

'Didn't people gossip after the suicide?'

'Course they did and right enough, the twins left. Couldn't cope, I guess, although Piran stayed.'

'Well, it wasn't his dad that committed suicide, and maybe he entertained hopes that his own father may yet return.'

'Fair enough, although after Roger disappeared, Paul took Piran under his wing. The poor lad went quite wild for a bit but Paul and his boys all helped him along. Ruth, as ever, had her church and forgot about her boy for a bit. Thank God the Trebethericks took care of him.'

'I suppose the murder and the suicide might not be linked?' said Mal, doubtfully.

'Agreed, but it still needs to be investigated. There's going to be hell up. For a start off, how the bloody hell did Roger get from his boat to being stuck behind the wall of a shop he had nothing to do with?' She put her coffee cup down.

'Now then, I wanted you to know the facts and a little about the background, seeing as you're new here. I imagine both women will come calling over the next few days and thought you could do with a heads-up. Here's my card if you have any trouble.'

'I think I can handle a grieving woman.'

'Probably, but an angry Cornish fishwife? Mind you, Ruth never saw herself as a fishwife, living up on Saints she always considered herself better than the other women. Could be a whole other level of trouble. Just call me if you need to. Or mention to them that I can come over and chat if they want. That should put them on their heels.'

Getting up, she walked over to the front door.

'I also came to tell you, you can let Dennis and his lads back in again. We're done here. And give me a call if you have any bother. I'm sorry your arrival at Golden has been so foul but give it a chance, this is a lovely place, really.'

She was about to leave when she turned and looked back into Mal's living room.

'And get rid of all those bits and bobs, it'll feel more like your place when you've boxed them all up.'

Mal was impressed with her insightfulness but wanted to test her.

'And how do you know those things aren't mine?'

'Give over. A statue of a seventeenth-century milkmaid, plates on the wall, horse brasses? If those are yours, I'll eat my stab vest.'

Laughing, she turned and headed back down the staircase.

Chapter Nine

Checking her outfit in the mirror, Mal smiled in approval. She would examine the state the police had left the shop in, then take a turn around the village. She had found a pair of red peep-toe sandals. The heel was only an inch high, which she decided would be safe on the cobbles.

After some rummaging, she was pleased to find a pair of white palazzo pants with red piping down either leg, and a matching jacket with small red poppers. She loved this outfit and was pleased her sister had packed it. She was even happier after she put it on that it still fit.

Heading downstairs, she wandered around the shop floor, her shoes making the plastic sheeting on the floor rustle. The police had left the place cleaner than the workmen who would be back tomorrow and she realised there was nothing for her to do. The front windows were still covered in paper and she decided to leave them up – she didn't want gawpers; the overhead lighting was good enough, if a bit sterile right now.

Looking around the large empty room, she could see the space held lots of potential, aside from the recent corpse. Admittedly, she didn't know the first thing about running a bookshop, but Gary had been helping her out and there was nothing she didn't know about profits and losses. She was about to head out for some fresh air, away from her feelings of incarceration, when a slight movement caught her eye.

Across the room, an enormous rat ran along the bottom of the wall. A second later, a cat exploded from the storeroom and sprinted after the rat, which in turn legged it as fast as it could towards the far corner newly exposed by the police. Mal had long enough to register that the cat was Mackerel when the rat disappeared, and the cat was now crouched in the corner, its tail flicking wildly from side to side.

Cautiously, Mal walked towards the corner and wished she were wearing boots or something she could tuck her trousers into. Her peep-toe sandals felt terribly vulnerable. Leaning against the wall was one of the builder's lump hammers and she picked it up, shuddering with the thought the rat had probably run over its handle.

'Hello, Mac. Where did you come from?' Even in asking the question, Mal decided the cat had probably come in through her bedroom patio windows. She enjoyed leaving those doors open as no thief would ever get in. So far, she'd had to shoo out a seagull, and now it looked like Mac was treating it like a hotel. Which was fine unless he was also bringing in rats to play with.

'Is this one of your guests?' she asked, addressing the cat. 'Because if it is, I'm not impressed.' She tiptoed towards the corner, her hammer held aloft, her toes exposed, and peered towards a tiny dark hole at the bottom of the corner. She leant forward. There was a loud bang from behind her.

Screaming, Mal almost bludgeoned the cat and sprang backwards, laughing in fear and embarrassment. Striding towards the front door, she wondered what was making her so jumpy, the rat, the dead body or the fact that so far, running a bookshop in a quiet fishing village was proving to be one of the most stressful things she had ever endured.

Unlocking the door, she threw it open, ready to fight whoever had caused her to completely lose her nerve. In front of her stood Jacques, holding her inflated red tow float. It appeared to be in a string bag. His smile had fallen almost immediately, and he had taken a step back. Mal wondered how fierce she looked.

'Do you want to put the hammer down?'

Mal blinked, then realised she was still holding the lump hammer, and glaring.

'Scared a little old lady could do you some damage?'

'If I see a little old lady, I'll let you know. You, on the other hand, could stop Genghis Khan in his tracks.'

It was an odd sort of compliment, but right now Mal was going to take it.

'I was trying to stop a rat.'

'With a short-handled hammer. He'd as like jump in your face before you got within a foot of him.'

'Dear God!' She shuddered, instantly appalled. 'Now, how am I supposed to get that image out of my mind? And what have you done to my float?'

'I fixed it.'

He stared at her and raised an eyebrow. Was he waiting for her to thank him like some desperate floozy? As far as she could see, her pristine tow float was now covered in black plasters and bits of rope. It was the only thing she had bought herself, beyond the haircut, and now it seemed even worse than before.

'How is that fixed? It looks like it has been dragged out from the bottom of the ocean.'

Mal was exaggerating, and she knew it, but she was still twitchy after seeing that rat, and now she was worried about rats invading upstairs. A soft body rubbed her ankles and Mal jumped a mile, dropping the hammer and swearing loudly, then laughing weakly as Mac sauntered out through the open door. She was about to apologise to Jacques when he cut her off.

'I'd be nervous as well if someone found a dead body in my home.'

Expecting a smirk, Mal was relieved to see a sympathetic smile.

'It wasn't that. I think Mac brought a rat in and now it's hiding behind the wall and honestly, the idea of a rat lurking freaks me out much more than a body.'

'Death and rats are both inevitable.'

'Doesn't mean I have to put up with them, though.'

'You're going to rage against rats? In a harbour?'

Now he was teasing her, and her back stiffened.

'I'll do whatever works for me. What do I owe you for the float?'

Again with the raised eyebrow. She was being rude, and they both knew it. He was also prepared to let it go and it irked her, and they both knew that as well.

'May I see where the rat went?'

Mal took a deep breath. He was a fisherman, maybe he was also a rat whisperer and could work out where it had gone. Inviting him in, she took the float from him and walked towards the back of the shop, then stopped a couple of metres away, gesturing to the corner where some rubble was piled up. Jacques looked thoughtfully at the point where the two walls joined. He moved a few bricks aside and pointed to a tiny gap in the bricks.

'That's where your rat went.' He stood up again and looked along the exposed wall. 'Where was the body found?'

For a moment, Mal didn't know what he was talking about. She was so fixed on flushing the rat out, but now she supposed it was inevitable that he would be curious. She pointed towards the back end of the long wall.

'Okay, this section is curious,' he said, pointing to the shorter wall at the back of the shop, constructed in brick.

'How so?'

'Okay, see this long wall here,' he pointed to the stretch that ran the length of the shop and had been boarded over. 'This is the original slate and mortar construction. This was how this building was built. All the old harbour properties were built like this, but this section,' he pointed to the back wall, that ran off the corner, 'is brick. And the brick section only runs for three feet. I'm guessing from the floor markings that was the width of the void space?'

Mal looked at the short brick wall that stopped at the door frame for the back storage room.

'I presume that was built when they wanted to partition off the back room from the rest of the shop floor?' said Mal, drawing the same conclusion as the police.

'Hmm,' said Jacques, as he studied the two walls. 'In that case, what's behind it?'

Mal cocked her head then caught up. 'Because if it were the end of the property, it would be slate and mortar like that wall.'

'Exactly.' Picking up a full-length sledgehammer, he grinned at her. 'Want to find out?'

What if it was another body? What if it was a nest of rats? Grabbing one of the builders' steps, she climbed up two rungs.

'If it's rats, I'm afraid I won't be able to save you.'

'Don't you worry about that. If it is rats, I'll tell them that Mac is on his way. I imagine he has quite the reputation amongst the rat population around here. Now, are you ready? This appears to have been put up in a hurry. Should come down as quickly.'

He swung the hammer at the wall and almost immediately it caved in. She didn't wish to disparage his strength, but she could have leant on it and it would have given way. A few more swings and all the upper bricks fell, leaving a pile of rubble on the floor and a dark aperture beyond. The smell of damp stone and seaweed rushed out into the light, mingling with the motes of brick dust floating in the air.

'Well I never.'

Chapter Ten

Jacques looked back at her with a massive grin. Mal was momentarily shocked by how it changed his countenance from supercilious to sunny. He struck her as nothing short of a schoolboy on an adventure.

'I think it's an old passageway. I believe without that rat, no one would have ever looked closer.'

'But the SOCO team were here looking for clues. How did they miss this?'

'A rat can crawl through the smallest of spaces and this gap was hidden behind an overhanging broken brick.' He smiled back at her. 'Shall we explore?'

Mal climbed down off the step ladder and peered into the dark. It was a rough corridor, both walls the same slate and mortar construction. The floor was lined with cobbles and a sandy mortar. Despite the air smelling damp, the floor and walls felt dry, and as she looked around, there were no rats to speak of.

Taking his hand, she stepped carefully over the bricks, then paused. Telling him to stay where he was, she returned to the shop. She dashed upstairs and came back in a pair of Chanel trainers with a flashlight. The trainers weren't perfect, but they were better than her peep-toes. Her next purchase was going to be a pair of wellingtons.

'Right, let's go.' Holding the torch aloft, the pair of them walked into the darkness. Jacques had offered his arm again, but Mal was perfectly capable of walking unaided and stepped away from the offer. The passage sloped gently downhill until they came to a short flight of steps. A rope tied to the wall was acting as a banister. They paused at the top of the steps and peered down into the dark.

'Shall we?' said Jacques. His voice echoed her excitement, all thoughts of rats now gone from her mind. As she nodded, she realised he couldn't see her face in the dark.

'Come on then. Where do you think this goes? Is it the sea? It smells like the sea. That would explain the rats, wouldn't it?' asked Mal, trying not to whisper.

'Rats go anywhere. But I'm not sure if this does lead to the sea, I can smell something else under the brine.'

Mal sniffed harder, but all she could smell was seaweed, ozone and that wet pull of distant shores. She was reminded of swimming out by the harbour and wondered what Jacques had detected.

'Take care of the steps now. The bottom ones are slippy.'

'Slippery,' corrected Mal.

'That is what I said.'

'No, you said—' Mal's foot shot out from underneath her and as her hand gripped the rope, she landed with a bump on the bottom step, a damp patch spreading through her palazzo pants.

'See. Slippy. Are you okay?'

Mal tried to glare at him but in the darkness he wouldn't appreciate it. Instead, she stood up. She hadn't fallen too hard, certainly she would have a bruise, but her dignity was more affronted. As she put her hand down to right herself, she touched a small cold lump. It had an edge that felt manmade unlike a pebble or a seashell, and she shone the torch on it.

'Pirate's treasure?' he asked with a laugh.

'An old button, I think.' She tucked it into her pocket to study later. 'You think this is a smugglers' tunnel, then?'

'Almost certainly. Shall we see? There's a bend ahead. And watch out, the floor here is slippier.'

Mal was going to correct him but decided to pay attention to her feet instead. The verbal tics of a French man living in a Cornish village were beyond the scope of her expertise.

As they moved slowly towards the bend, they kept bumping into each other as she slipped on bits of seaweed growing on the wet cobbles. Eventually Jacques tutted and stretched out his elbow.

'Take my arm before you break my neck.'

Mal tried an old-fashioned look and again realised that in the darkness, it was a waste of time. Grudgingly, she looped her arm through his and immediately felt more secure. He was wearing heavy working boots and had a sense of solidity to him that made Mal think of stone foundations, cathedral cornerstones, and flying buttresses. Something that stood firm, holding everything up, the very last thing to fall. She shrugged mentally. It was odd to compare someone to a piece of architecture, but it seemed appropriate down here in the foundations of the village. Still, walking arm in arm with a total stranger along a tunnel last used by a murderer felt foolish. But she was committed now and besides, she trusted him. It was one of her gut instincts that had served her so well in the City. She offered up a little prayer that down here in the darkness she hadn't made a mistake.

'Where do you think we are now?'

'Close to the harbour, I'd say. I think it was probably built at the same time as the first houses went up above it. If I had to guess, I'd say we were near The Cat and Fiddle. I can smell beer.'

Mal sniffed and indeed there was a faint aroma of hops.

'Do you think we're under them?'

'I think we might be walking alongside their beer cellar.'

As they got to the corner, the darkness faded slightly, and Mal saw the outline of the passageway again beyond the arc of the torch.

Turning the corner, it was lighter again and the smell of the sea was stronger still. Now Mal was picking up the smell of earth and trees.

'Is that running water?'

Jacques nodded and smiled down at her. 'I think I know where we're going to come out!'

After another hundred feet, they stopped at a rusted metal gateway whose bars blocked off the tunnel. Beyond them, she could see it opened onto a smaller one transporting an underground river. There was a door within the metal bars, but as she went to open it, Jacques stopped her.

'And if you slipped and fell into that river?'

It was a valid point. The river didn't look deep and the tunnel it ran in seemed as wide as the one she stood in, but it was lower and she wasn't sure she could climb back up. Plus, she had no idea where it ran to. She had visions of her being spat out of the top of a giant waterfall, a crowd of rats waving at her as she fell past them to a rocky death.

'Well, can we see if the door will open?'

Stepping forward, Jacques examined the rusty latch, then pointed to a padlock.

'That's not as old as the gate, but I don't think it's been used for years.'

In the gloom, Mal peered at the lock. Unlike the gate, it was free of barnacles but it was dull and covered in bits of mud and leaves. Peering to the left, she could just make out a small river rushing towards a source of light.

'So we're none the wiser?'

'Not at all,' said Jacques in an excited tone. 'I think I know exactly where we are. Come with me.'

'Hang on,' Mal looked out through the bars. 'If the killer had access to this route why not bring the body down here? Why not take the body away completely?'

Jacques paused. 'I don't know. Maybe he was panicking? Maybe where this tunnel comes out is too exposed at either end? Maybe he slipped out this way to the boats and came back later to wall in the body?'

'How would he get to the boats?' Mal thought the theory made sense in so far as it went, but that's all it was. Someone had taken Roger's keys and taken his boat out to sea, and then snuck back onshore without being seen. In Mal's eyes that could only be achieved by someone that understood boats and tides. The suspect pool was narrowing, although in a fishing village that didn't rule out a lot. In fact, she was standing in a dark secret tunnel with a perfect example of someone that fit the bill.

'Come on. Let me show you.' Taking her arm again, Jacques led them back through the tunnel, up the steps and along the passageway until she was once again standing in her barren shop. Stepping out onto the lane, she blinked in the light and took a deep breath. The passageway had been uncomfortably confining, and she was glad to be out in the fresh air. She was also glad that the sunlight and fresh air calmed her momentary suspicion of Jacques.

They headed toward the harbour and, turning right, walked towards the fishing boats.

'See there?' Jacques pointed down to the harbour wall. It was low tide and she could see metal bars in the wall where a large culvert was flowing out into the harbour.

'That's where a small river that runs under the village comes out. As the village grew up, the river was confined and channelled to help prevent flooding. I bet if we walked up that tunnel, we would find yours running off it.'

Mal looked around and tried to picture the route she had walked underground. The Cat and Fiddle was to her right and it felt like the same sort of distance.

'That's incredible.'

'Indeed. The killer must have been lucky with the tide and able to swim out through the harbour to the boat unseen. Set it off, swam back in through the tunnel and then finished bricking up the wall and tunnel.'

'But his clothes would be soaking.'

'He probably used the tumble drier upstairs. You will have to tell the police, you know.'

Mal pursed her lips. As much as she would have liked to keep the tunnel a secret, Jacques' scenario made sense. It was frustrating. She wanted to be done with this, a fresh start and no police, but she would have to inform them.

As they stood by the harbour's edge, she noticed they were attracting attention.

'Do you think they all know about the dead body?' whispered Mal. She didn't want to be the centre of attention.

Jacques looked down at her, his moustache twitching.

'Almost certainly, but for now they are wondering why such an elegant lady is covered in mud and seaweed.'

He laughed and plucked a piece of weed out of her hair and handed it to her. Alarmed, she patted her head and brushed off her trousers that had indeed borne the brunt of her fall on the steps.

'White is not the best colour, I think, for exploration?'

'You might have said I looked a state,' said Mal, sharply. Her previous excitement at the discovery had disappeared. Now she was preoccupied by thoughts of more police and appearing dishevelled in public.

'If you had told me, I could have changed,' she snapped. 'I don't want people to gawp at me. I've come to Golden to find myself. I don't want people staring at me while I do.'

Jacques raised an eyebrow. 'I thought you were clever?'

'What?'

'You strike me as an intelligent woman. Quiet, polite, a little too proud maybe, but not stupid.'

'In what way do you think I'm stupid?' asked Mal, aware her tone had become waspish.

'You say you want to find yourself? Well, here you are.' He pointed at her and laughed.

'It's a saying. I'm trying to turn over a new leaf. Be someone new.'

'But that *is* stupid. How can you be something new? You are you and always will be.'

'I know that,' she said, frustrated. 'I mean, I'm trying to find a new way of living. I have to start my life over and I'm trying to work out how to do that.'

'You are a little bit too old, I think, to start your life over? Maybe carry on with the one you had before.'

Mal was furious now. She was standing alongside a picturesque harbour, fishermen were tending to their boats, holidaymakers were taking photos and eating ice creams and she was being lectured to by a complete stranger.

'And how can I do that when I no longer have my job?'

'Your job was who you were?'

'No, of course not. Although, yes also.'

'See, stupid. I am a fisherman, but that doesn't mean I *am* a fisherman. It's something I do, not who I am. What you do is not who you are. Sometimes I wonder if the language is stupid or if it's the people using the words?' He shrugged.

'Maybe you are the one who is stupid for not understanding what someone is trying to say.'

'Yes, all things are possible,' said Jacques, in a manner that dismissed her idea as preposterous.

Mal stepped away from him. The open space, the people looking at her and the row with Jacques was making her anxious. She had only once had a panic attack, back in jail, but she remembered how it felt. The choking horror as wave after wave of fear paralysed her. Now she wanted to get back to the safety of the bookshop as her heart pounded.

'If you will excuse me, I need to call the police.'

She turned and walked away, but as she did, Jacques called out after her.

'The rope on the tow float. It's to protect it. If Mac jumps on again, he can grip the rope instead of the plastic. Better for both of you.'

Mal wanted to stop and thank him. She knew she should turn around, but no longer trusted herself. It was essential that she got away from the prying eyes and close her four walls around her.

In her distress, she completely forgot the button she had found as she shoved her outfit in the laundry bin and sat and shuddered in an armchair as the day closed around her.

Chapter Eleven

It was four-thirty, and the team were meeting in the Truro incident room to review the Golden case. Like every other incident room, Truro's was a large room with a low ceiling, windows that barely opened, and overhead fluorescent lights. The sort of environment that induced headaches even when Detective Inspector Hemingstone wasn't speaking. Sophie adjusted her trousers, hoping to find a more comfortable way to sit in them. She had started to need a belt with her last pair, so dropped down a size. Every time she dropped a size, she treated herself to a manicure. Now her nails looked lovely, but the waistband was digging in and she may have jumped the gun.

She was in the incident room because she had been the first officer on the scene. She didn't have any expectations that she could offer much to the team, but it made for a pleasant change of pace. Something to tell the family about when she got home.

She checked her watch. Clearly, the new inspector wanted to make an entrance. She yawned. God save her from men who needed their egos bolstered. Too often at the end of a night shift she'd be patching up blokes who'd lost the battle with booze and drugs and rampant egotism. The time-honoured chants: '*Do want a bit?*' '*D'you know who I am?*' '*Come on then!*'

Sometimes these out-of-control egos would get arrested, sometimes they'd be sent home. Now it looked like she was working with one. Still, nothing new there.

She glanced over at Donald, one of the older detectives, and tapped on her watch. He shook his head and grinned back at her. Donald had been around long enough to see most people come and go. He should retire soon, but Sophie thought he'd probably see her out as well.

The door swung open and DI Hemingstone strode into the room. All eyes turned to him and he paused, waiting until the silence bordered on uncomfortable, then cleared his throat.

'Right then. The lab confirms it. The body at Golden was murdered.'

'Not suicide or an accident?' quipped someone from the back. There was laughter in the room, but the joke sailed over Hemingstone's head.

'No, according to the report, the skull was indented and was the most probable cause of death. We were also able to identify the body as one Roger Jago. Jago went missing one night and his boat was found abandoned at sea. Everyone assumed the obvious, that he had fallen overboard and drowned.' Hemingstone tucked his thumbs into his waistband and stared around the room. 'At this point, I'd like to make it clear that I wouldn't have. Fishermen don't just fall overboard.' Someone coughed and Hemingstone stopped talking, looking around the room in annoyance. 'Yes. What is it?'

'Fishermen die at sea all the time,' said Donald. 'It's a bloody tragedy, but their bodies are often never found.'

'Seems unlikely,' dismissed Hemingstone, certain of his own opinion, but Donald persevered.

'Not unlikely at all. Check the figures. Industry with the highest number of workplace deaths in Cornwall is fishing. Mostly drowning. I dug up the report on Roger Jago's death and he couldn't swim. Drowning seems a logical conclusion for the team to have drawn.'

Hemingstone smiled smugly.

'I read that. Clearly, someone made an error in the report. Why wasn't that spotted at the time? That's something that wouldn't have passed me.'

'Sorry, sir, what error did you spot?' asked Donald, confused.

'A fisherman that couldn't swim!' Hemingstone chortled. 'Jumped out at me straightaway. That's the sort of attention to detail you can all expect from me now that I'm in charge. Sloppy reporting won't get past me. I'm a stickler for paperwork. That's where we'll catch the killer, here at our desks, not running around the streets knocking on doors.'

He paused expectantly. Sophie wondered if he expected applause or something, instead, like the others, she was wondering who was going to contradict him. Donald cleared his throat.

'Ah, well now. Not being local, I suppose you wouldn't know, but lots of fishermen can't swim. Even today.'

Hemingstone blinked, then looked at the rest of the room as everyone nodded.

'I had an old boy in the village once say to me, what's the point? Can't swim five miles back to shore. May as well go quick, as easy as slow.'

'But that's... What about health and safety?' he spluttered.

'They're fishermen. They don't have unions, they're mostly self-employed. It's a hard job and they get on with it.'

There was a general murmuring in the room. Growing up in Golden, Sophie knew better than most what a hard life it was being a fisherman, but they were a close-knit and stubborn community. Keeping food on the table, theirs and the country's, was a hard and dangerous job and they just got on with it. She wished more of them wore life preservers, though.

Having watched his morning briefing sliding out of his control, Hemingstone decided to wrestle it back.

'Right well, anyway, now we know he didn't drown. He was murdered, and whilst we already have our prime suspect, we need to cross the i's and dot the t's.'

Some of the junior detectives nudged each other at his mistake, but he glared at them and carried on.

'So, what do we know about the victim?'

A young detective lounged back in his chair, then started speaking. Sophie knew the type, fast tracked for leadership. Late twenties, well educated, knew the right people, looking for a quick rise up the ranks. She'd try not to hold it against him.

He read from his notes.

'Roger Jago. Fisherman. Married to Ruth Jago, from one of the big houses up on the hill the villagers call Saints. Church type, well connected. Their marriage raised a few eyebrows; Roger wasn't the right sort. Despite that, the marriage seemed steady although they only had the one child. Piran, aged fifteen when his father disappeared. Roger owned a fishing boat with Paul Trebetherick. They had been friends since childhood. Trebetherick was married to Sharon, another local girl, but not one with money. They had twins, Billy and Connor, in the same year as Piran. The boys and fathers were close, the wives not so much. Paul Trebetherick committed suicide five years after Roger's disappearance. The boys had turned twenty.'

The detective cleared his throat and looked up expectantly.

'Thank you, Williams,' said Hemingstone. 'I believe our chief suspect in the murder of Roger Jago is Paul Trebetherick. Trebetherick was Roger Jago's partner. Business not life.' He laughed and the room stared at him blankly, although Williams sniggered.

'Good one, boss.'

Oh aye, thought Sophie, *promotion, is it?*

Gratified his joke had been appreciated, he continued, although now he directed his comments to the junior detective.

'Five years after Jago's disappearance, Trebetherick commits suicide. Coincidence? I don't think so. Now, the two men owned a boat together. The boat is an expensive item. A good motive, I'd have thought.'

Sophie thought about what Malachite Peck had said and agreed that it sounded good for about five seconds, but didn't really hold up.

'It's much harder to be a solo fisherman,' she called out. 'A partnership is a good thing. It's safer. You have someone to share the work with. You make more money if you can stay out longer. I don't know a fisherman would kill simply to get a boat, otherwise they'd all be doing it.'

Hemingstone looked around the room angrily, trying to find the dissenter until he spotted Sophie standing at the back.

'Ah, uniform.' Sophie winced at the derogatory term beloved by the dicks in CID. 'I don't know if the others know you, what with you being an officer.' He addressed the room. 'Taphouse here, is with us today as first officer on the scene and no doubt feels that she needs more input into the investigation.'

'Take the exams if you want to be a detective,' jeered a voice from the other side of the room. Hemingstone beamed in their direction, then returned his attention to Sophie.

'When you've done this job a while, you see how easily people are motivated by greed.'

Sophie was certain her face was bright red and her palms were sweaty. Mocked and patronised was not what she had been aiming for. She didn't want to be a detective, but she had hoped she could offer some meaningful contribution.

'It's like Mal says, sir. Who commits suicide five years after the event? You either do it right away or learn to live with it.'

Hemingstone shook his head dismissively. 'And who exactly is Mal'

'Lady Malachite Peck, person who found the body,' said the junior detective, quick to impress.

Sophie didn't want to contradict him. She was pretty sure it was him who had heckled about the exams, but facts were facts and it was their job to get them straight.

'Mr Jenkins found the body, sir. And Malachite's not a Lady, she said that because she didn't like Miss, Ms or Mrs.'

Some of the women in the room laughed and said they wished to be known as Countess or Princess. One said she'd rather be a Doctor until her colleague pointed out she'd be expected to actually do stuff. The teasing, however, was light-hearted, and Sophie felt the camaraderie of the room lean towards her.

'So,' said Hemingstone, reflectively, 'she's a liar. A liar who found a body. That's curious.' He paused, waiting for the room to appear impressed.

'Do you want me to look into her, boss?'

Sophie was going to find out who that young detective was and spike his bloody drink.

'She's only just moved in! She can't have anything to do with this.'

The inspector gave a crocodile smile. 'In this game, you soon realise that people go to great lengths to hide their true motives.'

'But if she were involved, why would she comment that the suicide seemed unrelated? Why start with the renovations?'

'Why do people do anything?' countered Hemingstone, in an avuncular tone that made Sophie want to take a stapler to his face.

'Okay. Here's what we do. This is almost certainly an open-and-shut case, but let's tie up some loose ends. Williams, investigate our fake Lady Malachite Peck, see what we know about her. Donald, look into Jago and Trebetherick's financials, see if either of them had money worries. The rest of you, let's see if we can get some headway on these drug dealers operating out of Park Square. I know murder's always the cherry, but we're here every day, saving people from their own stupidity. Let's focus on our clean-up rates.'

Just as Hemingstone was about to dismiss them, Donald answered a call and waved his hand in the air, alerting the room. As he put the phone back down, he nodded.

'Well, now that's interesting. That was the lady in question. Seems she and a neighbour have discovered a false wall near where the body was found and a tunnel that leads down to the harbour.'

Everyone shuffled excitedly. Smugglers tunnels were often talked of, rarely discovered.

'Okay, settle down,' shouted Hemingstone. 'Williams, arrange for SOCO to go back down first thing tomorrow. We'll head down and have a look as well. It seems we now know how the murderer left the building unseen.'

As the team was dismissed, Sophie walked off, thinking dark thoughts about stupidity. Hemingstone's mostly, but her own for dragging Malachite into the investigation.

'Sophie, wait up.' Donald had jogged to keep up with her as she'd stormed out of the briefing room. 'Ignore him, lass. The man's an arse.'

'I know, I just feel terrible that I somehow dragged an entirely innocent woman under the microscope.'

'She'll be fine. As long as she has nothing to hide, job's a good'un.'

Chapter Twelve

Mal was sitting at the counter by the front door of the shop. The sun was out. She'd had a wonderful swim, Mac had joined her and not punctured the buoy. She was up to date with her letters, Dalgliesh had saved the day, and now she was waiting for a delivery of books from the wholesalers. Her wobble yesterday was behind her and she was determined to acknowledge that her rehabilitation into daily life would not be straightforward. There would be highs and lows, the trick was to wake up each morning and try again.

She was regretting coming to Golden, though. She had thought village life would be quiet. A place where she could pass unnoticed as she tried to start again. Instead, it was a hive of activity. Everyone knew everyone else and newcomers were scrutinised. On top of that, the tourists peered in everywhere, and Mal felt constantly exposed. The police investigation was not helping either, nor was the dead body. In London, no one would have blinked an eye. Here, they were taking notes and probably placing bets on how long she would last.

The SOCO team was investigating the tunnel, and the builders were working around them in another section of the shop. It was a day of industry, and Mal was determined to feel good. The only thing to mar the day was the collection of flowers building up outside the entrance to the shop. She understood their presence and could hardly begrudge them, but the place was resembling a mausoleum. It had only been twenty-four hours since the body had been identified. There had been no smell from the skeleton, but soon the shop would be overwhelmed by the stench of rotting blooms.

There was a rap on the glass and as it was still papered up, Mal couldn't wave the people in, or away. Getting up, she walked over to the door and smiled as she saw Collette looking concerned. Tucked under her elbow was a shoebox and Mal immediately deflated..

'Didn't they fit?'

Collette stared at her as if she were mad. 'Of course they fit. They fit perfectly; they're the most delicious shoes I've ever worn. Are you mad?'

Mal wasn't sure where to go with this conversation, but it was okay because Collette hadn't finished.

'Are these original? Do you know how much they cost? Because if they are original, there's no way I can accept them. Mandz looked them up online. They're practically vintage.'

Mal raised an eyebrow, she was old, but it seemed a stretch to call a pair of twenty-year-old shoes vintage.

'Honestly, Malachite. This design is collectable. Is it genuine?'

Collette finally paused and studied Mal with a mixture of anger and hope. *She doesn't want to return them*, thought Mal, *she loves them as much as I did when I first bought them.*

'Bad news, I'm afraid. They're real.'

The very idea that she'd bought knock-offs made Mal shudder, but she wasn't going to say that aloud, aware it would either sound rude or boastful in a village where disposable wealth stretched to a new winter coat for the wife and not much more.

'But I don't want them back. They were a gift. I couldn't afford the conditioner, and you did me a kindness. So I wanted to respond in kind.'

Collette looked momentarily stunned. 'But they're not remotely related.'

'No, indeed. Your gift was far more generous as you weren't really about to replace your conditioner, were you? You said that to make me feel better. I know in your business you can't afford to waste anything. Whereas my gift was something I haven't used in years and no longer have any need for. Your gift was better and kinder.'

'But yours is worth over a grand,' wailed Collette. 'There's no way I can accept it. Especially when you couldn't even afford conditioner. You should sell these.'

Mal thought about it, now that Collette knew the price of the shoes, she had caused an imbalance. But Collette's suggestion had given her an idea.

'How would I sell them?'

'On eBay, or any of the selling apps.'

'And do people have to come over and try them on?' It didn't sound feasible. Mal was no slouch with computers, but her area of expertise were spreadsheets and databases. Social media apps felt like a trivialisation of technology.

Collette laughed. 'No way. Just list them. Someone will buy them and you post it out. Where have you been living? Under a rock?'

Pretty much, thought Mal, then worked out a solution.

'Could you teach me how to do it?'

'Course I can.' Collette looked relieved and reluctantly removed the shoebox from under her elbow.

Mal shooed her hand back. 'No. I've already told you I'm not having them back. But I have others. If you show me how to sell them, you'd be doing me another favour.' She saw Collette wrestling with herself, indecision bloomed across her face. 'And whenever your samples bottles are running low. Properly low, though. You can give them to me. How does that sound? Fair?'

'You're proper mad, you are,' scoffed Collette, 'but yes, I can live with that. Shall I come over tomorrow to set you up selling online? Are you good with phones?'

Mal stared at her until Collette apologised, then with a grin, she showed the hairdresser her Instagram account. Collette flicked through the images.

'You've got a really good eye for the village.' She flicked her finger across the screen. 'Those are the best doughnuts, aren't they? Oh look, new hair!' Mal shrugged, she wasn't keen on selfies but she did look great. Now Collette laughed, pointing at an image. 'Lobster pots!

Everyone takes them, did you take it because of the coke can?'

'Yes, but then I removed it and put it in the bin. Or is it some ancient fishing tradition?'

'No, that's an ancient tourist tradition. Can't find a bin, can't be bothered to take it back to the car.'

Mal wondered if that was being unfair to most tourists but she hadn't lived here long enough to know the realities of living in a tourist spot.

'Where's that then?' asked Collette curiously, as she pointed to the metal gate she and Jacques had discovered under the shop.

'That's the end of the passageway we discovered running from the shop. Leads down to the river.'

Collette stared at her wide eyed. 'I swear, it would give me the total creeps thinking about that.' She shuddered and swiped again.

'Oh, I love Mac! Doesn't he look in control of everything from that angle?'

'He's in control of everything from any angle,' corrected Mal, and Collette laughed.

'He is that.'

Handing the phone back, the two women arranged the best time to meet up. If the shoes really could be sold online, she may have found an income source to see her through her first winter. The shop owner had warned her that the winter trade would barely keep her in salt. She had savings and a decent pension but that was it. She no longer had the high-earning income she had been used to and could no longer spend with impunity. She smiled thinking of the Paul Simon song, maybe the soles of her shoes were lined with diamonds after all.

Over the next hour, Mal made a fresh brew for the builders and was pleased to see the new floor going down where the old void had been. Soon the shelves would go up, just in time for her deliveries of new stock. According to Jenkins, they would be almost done by the end of the week. Right back on target. SOCO were beavering away in the tunnel, but so far they had found nothing of note; it was too much to hope for a murder weapon, but you could never tell.

Chapter Thirteen

She was about to head upstairs when there was another knock at the door. Mal opened it to see a woman dressed in black, leaning on the arm of a tall younger man. Looking at their faces, she would guess mother and son. It was hard to age the woman. Younger than Mal, but despite all her make-up, there was something about her that seemed worn out. She was tall, almost her son's height, and slim to the point of skinny, the flesh pulled tightly across her cheekbones. She was burning from the inside out and her sharp eyes flicked over Mal's shoulders, taking in the scene. The man was easier to predict, his eyes were also constantly on the move, alert to everything as he guarded his mother. She had only opened the door but Mal was already exhausted simply being in their presence.

She would guess he was in his mid-twenties and Mal presumed this was Ruth and Piran Jago. Sophie had said they were heavily involved with the church and indeed, a heavy gold cross hung around Ruth's neck. Piran wore no such paraphernalia but his devotion to his mother was crystal clear.

'Are you the owner?' Piran's voice was quieter and more respectful than Mal would have supposed and she nodded.

'I'm Piran Jago and this is my mother, Ruth. Would it be possible to see where my father was found?'

Ruth sobbed beside him and Mal could see that his own eyes were bright as he gave his mother a quick hug.

Mal had already stepped aside to let them in and the workers had fallen silent. Now Dennis walked over.

'Hello, Ruth love. Come with me.'

Taking over from Mal, he guided the pair of them to the back of the shop. As he did, the other builders left altogether. As Sean passed Mal, he stopped and whispered to her.

'We'll be back, just going to give her some privacy. Nice if the police could sod off as well.'

Mal rolled her eyes at that, fat chance they would be so sensitive. They had been popping in and out of the village asking questions and offending all and sundry.

She looked across at the small group, as Ruth placed her hand on the rough wall. Dennis then pointed to the hidden passageway the forensics team were currently searching for clues.

Piran's body was as stiff as a board, his fists clenched by his side. Mal remembered he had only been fifteen when his father had disappeared and her heart went out to the pair of them. So many years they wondered if he was dead. Whether he had done a runner. Now they could see the cowardly way in which their husband and father had been murdered and hidden.

She wanted to keep her distance but Dennis called her over, looking deeply uncomfortable.

'Mrs Peck. Mrs Jago wants to know if she can leave flowers here on the spot.'

It was a bad idea and both she and Dennis knew it. Unsurprisingly, Dennis had passed the buck as neither mother nor son saw a problem.

Mal took a deep breath and silently cursed her builder. He knew these people, knew the right way to say no. What was she but some posh incomer?

'Mrs Jago, I am so deeply sorry for your loss, but I'm going to say no.'

For a second, she was startled by the depth of hatred in Piran's eyes.

'Some bastard left him here to rot and you won't even let us leave some flowers?'

Dennis spoke quickly, trying to calm the distressed younger man. 'Let her say her piece before you reply. Alright, lad?'

Mal ignored Piran and continued talking to his mother. 'The police reckon he was moved to this spot. This wasn't where he was taken up to God. If you leave a flower here, you will give this place a power it doesn't deserve.'

Ruth nodded and looked at Mal. 'But he was here for so many years. All alone.'

'Only his body. All this time he has been in your heart and in heaven.' The words felt uncomfortable in Mal's mouth but Ruth made the sign of the cross, as did her son, and Mal wondered if she was actually helping.

'Making a shrine to your husband in a shop won't help you.'

'Won't be good for business either, will it?' jeered Piran.

'No, it won't,' agreed Mal, trying not to snap at the emotional young man. 'But right now, I'm trying to help your mother. Soon you'll have a gravestone that you can visit.'

Ruth sobbed harder at this and Mal wondered what she could say to help this woman. Dennis cleared his throat.

'Tell you what, Ruth, leave the flowers there and when me and the boys cover the wall up, we'll leave the flowers behind it. Is that okay with you, Mrs Peck?'

It wasn't, really. Mal thought it sounded a macabre gesture and still gave Ruth a focal point to grieve at, but she supposed she would always have that anyway. With or without the flowers. If the gesture brought her some comfort, then it made sense, despite Mal's misgivings.

'Of course that's okay. I'll leave you alone now.'

Mal retreated to the counter and watched surreptitiously as the three of them prayed in front of the wall and laid their flowers down. Piran helped his mother up off her knees, then they headed back to the front door. As they passed, he turned to her.

'Sorry about just now. That was unfair of me.'

Mal nodded and accepted his apology. Of course he was upset, but she had seen that flare of temper and bet he made for a nasty drunk.

The door closed and Dennis expelled a great sigh.

'That was an ugly business. I remember Piran was a handful when Roger first disappeared, we all thought he'd completely lose it, but the Trebethericks helped sort him out and the village all pitched in, and like Ruth, he found God. This is bound to bring up bad memories.'

'Course it is,' said Mal. 'What lad wouldn't be boiling with anger, seeing how his father had been discarded?'

'Right enough. Now, these flowers, do you want me to get rid of them when I put up the plasterboard?'

Mal looked at him in surprise.

'She won't know,' he continued, his fingers playing with a measuring tape.

'No, leave them be. It's what we agreed, plus it will be nice for me as well to think of flowers rather than bones.'

Although Mal imagined that in a week's time they would have wilted and she'd be thinking of old bones *and* rotting blooms. Dennis, however, seemed relieved, and she realised he had only made the suggestion to placate her for overriding her in the first place. The door opened as the builders came back in, quiet and subdued, and as they saw the flowers by the wall their tones grew even more hushed.

Chapter Fourteen

The meeting was reaching an end and still the Golden case hadn't been brought up. Sophie could have been back at her own desk catching up on paperwork but at least the coffee was better in CID. The team were getting closer to flushing out a drugs line and it would be a significant development when they finally stamped out the suppliers. The dealers were bad enough, but the up-country suppliers and hardcore crime syndicates were the root of the problem. Her job would be so much easier if the pathetic bastards addicted to the stuff got clean. It would make their lives easier too if they weren't addicted. Hell, it would make everyone's life better. And yet everyone focused on the pathetic crackheads and junkies as they sprawled across the streets. The suppliers were the issue – the businessmen making millions in this trade. Fingers crossed, the team in this room were about to sever another trade line.

Still, she wasn't here for that; she was here for the murder of Roger Jago, and it seemed like the new inspector had already lost interest in what he had dismissed as an open-and-shut case.

'Alright, team. Any feedback from the Golden case? I'm ready to shelve it with the note that the most likely culprit was Paul Trebetherick, now also deceased. That is unless anyone else has news.'

Sophie shook her head in disgust. Cold cases never attracted the attention they should, and yet she knew that this was blowing up the village. For decades, the Trebethericks would have to live with the suspicion that their husband/dad was actually a murderer with no evidence and no proper investigation. She had once liked Connor and Billy's mum, but over the years Sharon had become sour and bitter. Quick to take offence, slow to forgive. She spent her days telling everyone that her Paul didn't commit suicide. Even her lads had got sick of it and left. What would she be like when she felt compelled to say he wasn't a murderer either?

'I've got the findings from the financial checks you asked me to run,' said an older detective from the other side of the room. 'Their partnership was in a lot of financial jeopardy. They had a considerable debt to a Jacques Peloffy.'

'Why's that name familiar?' asked Williams.

'He's the bloke who found the tunnel in the bookshop,' called out another detective. Sophie shifted in her seat.

'Okay,' drawled Hemingstone, slowly, 'that's interesting. What else do we know?'

'After Jago's disappearance, Trebetherick continued to struggle with debt, but the three boys helped him on the boats and slowly it looked like he was turning things around.'

'I thought he only had two sons,' said Hemingstone. 'Twins, wasn't it?'

'The other lad was Piran,' called out Donald, 'Roger Jago's boy. Paul Trebetherick took him under his wing when his father disappeared.'

'Guilty conscience?' suggested Hemingstone to Williams. Sophie bit her lip. It might be a guilty conscience, but it was hard to explain to someone who hadn't grown up in Golden how things worked. Of course Paul took Piran under his wing. It was just how things were.

'How big was their debt?'

'They'd have had to sell the boat to clear it.'

Hemingstone shook his head in bafflement. 'Well, why didn't they do that then?'

My God, thought Sophie, the idea was so alien. She'd have to raise her voice, although God knows she didn't want to draw attention to herself.

'And what would they be then, sir? They'd have to go and work on someone else's boat. If they could even find a space.'

'I don't see the big deal?'

Everyone was now staring at Sophie who sat in her uncomfortable uniform looking like a square peg.

'Sir, the Jagos and Trebethericks have been fishermen all the way back. They don't sell their boats, they'd rather die.'

'Well, as you say, they didn't sell their boat and they are both dead. Maybe the debt and the guilt got too much for Paul Trebetherick and he killed himself?'

'Are we certain Trebetherick committed suicide?' asked Sophie hesitantly. She knew she was about to get shouted down, but it had never made sense. His life had been improving. Trebetherick had cleared his debts, his family were on the brink of moving into a new house, the children were doing well, it was a happy marriage by all accounts. His suicide made no sense. And the revelation of Roger Jago's body didn't change that – why take five years to be overcome with guilt?

'Bloody hell, woman,' shouted Hemingstone, 'why look for complications when there are none? This is obviously an open-and-shut case. Stop watching TV shows and start paying attention to the job of policing.'

Sophie wanted to die. She wasn't a confrontational copper, and getting shouted at in front of her senior colleagues was about as bad as it got.

'Sir, with respect.' All eyes turned to Donald. 'PC Taphouse has a point, the suicide makes no sense.'

'From what I've heard so far, nothing that fishermen do makes any sense.'

There was a general nodding of agreement. Everyone knew the fishing community were a law unto themselves.

'Right enough. Fishermen are tricky buggers, always unavailable or uncooperative. Always involved in fights.

Remember the fight over at Looe last year?' said Williams, snorting with derision.

Sophie jumped to her feet, past caring now. She had been utterly embarrassed, if she got kicked out of the room now, then so what?

'Of course they're unavailable! They're out at sea, risking their lives for your fish and chips. And yes, they fight, from time to time, but no more than anyone else on a Saturday night. And as for rivalry, within the village, a fleet pulls together. Those men rely on each other for everything.'

She knew she was flushed, her cheeks were burning with pinpricks, and she felt sick as everyone stared at her, but she didn't care. She knew the fishermen could come across to outsiders as surly and difficult, hell, half the time they *were* surly and difficult, but no one else here understood them and she needed to explain that.

'WPC from fishing village defends fishermen.' Hemingstone chortled. 'What a shocker.'

One of the other detectives cleared his throat. 'PC, sir, not WPC.'

Hemingstone looked at him and rolled his eyes. 'Of course, you don't mind though, do you, *PC* Taphouse?' He stressed the PC part this time. 'Not going to report me, are you?'

The room laughed, some jocular, some nervous. Sophie was glad to see not everyone was joining in.

Happily for her, she wasn't interested in advancement and didn't need to play along.

'Yes, sir. I do mind.'

The laughter petered away.

Sophie sat down as though nothing had happened, and everyone waited to see what the new inspector would do next. The silence became uncomfortable and Sophie had to clench her fists to stop herself from grinning a challenge at the man. This was better than bursting into tears.

'Right. Yes, well then. My apologies, PC Taphouse.'

Despite the sarcasm dripping from his words, there was an instant lessening of tension in the room. Sophie knew she didn't really have any friends in this room, excepting Donald, but they all knew what was right. But they also knew who they had to work with. Thankfully, the new guy had blinked first.

'Williams, could you run further background checks into this Frenchie? See when the loan was paid off. But if you ask me, he found the passageway, and I think maybe there's more to him than meets the eye, after all. Maybe Trebetherick is our killer, but maybe he killed himself for another reason. Let's find out.'

Sophie groaned. All she had done was wind up the DI and now he was going to prove a point in order to spite her.

'Right, if that's it?'

Williams cleared his throat again. 'There is one more thing. You asked me to investigate the woman in the bookshop who found the body?'

His smile was so smug that Sophie's heart sank. Whatever was coming was going to be bad news for Mal.

'We should have been calling her Prisoner Peck: our stuck-up clever clogs is a criminal. She's only been out of prison a month.'

Chapter Fifteen

Over in Golden, Mal was still downstairs signing for deliveries. The shop was awash with workmen and every time Mal blinked, it seemed like another piece had been finished. Tonight the floor would be sanded and varnished, then tomorrow the bookshelves would go in along the new wall. The paper had been removed from the windows and whilst the occasional person looked in, the returned glare of various trades was too much for the average rubbernecker. To complicate matters, she still had a team of crime scene officers working down in the passageway. Fingers crossed they would only be an hour more as promised.

The encounter with the Jagos had been difficult but now it seemed she wasn't done with grieving women. Coming down the street was another woman in black. This one was flanked by two young men, all three carrying wreaths, hers spelled out Roger. Mal rolled her eyes, who in their right mind would grandstand a widow? Slipping off her stool, she quickly opened the shop door and met the trio in the street.

The woman was dressed head to toe in black. A calf-length jersey dress stretched across her frame, and she was pulling the jacket across herself but failing to fasten it. Stout rather than fat but there was nothing jolly about this one. A shiny black handbag matched her patent shoes and Mal wondered if this was the obligatory mourning outfit.

Her two sons towered over her, both sporting black ties tucked into jeans.

'Are you the one that found our Roger's body?' demanded the woman, in a voice that struck Mal as unnecessarily belligerent. 'You know it had nothing to do with my Paul,' she continued as if Mal had somehow suggested it had.

'I'm sorry, I've only just arrived in the village.'

Mal was trying to remember the names that Sophie had told her and surmised that this had to be Sharon Trebetherick and her two sons, Billy and Connor.

'This has been a terrible shock for me. We were all devastated when Roger disappeared. No one was more heartbroken.'

Mal suspected his own wife and child probably were, but she wasn't about to comment, this woman was spoiling for a fight.

'It's all very sad.'

'And now people are saying that my Paul, God rest his soul, killed Roger, then couldn't live with the guilt. Well, where's the sense in that, eh? Five years later?' She glared at Mal as she swapped her bag from one arm to the other.

'My poor boys couldn't live with it. This village and its nasty gossip.'

Mal was confused. 'People were saying back then that he committed suicide because he killed his partner?'

'No, of course not,' replied one of the lads, taking a step forward. 'But you try living in this village when everyone is whispering about you and speculating behind your back.'

Well, Mal had some sympathy with that statement, and she was a stranger. What must it have been like at twenty to lose your father in such a tragic way, then have to cope with all the gossip from people you had grown up with?

'And why would he kill himself?' demanded Sharon again.

Now she stopped to cry, and her boys stepped closer towards her as she cried noisily into an embroidered handkerchief.

Mal knew she should appreciate the show that was being put on for her, but she found herself wondering who on earth still had embroidered hankies?

'Afternoon, Sharon.'

Mal was relieved that Dennis had come outside to join her. 'Come to lay flowers? Connor, Billy, nice to see you back in the village. Staying long?'

The taller boy stepped forward. It was clear they were twins, not identical but near as damn it. This lad was clearly one for the gym as he was well built and broader across the chest than his brother. That said, his brother was no slouch, and Mal reckoned they both played rugby at school if they didn't still. The lad nodded at Dennis, then cleared his throat.

'We've come to show our respect. And also to show everyone that Dad had no part in this.'

'Course he didn't, Connor. Come on, let's put those flowers down here.'

The boys laid the wreaths alongside the growing pile of flowers. Mal tried to remain sympathetic, but knew she was soon going to have to deal with a pile of rotting flowers. Overnight, candles had also started to appear. She was doing her utmost to keep this opinion to herself.

'I'll put Roger's name at the front,' said Sharon, there was no question in her voice. Mal shook her head in disgust, some people could make everything about them. This wasn't even *her* husband but the husband of a woman she apparently disliked.

'Nothing from Ruth, I see?'

That was too much bait for Mal, and she bit. 'Mrs Jago laid her flowers inside, where they found his body.'

Sharon instantly stiffened. She straightened up and looked down at Mal.

'Well,' she said, puffing herself up importantly, 'that's where this wreath should be.'

Good grief, thought Mal. This woman was appalling, did she think she was going to upstage the actual widow?

'I'm afraid, I can't have that.'

'And what the hell has it got to do with you? You have no idea how we grieved. My boys suffered. And you will not stop me from showing my proper respect for poor Roger.'

Sophie had warned her not to get in the way of an angry fishwife. Metaphorically, she rolled her shoulders.

This woman was in for a shock if she thought she could dismiss Mal so easily.

'Out here will do fine. Everyone can see your lovely big wreath. Indoors, no one will see it. Unless that's what you want? Something private? Only, it will get in the builders' way and then when the shelves go in, I'll have to remove it altogether.'

Sharon's eyes narrowed and her lips puckered in fury. Mal noticed the clumps of mascara, and wondered unkindly if the woman had put so much on so that when she cried it would run and make her look wretched.

Knowing she was beaten, the grieving woman paused and gave a little sob.

'Well, we can't have it getting in your way. Boys, place it there, where hopefully it meets your approval?' she said archly, sneering at Mal.

'Of course. And everyone will be able to see it out here.' Mal smiled back at her.

'Well, that's good, ladies.' Dennis now attempted to defuse the tension. 'Mal, I wonder if you can come inside? I have a question about the renovations.'

Leaving the trio outside, Mal watched as Sharon read out some cards to her sons. Mal wondered if they were taking notes. Some of those comments had been barbed: 'Now the truth will come out' 'Finally, rest in peace.' For a woman whose husband committed suicide, and that suicide was now being touted as evidence that he was actually a murderer, it must rake up awful memories.

Despite that, Mal was finding it hard to summon up any sympathies for the boorish woman. She dismissed them and turned back to Dennis.

'Okay. What did you need?'

Dennis looked rueful. 'Nothing. Just thought you could do with getting out of there. Sharon has always been tricky. Nothing good can come of spending time in her presence.'

Mal nodded in agreement, then bit her lip. She had met a woman at a moment of extreme stress and Mal was judging her through her own bias. In business, she had prided herself in being able to quickly sum up people and situations; she was in a new environment here, but she still felt she had misstepped. Thinking of Sharon, she now homed in on the fact that she had kept swapping her bag from arm to arm, pulling her jacket across her chest, constantly glancing up at her boys. The woman was unpleasant, but she was also an insecure wreck. Excusing herself, Mal headed back onto the street.

'Mrs Trebetherick.'

The three of them turned to look at Mal. Connor had been crouched down reading the notes on the flowers to his mother, now he got up and came to stand beside her. A united front.

'I'd like to apologise. If you say your husband didn't commit suicide, then I'm sorry you have had to live with that verdict for all those years. And I'm also sorry that with the revelation of Mr Jago's body, that suspicion has been cast on your husband and your sons' father.'

For a second Sharon watched her, waiting for the punchline, but when she decided Mal was sincere, she sniffed and patted her hair.

'Well, thank you for that. What are you going to do when all these die?' She waved somewhat dismissively at the bouquets.

Mal sighed and shrugged her shoulders. 'No idea. I thought I would remove all the notes and give them to Mrs Jago. Then find someone to compost the flowers.'

'I'll do that for you,' said the slightly shorter of the two boys. 'Roger was like an uncle to us. I'd be happy to help out.'

The other boy nodded, eager to help.

'You could also have a book of condolences in the shop. We had one for Dad and it was a huge comfort.'

'At the beginning,' said his brother, darkly.

'I was just thinking it might help this lady. All she's trying to do is reopen her shop. What do you think, Mum?'

'Ruth's already running a book up at the church. She doesn't care about anyone else's business.'

'Look.' Sharon opened her bag and pulled out a rolled-up set of A4 documents. Both boys groaned and Connor tried to snatch it out of his mother's hands. She slapped him and he winced like a little kid, not a strapping rugby player in his mid to late twenties.

'Mum, we've talked about this,' said Connor, his tone pleading. Billy's face was stony as he glared up at the sky.

'For God's sake, Mum. How many times?'

Sharon scoffed at her sons and waved the documents at Mal. 'This is my Paul's coroner report. I know it says he committed suicide, but he didn't. You read it and see what you think.'

Mal stared at Sharon's outstretched hand in horror. This was dreadful, why would she want to read a post-mortem? What was this woman thinking?

'For God's sake, Mum, you're embarrassing yourself.' He turned to Mal and appealed to her in anguish. 'Ignore her, please, she gets like this.'

'Don't talk about me like I'm not here. I'm not some foolish old nanny, sucking my gums. I brought you two up and I've run my business ever since your dad was taken from us. When you two both left as well, I managed perfectly fine.'

'Mum, let it go!'

Sharon turned to Mal again. She was breathing heavily now and her eyes were red with more tears threatening. Mal immediately felt the awkwardness of any English person faced with a public display of genuine emotion. And yet also a sudden empathy with this unpleasant widow being dismissed as a silly old woman. One that needed to be guided and checked by her sons. There was so little dignity as you got older. How mortifying it must be to watch the children who used to look up to you for everything, gradually change their gaze and look down on you with disdain or downright irritation.

She took the papers from Sharon's hand. 'I doubt I'll understand this, but I will read it.'

The woman's relief was palpable, and she snapped her bag closed with a shaky hand. Thanking Mal, she turned away and headed back up the lane, her sons following behind.

Mal was about to head back into the shop when Billy ran back to speak to her.

'Sorry about Mum. This has all been a bit of a shock. Brought it all back up again. Plus, she and Ruth never got on. Dad and Roger were thick as thieves, but not their wives.'

Mal cricked her neck. He had taken a step too close to her, and she felt uncomfortable as he loomed over her.

'Look, give me that post-mortem report, I'll put it in the bin for you.'

Mal dropped her hand down to her side. It was all she could do not to hide it behind her back, but she did move back a step.

'That's okay. Your mother asked me to read it and I will.'

Billy's smile dropped, and she was reminded again of how big he was. And angry.

'I'm sick and tired of Mum doing this. This is my dad,' he snapped at Mal. 'And she won't let it alone. None of us can get on with our lives when she keeps peddling it around to anyone that will read it. I bet nearly every person in the village has a copy of the bloody report. She's a bloody laughing stock.'

Mal didn't have any experience of angry young men and was at a loss how to defuse the situation. He had a point. This was his father; where was the privacy, the closure? No wonder he and his brother had left. His mother's daily refusal to accept the verdict of suicide must have been so painful to two young men barely out of their teens. But the aggression radiating off him made her pause.

Why was he so certain his father had committed suicide? Why did he want to quash his mother's hopes.

'I told your mother I would read it and I will.'

He took a step back and Mal let out an enormous sigh of relief; she hadn't realised she had been holding her breath. Contrite, he took a second step back.

'Sorry. I just get wound up about it.' He ran his fingers through his hair and grimaced. 'Look, read it, bin it, I don't care.' And with that he strode away in the opposite direction from his family and headed down to the harbour front.

Mal watched thoughtfully as he walked away – there were a lot of angry young men in this village, and a lot of old secrets.

Chapter Sixteen

Mal headed back into the shop and looked at the chaos. She trusted Dennis that it was all on course, but at the moment Mal couldn't see this being fixed before half-term. Especially as the builders had had to contend with a body *and* a hidden passageway. She wanted them all out. She didn't want to deal with anyone else's grief, and she was desperate for this to be over.

'When will you cover the wall?' asked Mal.

'Soon as the police are done in the passageway.'

Gary, Mal and Dennis had agreed that the passageway would be blocked off in the shop, but a new doorway into it would be opened up in the storeroom. That way, Mal had a second fire escape in case of an emergency. It would also be locked from the inside.

Mal looked at her watch. Time for lunch. Her parcels had been delivered, postie was late, but she'd come down and collect her mail later, for now she wanted to head upstairs. Sharon's misery and Ruth's grief yesterday, had taken something out of Mal. Their emotions made the body real, in a way that his bones never had. Maybe his son standing there yesterday in flesh and blood had made the man come to life. Today the shop was full of people and she needed to escape. Whatever it was, she was exhausted and needed to rest, away from all these interactions.

A rustle from the plastic sheeting that hung across the passageway informed her she wasn't done yet. The forensics team headed out into the body of the bookshop. The lead forensics examiner looked around at the workmen and spotted Mal, who had been on her way to the back room.

'Mrs Peck,' she said, in a bright and friendly tone. 'You'll be pleased to know that we are done. The inspector's on his way but I can tell you we found nothing to warrant further investigation. We've removed the padlock from the bottom gate to test for fingerprints so you might want to replace it. That lower door still works.'

Mal scowled to herself, more cost.

'No need for alarm,' said the woman, quickly, 'I doubt anyone can even get into the culvert, this would be for your own peace of mind.'

'I don't suppose you'll supply me with a replacement lock, will you?'

A loud voice boomed out behind her, making her jump. Feeling foolish, she turned to see the inspector and another detective had already arrived and not even bothered to knock.

'I'm sure you know someone with a line in locks, Lady Peck. Oh no, it's not Lady Peck, is it? It's Mrs Peck. Isn't that right, dear?'

Mal didn't like his reference to locks and knew she should bite her lip but honestly, his patronising tone was making her teeth itch. She was going to speak, then thought better of it.

'Oh dear, cat got your tongue? There's no point in trying to hide things from me.'

'The boss is too quick for you,' commented the inspector's sidekick, and Mal gave him a withering look.

'I wasn't trying to conceal anything. I simply don't like being called Mrs Peck.'

'You see that's the problem with the criminal type,' said DI Hemingstone to his partner, completely ignoring Mal. 'They can't stop lying.'

Mal's heart was hammering in her chest making her feel sick. She could weather this out but there were so many people looking at her. If she could only get upstairs.

'Now, hang on,' said Sean.

Oh no, thought Mal, *please don't make this worse.*

'Just because Mrs,' Sean paused, then started again. 'Just because the lady gave you a fake title, doesn't make her a criminal.'

'No, but five years detained at Her Majesty's pleasure does.'

The effect was immediate. Sean stared at Mal, his mouth open. Hemingstone and his sidekick smirked at her and the forensics team recoiled at the gross unprofessionalism.

Mal looked around the room. Her secret was out but oddly, now the worst had happened, she found she was all right. She wasn't happy, far from it, but she hadn't collapsed either, and as far as it went, she was going to count that as a win.

An unfamiliar voice broke the silence and Mal stared horrified at the postman, who had a bundle of letters and a small parcel in his hands for her.

'Sorry. The door was open, and I need you to sign for this.'

Despite his words, he wasn't remotely apologetic. His eyes were out on stalks as he took in the white forensic suits and the two detectives. Clearly he had heard every word, and whilst Mal had thought the builders might have kept her secret, she knew it was a forlorn hope that the postman would – he was practically texting.

As Mal signed for the parcel, he left, apologising again, no doubt in a hurry to share the latest revelation from the bookshop.

'Are we done here?' snapped Mal. 'Or would you like to arrest me for a murder that happened years before I ever arrived? I imagine that's about the level of your competency.'

Hemingstone's eyes narrowed and he flushed slightly. Remarkably, Williams took a step forward, and Mal snorted.

'What! Going to beat a confession out of me? I think you'll find they frown on that these days.'

Dennis had finally recovered from the shock and took a step closer towards Mal. 'No one's laying a finger on you, Mal. The boys and I will see to that.'

Hemingstone looked around the room and chuckled nervously. All the builders suddenly appeared to be holding crow bars and hammers.

'No need for the dramatics. We're not here for this little jailbird, we're already investigating other lines of enquiry. We're turning up all sorts of things. It seems you can't trust anyone these days.'

He turned and barked at the forensics team, telling them to run the lock for fingerprints, then swept out of the shop leaving an awkward silence.

'Would you like a cup of tea?' asked Sean kindly, and Mal was shocked by the tears that prickled her eyes. Shaking her head, she turned and headed upstairs in silence as the work in the room picked up again.

Mal floated in the sea. She looked at the blue sky above her, then closing her eyes, enjoyed the warmth of the sun on her lids. As soon as she had headed upstairs, she knew she needed to get out. Grabbing a towelling wrap and swim gear, she headed back out of the shop. The forensics team had gone, and the builders had all just smiled at her and told her she was braver than them for swimming. One of the guys had proudly proclaimed that two weeks a year in Tenerife was enough for him and the laughter continued as she left the shop. In an unwritten agreement, no one mentioned the inspector's revelation.

Now as she bobbed in the water, out of breath from her need to plough up and down, she smiled. Swimming was a perfect way to switch off, expel her energy and get into a blank zone. After a tense day in the office or a tricky merger she would go to her private club and swim until, exhausted, she had dispelled all her nerves and anxieties.

Sea swimming was proving a different beast though. Her fitness levels had fallen away and even a hundred metres drained her. The water was colder than she was used to, although five years of cold showers had helped. It was also more of a medium. In a pool it was simply water, here it moved of its own accord, and she rose and fell as the water gently surged back and forth. In one sense, swimming was easier because of the greater buoyancy the salt provided, but the undulation was throwing her rhythm.

She also had to be more alert to her environment. Not only did it move, but she also had to be aware of everything around her, rocks below her, seaweed, jellyfish. Above, a tern hung in the air, then flew away. Everywhere there was life and movement and she was a part of it. In the swimming pool she had been the essential element, the reason for the pool's existence. A pool was only there for its swimmers; here, her presence was utterly irrelevant. If she were to sink and drown, the waves and the weeds would carry on, regardless.

Turning back towards the harbour wall, she opted for the gentler breaststroke and sculled back towards civilisation. She'd hoped she might have had a chance for a fresh start here. Whatever Jacques said, she wanted to leave her time in jail behind her. Even if she would always carry it with her, she would rather it not be an item for public gossip.

As she headed back to the shop, she was certain everyone was looking at her. An older lady wandering through the harbour in a dressing gown, she probably was worthy of a second glance. Hopefully, that was all it was.

As she made her way off the harbour front and down her little lane, she saw that Dennis and Sean were up ladders at the front of the shop.

'Hello,' called out Dennis. 'The new shop name arrived, so we thought we'd put it up for you.' He climbed down his ladder. 'What do you think?'

The three of them stepped to the other side of the lane and looked up at the sign.

Mal's face lit up. The golden handwritten lettering across the red wooden boards was amazing, and framed the top of the shop window. Hanging from a swinging frame was a woodpecker in flight.

'I love it! Isn't it wonderful?'

Both men smiled at her and nodded in agreement.

'That's a fine bit of artistry there. What's with the name? Yaffle Books?'

Mal chuckled. 'It's a bit of a nickname. My name's Malachite Peck. At school, the other children – or maybe it was a teacher – noticed that my name could also be Green Woodpecker. And Yaffle grew from that.'

'I hadn't spotted that Malachite Peck is also Green Woodpecker,' said Dennis, with a grin. 'It's good, I like it.'

Sean continued to stare at the sign, then turned back to them. 'I don't get the Yaffle bit?'

'Professor Yaffle. From *Bagpuss*?' said Dennis, as Sean shook his head.

Mal looked at Sean bewildered. 'Have you never seen *Bagpuss*?' The idea was astonishing, and she felt ancient. How could there be adults who didn't know of Emily and her saggy old, baggy old, cloth cat?

A car drove past, and they all flattened themselves against the wall as it passed.

'They've all gone now, you know,' said Dennis, softly. 'It's just me and the boys in there now.'

Sean stepped forward and handed her a key. 'Here. I got a replacement padlock for you.' Mal looked at it and stared up at Sean. The young man studied his feet. 'Just thought I'd save you a job.'

'Yes,' said Dennis, 'and it so happens that one of my other jobs has hit a snag, so I'm pulling all the boys off that to come and work here tomorrow. We're going to make sure that by the end of the week your shop is going to be completely finished, looking wonderful and we'll get out of your hair.'

Mal felt sick and found her voice was shaking. She took a deep breath and tried to stand as tall as her five feet would allow her.

'I'm sorry if working for a criminal is embarrassing for you. I will keep out of your way until you are done.'

Both men recoiled and shook their heads violently.

'Oh, maid. I don't care about that,' said Dennis in a hurry. 'I just thought you could do with a break. You move into a village, keep your head down, try to do something nice then you find a body, then that policeman tells everyone your secrets.'

'I mean, that was bang out of order,' said Sean.

'Exactly,' agreed Dennis, 'so I thought we'd get this done for you as quickly as possible and give you back your privacy.'

Mal bowed her head and wiped her hands against her towelling dressing gown. Her face hurt from the effort of not crying in public and she patted her sides again. With her head still bent, she took another deep breath to steady her voice.

'Yes, well, thank you.' As her voice cracked, she smoothed the skirts of the robe again, and without another word, fled across the street and into the shop.

She was making a cup of tea to steady her nerves when there was a knock at the door. She didn't want to answer it, uncertain if she could handle any more kindness from strangers. In the end, she took a deep breath and checked her face in the mirror. Her make-up thankfully hadn't run, and she headed across and opened it to see Dennis standing in the hallway.

'Afternoon, Professor.'

'I'm not a professor,' said Mal, puzzled.

Dennis grinned. 'No, but you don't like Miss or Mrs and Mal feels too informal. So, what with Yaffle, I thought Professor was a good call. My kids used to love Bagpuss. Plus, all the books and how clever you are and all.' He paused and cocked his head. 'Unless you'd prefer Lady Peck?'

'Well okay.' Mal gave a short laugh, then cleared her throat. 'How can I help, Mr Jenkins?'

'Just to say we're going to varnish the floor now, so if you want to nip out for anything, do so now. Should be dry in the morning. And please, my friends call me Dennis.'

Chapter Seventeen

She walked back into the shop, laden down with doughnuts for the builders and a cup of hot chocolate for herself. Handing out the goodies, she headed upstairs and settled in for the evening after a long and draining day.

Sipping on her deliciously sweet hot chocolate, she opened the post-mortem that Sharon Trebetherick had handed her earlier and read through it in bafflement. How did that woman expect any layperson to make head nor tail of it? Mal needed an expert, and she knew just the person. In prison, Mal had met as broad a cross section of society as you might expect to find. The women were mostly younger than her, there were a few lifers and also some professionals. Veronica Wells was a pathologist who'd killed a cyclist whilst driving way over the limit. She had then tried to hide the body. A drunken murderer leaves a trail of evidence and in the sober light of day, she panicked and tried to flee the country. It didn't take long for the jury to find her guilty. Now she was inside, spending her time regretting every glass.

Mal picked up her pen.

Dear Veronica,

I wonder if you could help me with something. Please find enclosed a post-mortem report. I was given this by the deceased's wife and she asked me to see if there was anything untoward in the findings. I don't know if this will get through the censor, but I hope it does as it would be a kindness. Thank you for taking the time to have a look and I hope to hear from you soon. I will write you a second letter in case this one is stopped.

Yours

Mal

Having placed the report and letter in an A4 envelope she wondered how much it was going to cost to post. Since she had been inside, the cost of postage appeared to have outstripped inflation by an eye-watering amount. No wonder everyone texted.

Nonetheless, she would stick to letter writing. She finished the second letter to Veronica, minus the report, and flicked on the kettle. Pulling another sheet of writing paper towards her, she wrote a letter to all the women..

Dear Ladies,

Greetings from Golden. I said I would write, my address is at the top, and if any of you want to reply individually I will write to them privately. Stamps, I have discovered are now astronomically expensive. They went up again last month and I bet Nancy is now doing a roaring trade in them. Soon they'll be more expensive than cigarettes. Yes, Nancy, I can hear you laughing and shaking your head from here.

So, where is here? I ended up in this little fishing village and I am struggling once more to try and blend in. Ronny, do you remember how desperate I was at the beginning not to look at anyone, let alone speak? Well, I'm the same all over again here. And they are so inquisitive, just in a more subtle way. As Nikki said 'every effing scrote will want to know yer businesses' and, Nikki my dear, you were spot on. The lady in the post office is particularly nosey. Every time I go to buy stamps, she's at me with the questions. However, she's not a match for old Parky Nose Two-toes. (Hello, Warden, if you are reading this. I hope you are well and your begonias have managed to avoid this season's blight.)

I have had my hair done and I can't tell you what a delight it was. I had considered having it cut and dyed again so that I would look like my old self, but I have decided to own my grey. I hope, Gloria, you are proud of me: I have avoided the conformity of the patriarchy. Also I have a lovely new conditioner for my hair: Collette, the hairdresser, gave me a free sample. You ladies would love Collette, she didn't ask me a single question about myself. She's self-made, it's her own business, and she cuts hair for free for anyone who's homeless or short of a few bob.

Honestly, being a fisherman is an extremely tough job. These men, and it is all men, sorry, Gloria, fish because their fathers and grandfathers did, but it's hard and dangerous and when the storms blow they don't make much in the way of money. They are all self-employed so claiming benefits is an absolute headache. However, this community has lived like this for centuries and has a whole quiet network of systems in place to step in and help each other. Much like inside.

I suppose on reflection it makes sense for a closed community to need to know everyone's details, if only to help and support and also assess the threat levels the newcomer offers.

Anyway, that's me yaffling on again and I haven't told you the most curious aspect of my new life. Despite desperately trying to blend in and find my feet, "playing at being a little old biddy in a bookshop," thank you, Nikki, I have found myself at the centre of a storm.

During the renovations to the shop, the builders found a body hidden behind an old, partitioned wall! The body appears to be that of a fisherman who disappeared some fifteen years ago, and in the local vernacular "there's hell up".

I don't think I need to tell you ladies how distressing this all is. The police are here every day, and everyone keeps looking at me like I may be involved. It's beyond ridiculous. Most disappointingly, the detective in charge, who is an utter buffoon, has told everyone that I was in jail. He did it this afternoon in front of everyone, so I know by now it will race around the village. I must admit it has made me somewhat despondent; I can feel my head hanging and the idea of going outside fills me with dread. I don't mind admitting this to you as I know you will all understand that desire for a clean start.

I shall feel better tomorrow, simply writing to you all and picturing your faces has brought me a lot of comfort. I wonder, Jane, have you finished the blanket yet?

I am including a book that I just finished reading, I really enjoyed it and hope one or two of you do as well.

Mal

Mal put her pen down and winced at the thickness of the book. She would need to choose skinnier titles if she were going to make a habit of sending stories through the post, but the prison library was so small and so rarely restocked that a new book would be well received.

The radio had now switched over to the evening play and tonight it was about a housewife finding love in the hills of Dakota, Mal switched over to Classic FM to discover jazz. Frowning she flicked to Radio 3 and was pleased to discover a Brahms concerto she didn't recognise. She wondered, had her sister packed her CDs? Then she wondered if she even had a CD player. Was she ever going to unpack? Sighing, she poured another cup of tea and closed the curtains now that the last scraps of daylight had left the sky. Sitting down, she picked up her bundle of letters and smiled as she recognised the various hands.

Spotting Jasmine's neat round letters she opened that one first to get it over and done with.

Dear Malachite,

I was so happy to read that my little gifts had such an impact on you. I'll keep an eye out for more. I know when you first went away we were all so horrified. What you did was so wrong and so scary. I couldn't sleep thinking that people may come after me…

Mal scrunched the paper up in her hand. How typical of Jasmine to think of herself, but then she had a point, Mal's actions had had far-reaching consequences that affected the family in ways she'd never contemplated.

Smoothing out the paper, she read to the end, then placed the letter to the bottom of the pile to reply to.

Her next letter was from her sister and launched straight into her concerns.

WTF!? Shall I come down? I can. In an instant. I know you'll say no, but I want to be there. At least phone me so I can hear your voice and hear that you are genuinely okay. It is so unfair that this should happen to you. Please, please, please call me.

Mal looked around the living room with its boxes all packed and taped up. Her brother and sister's handwriting scribbled all over each box with notes as to the contents. The box with 'Open First' had been full of high heels and face creams, and it had made Mal laugh to think how much she'd changed, but had made her sob when she thought how much care her sister had taken to try to help Mal settle in. There had also been chocolates and a bottle of champagne 'To share with someone special. (So go find them!)' and Mal had laughed. That was the very last thing on her mind.

She picked up her phone and dialled her sister, and heard her voice before the phone had even rung.

Sipping her tea, she listened as her sister chatted on through her tears, and when she was finally convinced that Mal was indeed okay, the two sisters hung up with Oppy promising to write in the next few days. Mal knew her sister was unhappy that the two widows were treating her as a source of contention, that she was being targeted by the police, but she was more alarmed that Mal was heading off down tunnels with a stranger. Her exact words were: '*Are you mad or stupid? What if he had tried to kill you?*'

Mal had groaned, hearing the panic rise in her sister's voice, and tried to point out that killing her made no sense if he was the murderer. Come to that, neither did uncovering the tunnel. She knew Oppy would have more to say on that point and hadn't been reassured, but Mal hoped that when she next wrote the police would have solved the murder and her life could settle down.

The next letter was from Henry, her brother.

Hello Sis,

Fancy finding a body! I've been listening to the news, but it hasn't made the nationals. Have they worked out what happened yet? They should ask you, with your problem-solving skills you'd have this nailed in seconds.

Anyway, cool stuff! I've included a sheet of first class stamps as you are still indulging in this letter writing fad. Give us a shout if you need anything else. Can't wait to see you, let us know when. Love from all of us. Barney has news but wants to tell you himself; he loves getting your letters and now that they have money in them, they are even more treasured! Be warned he might start writing daily!!!

Love,

Hen

Mal blessed Henry for the stamps, then opened Barney's letter, smiling at his scrawl She could just see where he had rubbed out the pencil lines on the envelope trying to keep his words from wandering across the sheet. Inside the message was short and sweet.

Dear Aunty Yaffle,

I scored a goal!!!!! It was brilliant and Jamie sulked and Mr Fletcher told him off for being a bad sportsman. Our team one and everyone cheered. Mummy made cake to selebrate. How are you? I hope you are well. Here is a picture of your cat.

Lots and lots of love,

Barney

Mal took the drawing of Mac and placed it on the chimney breast. When she was next in town, she'd pop into the charity shops and see if she could find a frame. She read the letter again and decided that Barney got his love of exclamation marks from his grandfather. Henry had always approached life with a surfeit of excitement.

Finally, she opened the letter she had been saving for last.

Dear Yaffle,

I can't believe you are finally back in the UK, Mum said you have settled in Cornwall? I hope you've found somewhere lovely. I should love to come and see you? I bet you are going to be ever so popular in summer.

Mal had decided right from the beginning that none of her younger correspondents were to know she had been in prison. They would be told eventually but not until they were grown-ups, and not until Mal herself had decided how to explain what she had done. She wanted the children to be adults before they judged her. Most especially Miranda.

Halls of Residence is very noisy, and messy. I feel like I've finally made it to boarding school, although there are no magic owls here and the midnight parties are explicit rather than illicit. Illicit is my word for the week, I like how it sounds, if a snake could speak it would say illicit a lot, very sibilant. I like sibilant too.

The letter carried on with Miranda's new life at university and how much fun she was having. So far, the letter focused on her social life rather than her studies and Mal wondered if students ever changed. Her own university days sounded remarkably similar. Mal read every word with a smile on her face, then as she got to the *Lots of Love*, she read it all over again. After the second reading, she gave the letter a small kiss and slid it carefully back in the envelope.

The little clock chimed, and Mal was surprised how the time had flown. Reading and writing the letters had entirely calmed her, and as she made her way to bed she realised that her secret being revealed wasn't good but it needn't paralyse her either. If the villagers didn't want her, she would go. And that was okay. This might take a few fresh starts but eventually she would settle down and start a new life. She had hoped she'd be able to do it here, even with the screeching seagulls, mad cats and bodies in the wall.

Now if the police could only quickly resolve Roger Jago's murder, things could move on. Mal looked out onto the dark skies. How easy would it be to track down a murderer from fifteen years ago? Paul Trebetherick seemed the perfect scapegoat and maybe he was the killer, but it all seemed a bit convenient. The ghostly flash of a gull passed overhead and Mal was resolved to ignore the situation. It wasn't her business, and she wasn't interested.

Chapter Eighteen

The drop in the temperature overnight had forced Mal to close her bedroom patio doors. This had unforeseen benefits. She wasn't woken by the gulls, which meant she had her first lie-in since arriving in Golden. Mal stretched under the cool cotton sheets and reached over for the new book she was getting into, when she saw just how much of a lie-in she'd had. Cursing, she creaked out of bed and headed downstairs to the bathroom and tried to get ready before the builders arrived. She would have to swim later.

Lipstick in place, hair brushed, she swept up her letters and headed downstairs. Mr Jenkins had told her the varnished floor would be dry by now and today the shelves would go in. All the banging and mess had ended, and from here on in the bookshop would begin to re-emerge. It wouldn't be soon, it might never happen, but maybe people might also forget what was found when her builders tore the wall down.

Mal didn't want to damage the varnish or her shoes, so she crouched down to touch the floor. Running her hand across the surface, she marvelled at the soft tactile feel of freshly sealed floorboards. The low morning sun shone out from a passing cloud and the entire shop floor gleamed in the sunlight.

In the pretty motes that floated across the shafts of light, Mal stared at the floor again and frowned. There was a mark on the floor over by the counter. She craned her head so the light shone across the floor and saw it was a footprint, and not only one. Her eyes followed the footprints as they walked to the desk, then back away from it. She looked down at her own feet and shuddered as she saw she was standing on top of the phantom prints. Moving onto the shop floor, Mal looked back at the footprints. There were no two ways about it. Someone had walked up the tunnel and into her shop. As she traced their route, Mal shuddered as she saw the marks stopped by the door up to her flat. What did they want?

The builders pulled up on the street and Mal rushed over to the front door and all but dragged Dennis in, showing him the footprints.

'Alright, maid,' said the builder, calmly, 'don't panic. It was probably one of my lads at the end of the shift, forgetting the floor had been varnished.'

Mal visibly sagged in relief.

'Sean, nip down the passageway and check your padlock is still in place.'

Mal laughed weakly. 'Oh God, I had completely forgotten that. This is all taking its toll on me. I tried to get a good night's sleep but then I fall apart.'

Dennis cleared his throat and looked uncomfortable. 'What that detective said yesterday about where you were before here? I want you to know that none of us cares. It's who you are that matters, not what you did.'

Mal was going to thank him when Sean returned from the passageway, his face pale. In his hands, he held out the padlock that had clearly been cut in half by a pair of bolt cutters.

Having called the police, Mal grabbed her letters and headed out of the shop. She and Dennis had spoken and, whilst he argued for her to stay, she was resolute. This had nothing to do with her. She was unnerved and wanted out of there. Her plans for a new beginning were falling apart. She knew she was only delaying the inevitable interview, but after the inspector had publicly outed her yesterday, Mal wanted nothing more than to smack him in the face. Knowing that police officers frowned on that sort of behaviour, she decided it was better to post her letters, then head out for a long walk. She had no idea why someone had broken in or what they were after. This was not her problem, and she would not lift a finger to help that buffoon sort it out. Maybe she should give up. Stay with her sister until this was all over.

Mal had packed a small plastic shopping bag and thought if she wandered along the coast path, she might find a new beach to swim from. The fine weather was holding and everyone was referring to it as an Indian summer. Looking at her supermarket bag, she vowed to continue unpacking. Surely her sister had included some of her sports holdalls. She couldn't keep wandering around advertising for supermarkets. God, it wasn't even

Waitrose. How she had fallen. She chuckled to herself. It was a weak laugh, but it was a start.

She was only halfway along the lane when she noticed Jacques walking towards her. The last time she'd seen him, she had been unfathomably rude as she all but ran away from him. How could she explain the surge of panic that had caught her out? She hadn't seen him since and hadn't found the opportunity to tell him how well the float worked.

Her smile was met with his frown. Maybe he hadn't forgiven her lack of manners?

'Is everything okay? Dennis looks concerned back there.'

Mal glanced over her shoulder to see that Dennis had watched her leave, and now raised an arm to Jacques. She didn't want to discuss the break-in with him. She had stepped out of the building and wanted to leave that nonsense behind her.

'Everything's fine. But I have to post these and then I'm off out for the day. Exploring.'

Jacques studied the sky. 'It's a good day for it.' She noticed that lots of locals looked about them when discussing the weather. It had struck her as superstitious at first until it dawned on her that they could simply examine the clouds and the environment around them and actually knew how the weather would develop. After decades of working in the City, passing from taxis to tower blocks, she'd simply become reliant on whatever her app told her.

He looked at her bundle of letters. 'The post office is in the wrong direction, though. If you like, I could drop those in the letterbox for you. Let you get off?'

She considered it, then remembered that the post-mortem report for Veronica would need to be weighed. She glanced at the large brown envelope. Could that be what the intruder was after?

Mal frowned and shook her head. 'Thanks, but I haven't worked out the postage for this one. I'll do it myself.'

Plus, she knew sending mail to a prison was going to cause speculation, and she'd rather Jacques not be a part of the gossip machine surrounding her. She knew it was coming. In a village this size it wasn't going to take long before word got out that they were harbouring a jailbird. Mal liked Jacques and wanted to get to know him better. She had spotted a kindred spirit as they explored the tunnel together but then she'd spoilt it by overreacting to a pair of muddy trousers.

However, now wasn't the time. She also didn't want him to view her as an ex-convict. Even if she was.

'Oh dear. This doesn't look good,' muttered Jacques, as two men walked towards them. In their suits, they stood out like a sore thumb and Mal's heart sank as she recognised the detective and his pet sidekick.

'I'll distract them and you make a run for it.'

The absurdity of his suggestion and the absolute accuracy of it made Mal stand still and burst into laughter. She had never run from her problems.

'Mrs Peck. What's so funny?' Hemingstone was already taking offence at her very presence. 'We were just on our way to your property.'

'And I was just on my way out.'

The detective looked at Jacques curiously and rather than drag him into the situation, Mal made a quick decision. Turning to Jacques, she shrugged her shoulders.

'It seems I will have to take you up on your offer after all. The big one needs stamps. I have a twenty.'

Waving her off, he told her to keep her money. 'I'll let you know what you owe me next time.'

Taking the small bundle of letters, he nodded at the other two men and left.

'Who's that then?' said the detective, somewhat belligerently. Although, by now, she thought DI Hemingstone said everything in a belligerent manner. An incompetent oaf, raised above his station and aware of it.

'A friend.' She turned and headed back to the shop. So much for a quick escape.

'Does he have a name? This friend of yours.'

Mal looked over her shoulder. Both men were watching Jacques as he turned the corner and walked out of sight.

'Yes, he has.' She walked towards the shop as the two men moved to catch up with her.

'What is his name?' Now there was no mistaking the belligerence.

'It's nothing to do with you.' Mal was aware her own tone was no more friendly than the inspector's.

'This is a murder investigation and I'll be the judge of what's important or not. Now, what's his name? Was that Jacques Peloffy?'

Mal paused, his accent had probably already given up his identity, but she wasn't about to help them. Plus, why did they care? He wasn't involved in this. She stared at the inspector, shrugged, then continued her walk back to the shop. Once inside, she headed straight for Dennis to let him know the police had arrived.

'If you want to be charged with obstructing justice, that's what I'll do,' called an angry voice from the other end of the shop. All the builders fell silent as Hemingstone continued shouting. 'I reckon your parole officer will have something to say about that. Now, who was that man you were talking to out on the street?'

Mal shrank inside. She had met her parole officer, a well-meaning ninny who spent half the time warning her not to take drugs. The woman had a script that bore no resemblance to the person sitting in front of her. Mal had wondered if all ex-offenders got the same speech, regardless of circumstances. She had also made it clear that Mal was not to step over any legal lines and, in fact, Mal realised that she should have probably informed her of her involvement in this investigation. Now the leading detective was haranguing her in her own property and threatening her with the loss of her liberty. Mal's breathing was fast and shallow. She was a fool. She had lost the right to be strong-willed and opinionated five years ago. When was she ever going to learn that?

'Do you mean Jacques Peloffy?' Sean, who had been working in the bay window, spoke quickly. 'The prof here has only just moved into the village. You can't expect her to remember everyone's names.'

There was a general chorus of agreement from the workmen in the room. Their expressions were sullen and Mal was aware of the tension. Detective Inspector Hemingstone might not be the smartest tool in the box, but even he could see that hounding an older lady was not going down well.

'Right enough. Williams, go after Monsieur Peloffy and ask him when we can drop by for a few words.' He said the word monsieur in a sneery accent.

He turned and sneered at the builders.

'I'm sure it was a complete coincidence that Monsieur Peloffy somehow found a passageway that all of you had missed, as well as my SOCO team. Then last night, someone apparently used the passageway that no one but you, him and the killer knew anything about. And in case everyone has forgotten, Jago once owed Peloffy a considerable debt.'

There was an uneasiness in the room as everyone considered the implication of the detective's words.

'I'm sure you all knew about that. A place like this, everyone knows everyone else's business. Maybe I should interview some of you?'

Dennis cleared his throat and walked towards the inspector.

'Now, look here. This is a small village and we all get along best by minding our own business. If something is known, we don't talk about it. And we don't care much for those that do.'

'Closing ranks?'

'Taking care of our own. None of us here know anything about Jacques' dealings with Paul and Roger. Malachite Peck knows the least of any of us.' He paused and continued to stare at the inspector. Mal was surprised by his tone. He had always come over as a quiet, respectful man. Never dangerous. 'Now, the lady had a break-in. I suggest you investigate that and leave chasing red herrings to the fishermen.'

Hemingstone blinked furiously, trying to think of a reply. In the silence, Williams returned.

'Couldn't find him, boss. If I were suspicious, I'd say he'd done a runner when he saw us.'

Mal bit down on a reply. She wasn't helping herself or Jacques by making smart retorts, but honestly, *done a runner*. These clowns thought they were on TV. Still, at least he had broken the tension.

Now the SOCO team walked into the shop, and again the workers were ordered to down tools and were sent outside. Mal wanted to protest, but she knew it had to be done. Deciding she'd had enough, she turned tail. The inspector and sidekick went off to talk to a few people, scowling at the builders as they did. She headed back upstairs and looked out of the window, unable to concentrate on a book or her letters.

An hour later, it had been established that someone had entered the culvert upstream. They then made their way down the river tunnel to the gate in her passageway, broke in, examined the shop counter, tried the locked door up to the first-floor flat. And then left again.

Mal had come back downstairs where the inspector was talking to the lead SOCO. As she entered the room, he turned to study her.

'So, he was looking for something. Mrs Peck, any ideas? You never seem short of an opinion.'

Mal glared at the detective. 'For the umpteenth time. This has nothing to do with me. I moved in here a fortnight ago. Maybe this was a village kid on a dare?'

'With a bolt cutter and size nine feet?' His sarcasm dripped onto the floorboards and he bobbed down to take some photos of the footprints. The SOCO team looked over and shrugged. They had already taken proper photos and measurements, but sometimes the detectives liked to interfere.

'Inspector,' said one of the SOCO officers, 'We're done here. We'll send you the full report. The builders can carry on if they want.' Apologising to Mal, they headed out of the building and Mal prayed this was the last time that she would ever see them.

Chapter Nineteen

The bell above the door rang and Mal looked over from the corner of the bookshelves where she had been filing some new stock. Dennis had been as good as his word and the team worked double time to finish her shop before the weekend. The police investigation, as far as she was concerned, had gone quiet, and now she was finally running her bookshop. There had been no more incursions, and she could finally sleep without nightmares.

Despite not really being ready, she had opened the doors and enjoyed welcoming customers into the shop. Some were clearly only there to have a nose, so she put them to work. She made sure they helped her move boxes around and bring the books from the storeroom out onto the shop floor for her to shelve later. It was a happy little buzz. Each morning so far there had been deliveries, boxes and boxes of new books. Some she had chosen because she knew they were great, others she picked on recommendations.

It was like entering Aladdin's cave and slowly but surely, her shelves were filling up nicely. Where there were gaps, she put in jars of seashells and pebbles. She'd tried some dead starfish she found, but woke to a shop smelling of rotting fish and had to spend the entire day with the front door open. Mac also tended to sleep on the empty shelves, to the delight of the customers, and she had to warn anyone with a dog to keep it on a tight lead. There were days she wished she could say the same about their children.

Now as she looked over, her heart sank. Piran Jago had walked in and was standing by the counter. Mal rose slowly from the floor and summoned a smile.

'Hello, Mr Jago. Can I help?'

The young man shook his head quickly. 'Piran please. Mr Jago is my dad, and I don't think I'll ever fill his shoes.'

The direct reference to his father, who had lain behind the wall for fifteen years, threw Mal and she wasn't sure how to respond.

'Can you help me?' He tipped his head and appeared anxious. She could see that, when he wasn't full of anger, he was actually quite a charming looking individual. Life had thrown him a very tough path.

'I would be happy to.' She meant it. If she could do anything to make this young man's life easier, she would.

He nodded to himself, then took a deep breath.

'Firstly, I would like you to accept my apology. My behaviour towards you when I was last in here was unforgiveable.'

'Totally under—'

He held his hand up. 'No, it wasn't. There are no circumstances where I should have lost my temper with a stranger. Especially one who also found herself in a dreadful situation.'

He had stopped smiling and looked so worried that Mal rushed in and told him not to be ridiculous. She could imagine Charlie, one of her more boisterous nephews, in the same situation and agreed that he may just as easily have lost his temper.

He breathed out deeply. 'Thank you. I'd have hated to be banned from a bookshop.' He laughed weakly. 'Now, my second favour. Can you tell me where the sci-fi and fantasy section is? And do you have any recommendations?'

Mal grinned and walked with him to the rather empty section. 'I'm afraid there are more jam jars than books at the moment. I don't know many titles in this section.'

Piran read along the books until he paused on one and pulled it out. 'I haven't read this. The rest, by the way, are excellent. But you're right, you are missing a few standards and some great new titles.'

Mal shook her head. She knew running a bookshop was going to be a steep learning curve, and she was studying each section as she went, taking advice from reading groups and librarians. It was incredible how much information there was online, but in honesty she had left fantasy and sci-fi until the end. She didn't know where to start with it.

'I could help if you want?' He spoke hesitantly, and Mal was surprised by the offer. God knows she needed help in this field.

'Well, if you could drop me a list of the titles I must have on the shelves, that would be incredibly kind. I can even offer you a discount on your next purchase?'

He laughed now, more relaxed. 'No, this will be fun. I'm always boring on about books I like, so this will spare people my sermons.'

They had got to the till now, and as Mal rang up the sale his talk of sermons seemed to nudge a memory in him.

'Speaking of which, I do have another favour. But this time it's from my mum.' His voice rose questioningly and he dipped his head, as though half expecting Mal to shout at him. She looked at him and held his eye. If this was going to be a memorial plaque or some sort of marker, then it was going to be a hard no. She would not turn her shop into a mausoleum. Piran clearly interpreted her thoughts and rushed on.

'She wants to know if you'd like to carry a bucket at the festival. She said what with being a newcomer and having had a tough start, you might like to get involved. Besides, it's for a good cause. And it's always a laugh.'

Mal looked at him blankly, trying to work out what he was asking until she gave up.

'A bucket? For what?'

'For the money. You'd walk along the floats as the procession weaves through the village. Rattle your bucket, people drop money in.' He shook his hand, miming a clattering collection bucket. 'It's for the village harvest festival. Goes back centuries. Only these days we also have fancy dress and bands and probably more making-merry than back along. Although never let it be said that a Golden resident doesn't know how to celebrate. So, what do you say?'

Mal wanted to say no. And also yes. She wasn't really ready to join the community, but it was only helping out. She wasn't inviting people over for coffee and cake.

'It's for charity? The money helps village projects?'

Piran gave what was probably his most beseeching smile and Mal laughed despite herself.

'Tell your mother I said yes. But someone will need to fill me in on the details.'

As Piran left, a small family came and headed straight to the railway set. She watched them, pleased with the smiles on their faces, and wondered what the hell she had let herself in for.

Chapter Twenty

Mal put the shop phone back in its cradle with a shaky hand and took a deep breath. She had been expecting this and finally it had happened. The village was rejecting her. This past week she had filled the shelves with a mix of the new and old stock, zoned the areas of the shop and dressed the windows. As far as she could see, it looked like a proper bookshop. Her first few days trading had been good as locals and tourists all came in to have a nose around. Questions about dead bodies had been deflected for 'the sake of the family' which no one could argue with, and the trade had been decent.

Tomorrow was Friday, her first parent and toddler session, and she had been so looking forward to it. Not having her own children had been a conscious decision and one she had never regretted, but she did love having children around. Mal was thrilled to be an aunt and a godmother, and was known as Yaffle throughout the younger generations. Her friends and family had so much privilege she hadn't even been aware of until she went inside.

Whilst in prison, she had discovered what life was like for young women with no family network to support them whether they were children themselves, or when they grew up to become mothers. She knew how tough life could be for parents and had been looking forward to offering a session where mums and dads could relax with others and read stories. She'd bought some beanbags and a wooden train set and was anticipating the laughs and the rapt expressions as they listened to a great story. Now that wouldn't happen. She had wondered if the body would put them off, but it turned out it was her record that was the problem.

'Morning, lover, you look like you've swallowed a fish hook. What's up?'

Collette breezed into the shop with a bottle of shampoo. 'Here. Good for surfers apparently. Consider it a freebie.'

Mal rolled her eyes fondly at the younger woman. 'I've told you. The shoes were my gift to you. Stop paying me back!'

Mal fully understood that Collette wouldn't. The value of the gift outweighed the intention and Mal felt stupid for not appreciating that when she had first given her the shoes.

Collette put the shampoo on the counter. 'So, what gives? Is it the police?'

Mal sighed. 'No, Sophie said the investigation has gone quiet. I suspect the inspector is disappointed that his first murder is a cold case. It's all a bit boring.'

She wondered about the wisdom of telling Collette about the phone call she'd just had, then shrugged. What was the point in trying to protect her privacy? This would sprint around the village.

'The toddler session tomorrow is cancelled.'

‘What! Why?’ Collette looked around the shop, trying to see a physical issue with the space, but everything appeared fresh and inviting. ‘Mandz will be gutted. I know she was desperate for it.’

Mal gestured towards the phone. ‘That was the head from Golden Primary. She said they have taken down my posters. They can’t be associated with a criminal.’

Mal said it carefully. This may be news to Collette, but she simply nodded. Mal shrank inside. Everyone probably knew. It was like Dennis had said, people might know each other’s secrets but they didn’t talk about them. Except when they did. So far, Mal didn’t know the difference between unspoken common knowledge and rampant gossip.

‘I guess she has a job to do,’ said Collette, acknowledging but not referring to Mal’s past. ‘But why cancel?’

‘Well, won’t everyone keep their children away?’

Mal felt the weight of Collette’s consideration. She tried to start a sentence several times until Mal could bear it no longer. ‘Spit it out. I’ve heard it all before.’

Collette took a deep breath. ‘Did you kill anyone?’

‘No.’ Mal was shocked, but on reflection five years was a long time served. She knew killers had served less.

‘Would you do it again?’

Mal thought back to the shame and humiliation of the trial, her exposure in the press. Those cold nights in prison, her first black eye, the fear and the loneliness.

'In a heartbeat.'

Collette looked at her closely, then nodded her head. 'Fair enough, I won't ask what. Just tell me it had nothing to do with children.'

Now Mal felt impotent rage pouring off her, but she couldn't answer. This wasn't just her story. She watched Collette's face as she looked at her closely.

'Were any children hurt by what you did?'

Mal recoiled. 'Christ, No!'

Collette studied her for a few seconds, then nodded. 'Okay then. Whatever you did, you've been punished for it. I'll tell Mandz tomorrow is still on, in case she hears to the contrary. Some may stay away, but I think you'll be surprised how many exhausted parents don't care about what you did in the past.'

As Collette had been talking, Mal had seen the postman walking towards the shop. She was far from reconciled to the fact that he had told half the village she was an ex-convict, but he was also the person who brought her her letters. As he stepped into the shop, both women glared at him and he took a laughing step back under the wall of unwelcome faces.

'You've a nerve, Bill,' snapped Collette. 'You're supposed to deliver mail, not gossip.'

'It's not gossip if it's true.'

'It is gossip if it isn't yours to tell. Give me those and bugger off.'

As he left with his tail between his legs, Collette handed the post over.

'He's not much liked around here. Noses through everyone's mail and probably steams some open as well. Plus, sometimes birthday cards with money in them go missing. And last year he told everyone Mary was pregnant before she'd even announced it.'

'Why don't you complain?' said Mal, in horror.

'Oh, we did that, girl. He isn't our regular postie anymore, but he covers for holiday and sick. You were unlucky. Ted, our regular, he'll take your secrets to the grave. He takes the responsibility of the Queen's postal service very seriously indeed.'

She studied Mal critically. 'Now, are you alright? If you don't mind me saying, you look a little tired?'

Mal sighed. So much for the extra make-up.

'Not sleeping well. After the break-in the other day, I've been a bit on edge. I don't mind dead bodies, but live ones?' She gave a small shudder.

'Yeah, sorry about that. The police were all over me about it.'

Mal groaned. 'The photo I showed you.'

'Right enough. They came in asking questions like they were bloody Sherlock Holmes. Who did I tell? Had I investigated it myself? Did I know anyone with size nine feet?'

Mal was horrified. The police had asked her who knew about the tunnel and she had mentioned that she'd shown

Collette the photo of the gate. It hadn't crossed her mind that they would give her a hard time as well. She tried to apologise, but Collette laughed it off.

'Don't fret. We had a right bloody laugh. *Do I look like the sort of person that clambered around drainpipes*? I says, and then when he asked if I knew anyone with size nine feet there was a lot of laughter. *Hair, mate, I'm looking at their heads, not their feet!* Then I got all the girls to wave their feet and asked the police if they thought any of them were size nines.'

Mal laughed. She could picture the scene.

'But did you mention the picture to anyone? Not that I'm blaming you. I'm not. Honestly. But I can't get it out of my head that someone from here broke in.'

Collette's smile fell. 'Yeah, I did mention it and I have cursed myself every day since. It was just so interesting that I mentioned it that afternoon when I was working. We used to love it as kids, trying to find tunnels and pirate's treasure. I wasn't thinking. And I am so sorry.'

Now it was Mal's turn to apologise. Honestly, everything about this investigation was upsetting.

'Of course, finding a tunnel is exciting. I was thrilled. It didn't occur to me to keep it secret, otherwise I wouldn't have shown you the photo. So, who was in when you mentioned it?'

Collette rattled off a few names, none of which she recognised until she said Eden Jago.

'Jago?'

'Piran's wife. Nice girl, local, but I think she's out of her depth in that marriage. Ruth is a tricky mother-in-law.'

Interesting. No doubt the police had thought so as well. Not that they had mentioned it to her.

'Was Ruth there as well?'

'In my place? Give over.' Collette shook her head. 'Ruth gets her hair done somewhere fancy in Truro. No doubt pays twice the price and gets to drink fancy coffees whilst they fleece her. Our Ruth is not one for getting down with the locals.'

'I thought she was local?'

'She is right enough. But she's from Saints, and there's them up there think they're better than the rest of us. Ruth is one of them.'

'What size feet do you reckon she has?' asked Mal, idly. Collette looked at her shrewdly.

'Well, she's tall enough. I can't see her in a tunnel any more than me, but maybe she wanted to see the place for herself. Was there any damage?'

'No, it just seemed like someone wandered about the place.'

Collette nodded, then tilted her head, her nails tapping on the countertop. 'Could that be it? Just a grieving widow come to have a look for herself?'

Mal thought about it. The idea of it being a woman hadn't even occurred to her, but it did make a weird sort of sense, and if it would help her sleep at night it was a theory she was happy to embrace.

Telling Mal that she'd be fine, Collette headed back out of the shop, shouting to someone further down the street.

That young woman was so self-assured. Mal wondered if that came from a sense of place. She was born here; her grandparents, and theirs before them, populated the graveyard. Her family name was everywhere in the history books, she went to school with half the village, her children were born here, like as not she'd die here. Mal wondered what that did to a person. You could get confidence from being loved, from being right, from being good. But was there a confidence developed in knowing you were where you belonged? Whatever the reason, Collette was an impressive young woman and Mal imagined she probably ran half the village. By the time she retired, Mal suspected Collette would rule the entire place.

'Excuse me?'

A couple stood in the doorway, interrupting her thoughts. They were wearing walking boots and matching jackets, with a small dog pulling on a lead.

'Yes?'

'Do you know where the sea is?'

Mal looked baffled. 'The sea?'

'Yes, big wet thing with boats in it,' said the man, with a hearty laugh. Mal imagined he also called the landlord 'my good man' as he ordered a pint. She continued to look at him. The village was not what could be described as large. Surely if they simply walked downhill, they'd find it on their own. Deciding to bite her tongue, she tried to be helpful.

'Carry on down this lane.'

'Downhill? I wasn't sure we were heading in the right direction. That's why we thought we'd ask. Always good to stop and ask the natives.' He was one stereotype away from ending his sentence with a *what.*

'You thought walking uphill might take you to the harbour?' Mal was certain that her derision was clear, but the man continued to beam at her.

'Which way then?'

'At the bottom of the lane you'll see the boats.'

'Very good.' He paused. 'And then do we go left or right?'

Mal stared at him. 'The boats are in the harbour.'

'And that's the sea then?'

Mal's eyes widened. Was this a prank?

'Yes, that'll be the sea.' She spoke cautiously, uncertain if she was dealing with a total imbecile.

Tipping a non-existent cap to Mal, he and his wife were pulled away downhill by the little dog. Mal decided the dog may well have more brains than its owners.

Shaking her head in bemusement, she looked at the letters Collette had passed over. She tore opened the largest of the lot. Given the size and the postmark it was clearly from Veronica, returning the post-mortem report.

As Mal slid it out of the envelope, she saw Veronica had attached a note to the document. Mal read it in dismay.

'Not suicide.'

This changed everything. Dialling Sophie's number, she wondered if she should leave this monstrous village and its murderous inhabitants and settle somewhere safer, like Colombia.

Chapter Twenty-One

Eden Jago closed the car door and stretched. Travelling the back roads home from Truro was always dicey. She'd avoided the traffic jams on the main roads but you never knew when you'd meet a caravan, the drivers panicking at the route their satnav had taken them. She thought some roads should have signs on them saying 'Locals Only'. Or at the very least: 'No caravans, and if you can't reverse, turn around now'.

Still, you went where the work was and Eden liked her job in Truro. It wasn't glamorous or even taxing, but it had flexible hours and paid a decent wage. She was lucky to have it. She was also lucky she didn't have to pay for childcare, but as she looked across at her mother-in-law's house, she knew she paid in other ways.

The Jagos lived up on the east side of Golden, on the fringes of the village. Up here the houses were detached and spacious, each sat in large gardens with glorious views across the bay. When Piran had first brought her home, she had been slightly overwhelmed. Her own folks lived over on the other side of the river, back up the valley on a purpose-built housing estate. No views, precious little parking, and postage stamp backyards.

Ruth had been charming and was dressed so nicely that Eden found herself apologising the whole time and tried to find a scruffy chair to sit on so that she wouldn't somehow mess things up. Of course, Ruth Jago had no such thing as a scruffy chair or a comfy sofa. She even had a cleaning lady. For just her and Piran. Plus they both had cars, and not hand-me-downs but brand-new models. Eden had been easily impressed by the trappings and Piran's fancy manners. When they had been at school together, he was wild, but after his mother sent him away to a sixth form boarding school he came back polished.

Eventually, after a few years of engagement, Eden got pregnant, and the wedding was pulled into focus. The wedding had been a huge village affair. Her folks wanted it at the chapel but Ruth insisted it take place in the church. Given that she was footing the bill and had bought Eden the most amazing dress, Ruth won the day.

She also put the deposit down for Piran and Eden's cottage, a pretty little place down near the harbour. Eden had suggested a garden but Ruth said this was a better investment and Piran backed his mother. Now Eden lived in an idyllic little fisherman's cottage, with barely any room for a buggy let alone a tumble dryer. There was no garden to hang the washing, so she had to traipse over to the launderette. Obviously, nearby parking was non-existent, so she'd clatter along the cobbles with the buggy and a shopper, as tourists asked her to move out of the way whilst they took photos of her lane. And, in winter it was as dark as a mine.

Piran would admonish her for the state of the electricity bill, but it was okay for him; he was hardly ever in the cottage, working every hour that God sent.

Eden sighed and headed across the gravel driveway. She sounded so ungrateful. Letting herself in, she called out and heard Ruth call back from the conservatory. She and Sam were sitting on the floor playing with building bricks. As Sam looked up at Eden, she knew it was all worth it. With a yell and a laugh, he ran over and jumped into her arms as she swung him around.

'Will you stay for a drink?' asked Ruth. Her cultured voice always made Ruth feel out of place, even here in her own village.

Ruth always asked and Eden always said yes. She felt sorry for her, despite her critical ways, she must be lonely up here on her own. Notwithstanding the gardener and cleaner, but Eden guessed it wasn't the same. As Sam continued to play, the two women resorted to stilted small talk until Eden mentioned the bookshop was running a new reading group for families.

'Are you insane? You can't go!'

Eden Jago gazed at her mother-in-law with weary resignation. Her own fault for mentioning the subject. Of course Ruth was going to object.

'I didn't say I was going, I said it's a shame I can't go. It would have been nice to have somewhere to take Sam.'

Ruth continued to wipe down her already clean kitchen worktops. She had been taking care of Sam whilst Eden worked an early morning shift at the supermarket. Ruth was always up early and refused to take any money, what sort of grandmother had to be paid to look after her own grandchild?

One who likes to make a point of it, thought Eden, every time she heard Ruth mention it in the village, at church, in the bus queue.

'What about the mother and toddlers' group? You always enjoy going there.'

I don't, thought Eden. 'It's not really the same, is it? A bit more churchy, isn't it?'

'Not at all.'

'You make them pray at the beginning and end of the session.'

Ruth threw her cloth on the surface and looked at Eden in horror. 'Make them pray. You make us sound like the inquisition. No one makes them pray, children love to join in. They are naturally closer to God; it's easier for them. It's we adults that struggle.'

You don't seem to struggle with your faith, thought Eden. She relished it, it was all that kept her going. That and knowing everyone's business and telling Eden how to run hers. Eden knew from friends how Ruth had all but abandoned Piran when Roger died, or so the village gossip went. Piran refused to talk about it and only said it was a dark time for both of them. Typical Piran, forgiving to a fault, to a mother that could do no wrong.

'I just thought the idea of a new venue and a little story time with friends would be fun.'

Ruth gripped the cloth and twisted it through her hands. 'Where Sam's very own grandfather lay?'

'The church hall is in the middle of the graveyard! All his great-grandparents are in there!'

Ruth looked at her, shocked, and started wiping down the surfaces again.

'How can you possibly compare them?'

Eden was instantly contrite, as Ruth's voice broke. Of course it wasn't the same, and although Ruth was an interfering pain in the backside, she had gone through a massive shock this past fortnight. Apologising, she picked up Sam's things and loaded him into the buggy.

'I'll see you on Sunday. If I come over early, I can prepare the food while you play with Sam?'

Normally, Ruth would see Eden to the car and wave goodbye to Sam, but now she simply turned her back and walked out to the conservatory. Another black mark against her.

Chapter Twenty-Two

Sharon Trebetherick was watching TV when there was a knock at the front door. Grumbling, she paused the show, the tiles were about to fall and they were on for a jackpot win. No way was she missing that. She headed through the hallway and could see the outline of more than one person through the opaque glass. That took her back, it was either officials or religious sorts. She prayed it was the latter. Them, she could get rid of. Wiping her palms on her jeans, she opened her door and glared at the police – the bloke leading the investigation into Roger's death, his sidekick, and Sophie Taphouse, the only one in uniform.

'What do you want?'

'Hello, Mrs Trebetherick,' said Sophie, with a smile. 'Can we come in for a chat?'

Sharon didn't want the police in her house. But it was better than them saying what they had to on the doorstep, with the whole world watching. She looked at Sophie.

'Since when did you start calling me Mrs Trebetherick again? You're not a schoolgirl anymore.'

Waving them in, she turned and opened the door to the front room. As she walked in, she stared in dismay. The boys had left all their dishes in here and kicked their shoes off wherever. She stepped forward quickly, tidying things up. Thank God she had dusted at least. Sophie followed her in tutting and helped to straighten the place up.

'Bloody kids are the same the world over, aren't they? Mine would shame me to the devil. They can walk into a tidy room and five minutes later it looks like the place has exploded.'

Sharon straightened a pair of shoes and placed them alongside a wall. 'But yours are still in little school. Mine are in their twenties. You think they'd know better.' She grinned across at Sophie, as she stacked some bowls.

'And when exactly do men grow up, anyway?' asked Sophie.

The two women laughed, but the inspector cleared his throat noisily.

'You can leave that, we need to talk to you.' And without invitation, he sat down. She was grateful that his sidekick looked across to her and she nodded. At least one of them understood the importance of a best room. The boys always teased her for it, but it was a matter of pride, or maybe a generational thing. In fairness, she remembered thinking it mad that her parents had a room that no one could use. Maybe you simply got to a certain age and discovered the old ways were best.

'Constable Taphouse,' said the inspector, 'would you like to find the kitchen and make a pot of tea?'

That was a step too far for Sharon. Who was this man to arrange tea in her own home?

'Young Sophie knows where the kitchen is well enough.'

'That I do. Do you still hide the milkshake powder behind the flour bags?'

For the first time since she opened the door, Sharon relaxed. 'Oh my days. You lot could drink me out of powder quicker than I could buy it.'

'But you made the best milkshakes. I still think of them.'

Sharon smiled fondly, remembering all the children traipsing in and out of her house. The noise, the mess, the laughter, she loved every minute of it.

Sophie continued, 'I try to make them for my own kids but they are never as good.'

'Memory makes everything taste better.'

The inspector cleared his throat again. 'So, if you could put the kettle on, PC Taphouse?'

Sharon glared at the man and shook her head. 'Not in my house. I'll make the tea. Thank you very much. In fact, just say your piece and get on.'

Sharon sat back in her chair and crossed her arms. She had noticed the worry in young Sophie's face and knew what was coming would not be good news. The inspector looked uncomfortable, then destroyed Sharon's life.

'We have reinvestigated your husband's post-mortem, and the evidence suggests that the initial verdict was incorrect. The evidence suggests that your husband was strangled following a fight. The hanging was an attempt to cover it up.

'It seems the pathologist who examined your husband was later found to have made other errors in judgement. No doubt this new finding will trigger an investigation into—'

Sharon zoned out. She had been telling them for years that he hadn't killed himself. She had always known the pathologist had got it wrong. How many other families had pleaded that his findings were wrong? How many other families had been dismissed? And dear God, as she sat in her armchair, she realised that someone had hated her beloved Paul enough to kill him. The policeman was still talking, but she stood up.

'When you know who killed him come and tell me.' Her face twisting into a sneer. 'That is, if you think I'm worthy enough.'

'Sharon—'

'That's Mrs Trebetherick to you.' God, everything about his patronising manner made her want to scream.

'Mrs Trebetherick, we still need to ask you questions.'

'Then go read what I said when Paul died. Now go on. Get out.'

Both men were still sitting, but Sophie had risen when Sharon did and now looked really upset. The junior detective was taking notes of everything thing that was being said. She flinched, remembering in the past when the police officers had stopped taking notes, bored with the desperate rantings of a widow refusing to accept the truth.

'Can you think who may have wanted to harm your husband?'

Sharon choked back an ugly laugh. 'Harm? They didn't bloody harm him, did they? They bloody murdered him!'

She was beginning to lose it and needed these men out of here. Sophie walked across and held her hand.

'Boss, how about you call in again tomorrow? Give Mrs Trebetherick time to adjust.'

The young man had also finally risen to his feet. 'That sounds like a good idea.' He looked at his boss, then turned to Sharon. 'We are terribly sorry for the loss of your husband and the fact you weren't listened to. DI Hemingstone here, however, is a new broom and he will get to the bottom of this.'

Grudgingly, the older man pulled himself forward on the couch and slowly got up.

'Yes, as Williams says, I will solve this for you. I'll leave you with PC Taphouse here, and when you feel a little better, I'll call tomorrow and we'll see what's what. In the meantime, I'd be grateful if you could keep this piece of news to yourself.' He gave her a patronising smile that didn't quite make it to his eyes. 'We don't want you hampering our investigations, now, do we?'

Sharon wondered if they'd put her in a cell for hitting a policeman. Clearly Sophie spotted her intent as she quickly ushered the men out of the room. By the time the front door closed, Sharon was in the kitchen. The kettle was on and she was washing the boys' dishes. Sophie walked back into the kitchen and pulled bits out for a brew.

'Alright, Sharon? Where's your tea towels? Surprised you haven't got yourself a dishwasher.'

'Give over. Just for one? It's not like I make much mess.'

Sophie dried the bowls as the kettle came to the boil. 'Bet you're loving having the boys back, even if it is under such shitty—'

'Sophie Taphouse! What would your mother say?'

Sharon watched in amusement as Sophie blushed to her roots. She was always the same as a child, if anyone so much as raised their voice to her, her skin would flush red. It was a wonder she had made it as a police officer. But she had, and she was a good one. She cared about people and that was a rare skill these days.

'Sorry, Mrs Trebetherick.'

Both women stopped and laughed.

'Oh God, is it wrong to be laughing?' said Sharon, wiping a tear from her eye.

'Shows you're human. Come on, let's have that tea, I'm parched and you can ask me any questions you've got.'

The two women sipped their drinks at the kitchen table. 'I'm surprised you didn't make us take our shoes off when we came in. I was ready.'

Sharon laughed at Sophie. 'You children were the very devil with your dirty shoes. New house, new carpets, and you lot treating it like a playing field.'

Sophie looked back into the hallway. 'Well, you've kept it lovely.'

'That's because no one ever visits now. After Roger disappeared, you all fell apart. Fifteen is such a tricky age, anyway. Then when Paul died, that was the end of any visitors.'

Sophie gulped at her tea and Sharon realised she was making her feel guilty and that wasn't fair.

'Do they think the two murders are connected?' she asked, sipping her tea.

'Hard not to,' Sophie said, shaking her head. 'Two violent deaths in the same village, and those two men working together.'

'But it's five years apart.'

'I know, that's the bit that doesn't make sense. But we'll work it out.'

'You have faith in that inspector then?'

'To be honest, not much, but he has a good team. It'll be them that solve it.'

'And you,' said Sharon. Her voice brooking no contradiction. If there was one thing Sharon had faith in it was Golden and the people in it. Even if she thought of Sophie as a schoolkid, she knew she had children of her own. Everyone grew up and moved on. It was just her, sitting alone in her pristine house with her bittersweet memories.

'Oh, I'm not involved much. The local village bobby, is how they see me. I've sort of been co-opted, but I don't think the inspector thinks much of me either.'

Sharon poured another cup and offered Sophie a biscuit.

'He can't be that useless. He did look at the post-mortem like I asked.'

Sophie put her cup down and cleared her throat. 'That wasn't him. That was Malachite Peck in the bookshop. You gave her a copy of Paul's report? Well, she sent it to a friend of hers who is a retired pathologist. She spotted some irregularities. Mal told me and I told Williams. He then ordered a formal investigation.'

Sharon thought about it and shook her head. 'So that's how your inspector works, is it? Doesn't listen to women.'

'That's about the long and short of it.'

Sophie was about to drink again when Sharon finally burst into tears and Sophie dashed around to her side of the table to give her a huge hug.

Chapter Twenty-Three

Mal's smile grew more confident as each new parent and toddler arrived. It was mostly women, but there were a few men, and the scene was lively and noisy. There were eleven adults and it occurred to her that she might have to mention a limit to numbers. She hadn't dreamed so many would turn up and was thrilled by the response. Each time a parent arrived with a baby or toddler in a sling or backpack, Mal cheered. Some of these buggies took up a huge amount of room. One of the dads had offered to read the first story, and almost immediately the group quieted down.

The rest of the shop was open to customers but there weren't many people about. Mal was calculating the cost-benefit analysis and would do so over the next few weeks to see if this made sense, but the benefits of the children's rapt faces and the parents' relaxed smiling ones were going to take a huge cost to outweigh. This already felt like a good thing. One mother wasn't smiling though and kept glancing around the room, the little boy on her lap entranced by the tale of a naughty dragon that liked to get up to mischief with a princess. If Mal was any judge of character that princess was a born troublemaker: all that sitting around brushing her hair, that was no way to raise a girl. The mother kept surreptitiously looking around the shop and out the window, shuffling around so she wasn't instantly visible from the street.

Mal wondered if she was ashamed to be here. Her behaviour was distinctly uncomfortable, and as the story ended, she muttered an apology to a friend and gathered her belongings. The little one was less impressed at being removed and made his feelings clear. Everyone else in the group seemed sympathetic to her situation.

Whoever this was, most of the group understood why she was leaving. Mal stared out the window, the rain had stopped so at least the young mum would have a dry walk home. She groaned as she saw Ruth Jago enter the lane and head down. So much for a day without drama, and suddenly all the pieces fell into place. She looked at the young woman and wondered if she should interfere. This wasn't her issue after all. However, it was her shop, and she hadn't taken to Mrs Jago when she first met her. All that obvious kneeling and praying. She called out to the young mother, 'Mrs Jago is heading down the street.'

The blood drained from her face, confirming Mal's suspicions. 'You can go and wait in the storeroom if you want.'

The woman stared at Mal, her eyes wide with horror, then almost ran down the length of the shop pushing the buggy and closing the storeroom door behind her. As the door closed, the bell rang over the front door and Ruth Jago walked in.

'Good morning, Mrs Jago.'

Mal had turned to regard Ruth, who was still wearing black. Mal tried to be sympathetic but there was something very public about her grief.

'Good morning, Mrs Jago.' Mal tried again. Mrs Jago was studying the bookshop in disgust. 'May I help you with anything?'

'So you've gone ahead with this then?' She looked over at the rather nervous group that had fallen silent.

Mal decided deflection would work better here.

'I see you missed the rain.' Inane, but it might remind the woman that this was not the place to start a scene, in front of all these children.

'Don't change the subject. I think it's shameful what you are doing here. Babies at a crime scene, a bookshop run by a criminal.'

Mal took a deep breath, she hadn't asked for this. God knows she was desperate to avoid this, but if this woman wanted a fight.

'We're going on a bear hunt!' One of the mother's voices rang out and all the small heads turned towards the sound of their favourite catnip. The parents leant into the story and the group studiously ignored the situation at the desk.

Mal took a step back and decided they were right, this wasn't the time or the place. She had this foul woman's daughter-in-law hiding in the store cupboard and a shop full of children.

'If you've said your piece?' Mal asked, coolly. She might be short but she was never overlooked. Even after five years in jail, she could still clip out a sentence so dismissively that no one was under any doubt as to who was in charge.

Ruth took a deep breath.

'Don't even think it,' hissed Mal. 'If you think you can come into my shop and bad-mouth me, then I'm going to come into your church on Sunday and denounce you.'

'You wouldn't dare!' Ruth took a nervous step away from the counter.

'Try me. Never start a fight with someone who has no reputation to lose.' Mal paused and smiled at Ruth. 'Especially when you care so much about your own.'

Ruth fled and the parents burst into rowdy applause. One of the mums dashed down the length of the shop and let the hiding mother know she could come out, to more applause. Clearly Ruth was not a favourite amongst these young parents.

Mal was waiting for that little shudder of fear that she had been getting used to, but realised she was still smiling. For the past few weeks, she'd felt unsure of herself and out of place, but something in Ruth's direct attack and the inspector's constant digs was waking her from her torpor. She hated bullies, but she bloody loved a fight.

The villagers could like her or lump her, but on the whole, they seemed a decent lot. She liked her morning swims, her daily photos, she loved waking to the sound of freedom and fresh air. In the evening she said goodnight to the books and headed upstairs to her radio and writing desk. Life was good, and if that inspector expected her to tug her forelock and quiver in terror then he had failed to notice that she was Malachite Peck, and she was hewn from granite not sand.

Chapter Twenty-Four

Roland Hemingstone looked across his desk out onto the work floor beyond his office. All those policemen looking to him for leadership. It had taken a long time to get to this position, too long in his opinion, but now he was here he could feel the rightness of it. Rita had always told him he'd been born twenty years too late. In a different era, he'd already be a commissioner. He knew a wife was going to be biased, but he thought she had the right of it.

Too much policing these days was kowtowing to the woke mob, and he wasn't interested. He was a thief-taker, plain and simple, and if people didn't like his methods, tough. He wasn't going to change. Still, he knew his attitude had held him back in Coventry – cases were passed on to colleagues who were more touchy-feely. Gradually cases were being passed on to men younger than him, even women, and he wondered if he was ever going to get the promotion he deserved.

He had written in protest to his boss after the most recent travesty, where he had actually been taken off a case. Soon after that he had been encouraged to apply for a promotion in Cornwall. It seemed that the powers in Cornwall knew a good thing when they saw one. Now he was here and making waves.

A double homicide. A drug ring. All he needed was a serial killer, and he'd be laughing. His boss had dropped in the other day and made a point of praising him in front of the team for the work they were doing on the drug ring. If they made a big enough bust, he should make it to the local papers, which reminded him to find out who was in charge of PR around here. A couple of women had got in touch but he'd wait until he had something important to announce, then take their boss out for drinks. Man to man, work out the best way to make the announcement. One thing he did understand about this day and age was that image was everything.

Out on the floor everyone was working hard, all performing tasks that he had set them. It was a good feeling. Williams stood up and looked his way; waving his arm he beckoned him in. He wanted the team to know he was always available to them. It was important to make them all feel included, no matter how big a waste of space they were. DS Williams however was not a waste of space, he had already clocked him as a diligent worker and someone he could depend on. His first lieutenant.

'Hey, boss, got a minute?' Williams leant on the door frame.

'What have you got for me? How's the sting coming along?'

Williams looked over his shoulder back onto the floor, then back at his boss.

'It's good I think, but Donald's on that. I've been looking into the Golden murders.'

Hemingstone tried to hide his disappointment, clearing up a cold case would be good work but it wouldn't get him on telly.

'Okay, let's have it.'

'Two things. I've had the results back from the coroner's report and the financial investigations.'

'We know the coroner's report was a cock-up,' pointed out Hemingstone.

'Yes, so I've been going over the old investigation, what there was of it. The post-mortem found some hair on the body that didn't belong to the victim, but as it was a filial match they dismissed it.'

'Was that smart? How old were his sons at the time?'

He'd had both sons shouting at him in the street, accusing him of corruption and cover-up. He'd tried to explain he hadn't even been in Cornwall back then, but they weren't interested. All they wanted to do was embarrass him. It would be good if he could prove their involvement.

'They were twenty when their dad died, but it's a non-starter. They were up playing rugby in Bath. They were gone for the weekend.'

'Could one of them have snuck out?'

'It's a six-hour round trip. Plus, each brother alibis the other, as did the entire team.'

'Bugger. Well, what else have you got?'

Williams smiled. 'Now this looks more promising, you told me to look into everyone's finances.'

He nodded sagely and leant back in his chair, making a steeple of his fingertips. 'Always follow the money, son. Won't go too far wrong if you follow the money. DNA evidence will always send you running in circles. The money's where it's at. So out with it, you're smiling like a kid at a theme park.'

Williams shuffled his printouts and handed them to him. Hemingstone took one look at the figures and promptly handed them back. He didn't have time for spreadsheets and computers.

'Just the headlines, hey?'

Chastened, William tidied up the papers and carried on. 'Well, I started looking into everyone's finances and I noticed a few oddities. Jago and Trebetherick had a loan from Jacques Peloffy with their fishing boat as surety against it. A few months before the loan was due to end, the payments stopped. Now I'm thinking either Jacques cancelled the loan and if so, why did he do that? Was Trebetherick blackmailing Peloffy over something? Had Peloffy discovered something? Or maybe it's the other way round. Maybe Trebetherick paid the loan off early, and if so, where did he get the money from? He also put a deposit down on a bigger house.'

Hemingstone stretched back on his chair. Both were interesting leads, and he liked that Williams had focused on the Frenchman; why waste time looking elsewhere?

'The thing is, boss, I think I might be onto something. At the time of Roger's disappearance there was a rumour going around that the two fishermen had found the *White Maria*.'

Hemingstone shrugged his shoulders and looked at Williams with a frown. What was wrong with these people? They assumed that because it had happened in Cornwall, the entire world must know about it.

'Sorry, boss. The *White Maria* was a treasure ship that sank during a storm off the south coast. She was never recovered but was said to have a cargo of gold and revenue money on her. What if they had found her? Was that why Roger Jago was killed? Did Paul Trebetherick think his partner had run off with the treasure? Did they have the treasure, but he got spooked when his partner disappeared? He waited five years before he started spending it, then gets killed?'

Hemingstone leant forward, his elbows on the table, and his eyes sparkled. A lost treasure ship would make national headlines, maybe even international ones.

'There wasn't any evidence that Trebetherick was tortured was there?'

'No, but the pathologist thought it was a suicide, God knows what else he missed.'

Hemingstone slammed his hands on the table. This was something, he could tell. Jumping up, he strode out of his office and shouted to the rest of the team.

Sophie looked up from her monitor. She'd been asked to read through witness statements and see if anything struck her as out of place. So far it made for entertaining reading as she could hear the voices of the people being interviewed in her head. There was Phyllis with her gossipy innuendos, Ruth with her self-pitying tears, Morris down by the boats, surly and opinionated as ever. Now she stopped to listen to DI Hemingstone, another man who loved the sound of his own voice.

'New leads, everyone. I want us to look into the finances of everyone named so far. Any sudden windfalls, any unexpected patterns of spending. Any unexplained wealth.'

One of the women looked up from her screen. 'Is this for the county lines, boss?'

'Bloody hell, woman, keep up. The Golden murders. We might be on the hunt for a fortune. Right then,' he continued, 'here's where we are so far. As I suspected, we are looking at a double homicide.'

Sophie tried not to snigger, no self-respecting copper said homicide, not unless they'd been watching too many movies. Still a double murder was no small thing, even if it was still a cold case.

'You all remember how suspicious I was about Paul Trebetherick's suicide.'

Sophie was going to have to leave the room, this rewriting of history was ridiculous. He had publicly humiliated her for daring to suggest the suicide was suspicious. Now he was claiming credit for it. Across the briefing room Donald rolled his eyes at her, at least the inspector's charade was not going unnoticed.

Hemingstone continued to spin his yarn. 'Yesterday I visited Trebetherick's widow, who was uncooperative to say the least. She always insisted that her husband was murdered, and now I'm wondering did she know more than she was letting on? Did she know why Trebetherick was murdered?'

Hemingstone waited for the muttering in the room to die out whilst he bathed in the drama.

'So, two men, two business partners, two fishermen, both murdered. The first's body was hidden, the second staged to look like a suicide. Someone out there thinks they've got away with this, but they weren't banking on me. Now, here's what I want.'

Hemingstone turned towards the blackboard and Sophie looked over at Donald, waiting to see his reaction. She smiled when she noticed he wasn't the only one rolling their eyes. She wondered if it was worth pointing out that she was the one who had brought the post-mortem notes to his attention, and had only done so because Mal Peck had got a friend of hers from inside to have a look. The irony of a convicted criminal doing the work of a detective inspector was not lost on her, but she thought if she mentioned it she might get kicked out of the room, then she'd be no good to anyone. Still, she was certainly going to tell her partner about it in the canteen.

'You mentioned something about a large sum of money?' prompted Donald, trying to move the investigation on from Hemingstone's tirade of self-congratulation.

'I want background checks into both men, their families, and their bank accounts. I know this is a cold case and might take some time, but get down to the village and start chatting to the locals, see what you can pry out there. A place like that is probably a hotbed of gossip.'

He looked around the room making sure he had everyone's attention.

'Williams here has kept his ear to the ground and found a whisper connecting the two men to a lost treasure ship.'

There was some groaning from the room as some of the older detectives had had a lifetime of rumours of missing treasure ships.

'No, hear me out. Williams thinks this is a good tip-off and one worth investigating. It's a shame that local uniform didn't spot this.'

All eyes turned to Sophie, and her cheeks prickled again.

'That's because every child in Golden has grown up with this fairy tale, and there has never been a single scrap of evidence that it sank off our shore. It's just tale for the red lips,' she paused, then added 'sir' in case she had sounded too dismissive.

'And yet, we suddenly have a double murder. Oh, and here's a thought,' his face lit up as he realised something, 'right in the middle of this sits a convicted criminal. Is it a coincidence that our Malachite Peck arrives to the scene of two murders and lost treasure?'

The room stirred in anticipation.

'Her conviction fits, boss,' called out one of the junior detectives, and Hemingstone nodded, seeming pleased that they were catching his train of thought.

Sophie listened in dismay. The idea that Mal was involved was ridiculous, unless she was some sort of criminal mastermind. Sophie felt uneasy. Mal was certainly smart and probably well connected. And she had been inside. The conversation carried on as Sophie fretted.

'What are you doing, boss?' asked Donald.

Everyone paused to listen. They knew that whatever he was going to do was where he felt the investigation was going. It was the same in any department, the lead detective always followed the hottest trail.

'Williams and I are going to bring Peloffy in for questioning. I don't like how he's been a part of this case from the beginning. He lent them the money for their boat, maybe he expected them to fail so he could grab the boat for himself. Maybe he was having an affair with one of the wives? He is French.'

One of the younger female detectives cleared her throat. 'That doesn't explain why the deaths were five years apart, also I don't think we can talk about the French like that these days, sir.'

'Never underestimate the obvious. You won't get far in this line of work if you are too busy being politically correct.'

Chastised, the woman started writing notes, but the tension in the room had changed. She was in the right and the rest of the room knew it. Clearly, Hemingstone also knew it and decided to remind everyone who was in charge.

'And don't forget it was him who found the tunnel and was also on the scene the following morning when the prints were found. He was hanging around Mrs Peck, the owner. No doubt trying to get information out of her. And I want more details on Mrs Peck. Let's dig deeper. Taphouse, you can do that. You've been talking to her. See what you can wheedle out of her.'

Sophie closed her notebook with a snap. She didn't like the direction this investigation was heading. Mal didn't strike her as anyone's fool, but Jacques had too many connections to this case and that was going to have to be investigated. Still, that was the problem with Golden: the more you investigated, the more you discovered everything was related. It was going to be a nightmare to follow the right lead.

'But before we talk to Peloffy, I'm also going to talk to Billy and Connor Trebetherick.'

‘You think they may be involved in their father’s death?’ called Donald. ‘What were they, twenty? They also have an alibi. They were up in Bath. Seems a long shot.’

‘After ten years, everything is a long shot,’ said Hemingstone, tucking his thumbs into his belt. ‘But their dad was up to something. Him and his partner, and I intend to find out what it was.’

Chapter Twenty-Five

Hemingstone and Williams were back in the Trebetherick front room, on the same cheap couch as last time. The two boys were sitting awkwardly together on the other couch, their large frames swamping the little two-seater.

'Thank you for talking with us today,' began Williams. The two detectives had already agreed that as the younger man Williams might get them to open up more.

'You should have made sure we were here when you told Mum yesterday,' growled Connor. 'Can you imagine what that was like for her?'

'We wanted to let your mother know as quickly as possible. We wanted her to know we were taking her seriously,' said Williams.

'The old woman in the bloody bookshop found it out, is what I heard. Had nothing to do with you.'

Hemingstone looked crossly at the men. 'We have asked you to keep the findings private and not discuss it outside of the home.'

'Stuff that,' said Billy. 'Connor, and I went down to the pub last night and put everyone right about all the rumours that have flown around the village these past years. Mum can finally hold her head high now she's been proved right.'

'But you may have alerted the murderer.'

'That's not my problem. Maybe if you lot had done your job properly at the time, we wouldn't have had to suffer so long. Do you know what our mother has been through?'

He broke off as Sharon Trebetherick entered the room and placed a tray of mugs on the side table and handed them out to everyone. She then placed a plate of biscuits on a side table beside the two detectives and sat on a chair next to the boys. Hemingstone looked at these three Cornish villagers. What were they hiding? They had insisted this wasn't a suicide all along. What did they know?

'Tell me. At the time, did you have any suspicions? Anything you didn't mention to the police but felt was concerning?'

Now Billy looked at him, his mouth ajar. *Ha,* thought Hemingstone. Thought you could hide something from me? Wondered how I could be so perceptive? I'm not one of your local coppers. I'm Detective Inspector Hemingstone.

'Are you bloody stupid?' Billy interrupted his thoughts. 'We told the police everything we knew. Which was nothing! Dad was one of the village; we're related to half the families here. Why would anyone kill him?'

His mother stretched over to him and patted his knee. 'It's okay, love. At least now everyone knows the truth. We'll get through this.'

Hemingstone nodded to Williams to resume questioning. They were clearly hiding something and reacting to Hemingstone's natural authority. A junior officer, more their own age, might lull them into a false sense of security.

'Mrs Trebetherick,' began Williams, 'on behalf of myself and all my colleagues in the force we are incredibly sorry that your concerns were overlooked. But,' now he leant forwards and dropped his voice, 'we are listening now, and we will find who did this to your husband,' he looked across to the boys, 'and your father. And we will see them behind bars.' He leant back again. 'Now, Mrs Trebetherick. As you know, we've been looking through your finances and noticed your husband was paying a regular amount of £200 a month to Jacques Peloffy, but the month before he died there was no payment. Do you know what that was about?'

The boys looked at their mother in confusion. 'Mum, why was Dad paying Jacques?'

Sharon waved her hand in dismissal. 'He and Roger were in trouble a few years back, and Jacques leant them some money for a new engine and a new refrigeration unit for the boat.'

'Bloody hell, that must have cost a lot?' Billy whistled. 'Why didn't we know?'

'You were children and you know how your dad was about money.'

Williams was nodding along, then stepped in. 'And why did he stop paying, Mrs Trebetherick? Had the loan been paid off?'

'I don't know about that. All I know was Paul came home one day and told me the loan was finished. Which, given the baby on the way, was a blessing.'

'A baby?' Both boys turned and looked at their mother. 'You weren't pregnant.'

Billy held his mother's hand. 'Were you?'

Hemingstone narrowed his eyes. Was this a scam? Fake pregnancy, blackmail?

'I lost it after your dad died. I was early stages but quite old, the doctor said.' She sighed deeply, lost in old memories. 'Ah, what does it matter what they said? Your dad was murdered, I lost the baby, your lives were falling apart, and the village was all saying it was suicide.'

Billy squeezed his mother's hand whilst Connor got up and came around to the other side of her chair and hugged her. Hemingstone watched on, ignoring the little charade, and thought how smart he had been to put Williams onto the questioning. He must have picked up those soft-soap techniques at Hendon.

Now the woman turned back to the officers, her face hot and angry.

'Our money worries were behind us, the boys were working on the boat pulling their weight, a new baby was on the way. We had just bought a new house. Everything was going great. Why would he have killed himself?'

Williams cleared his throat. 'Maybe we'll come back another time.'

The three were nodding, but Hemingstone wondered if Williams had the stomach for this after all. He had been doing so well, but now he was falling for the sob story.

'We still have questions,' he tried to match Williams' friendly tone. 'On your father's clothes, the coroner reported finding a hair that turned out to be a filial match.'

Three pairs of hostile eyes glared at him but remained silent.

'A filial match means—'

'We know what that means. Are you seriously suggesting there is something suspicious about one of our hairs being on our dad's clothes?'

Connor now got to his feet as his brother looked up at him.

'Wait,' said Billy, looking astonished at the detectives. 'Are you suggesting that we were involved? That we killed our dad. What the f—'

'Enough!' Sharon stood up. 'Get out of my house. The next time you knock on my door it had better be to tell me you've made an arrest.'

'We haven't finished yet,' blustered Hemingstone, as Billy stood up beside his mother and brother, looking down on him.

'You bloody well have, mate,' snarled Connor. 'If you don't get out now, I'll kick your arse out.'

Hemingstone moved with a speed that amused the Trebethericks, and within seconds found himself out on the street as the door slammed loudly behind him.

'That was interesting. Why would a man not tell his wife why the loan was paid off?'

'Some guys are like that,' said Williams, but Hemingstone ignored him.

'And a pregnancy at her age. His?' He looked across at the younger detective. 'Come on. You need to think this through. She's hiding something.'

Williams looked at him dubiously. 'Are you sure, boss, she looked genuine. So did the sons.'

'You know what I saw? I saw three people hiding secrets.' Hemingstone looked down the street. 'But let's leave them for a minute. I want to know why Peloffy cleared the debt. Was it his baby? If not, why cancel the debt?'

'Seriously?' Williams looked at him puzzled.

'Place like this. Don't let the cute cottages fool you; sex and money are the root of most things, and we have a lot of that around here.' He headed towards the car. 'I think it's about time we ask a few more questions about our mysterious Frenchman before we question him. The postmistress seems something of a gossip, let's see what she knows.'

Chapter Twenty-Six

Dear Oppy,

Please don't panic. I have no intention of getting involved. I only asked about the post-mortem because I felt sorry for the widow. I didn't realise it would open such a can of worms. And yes, you were right, village life is more complicated than I had understood. And yes, you were right, it is unnerving to have two unsolved murders in a village and me living at the scene of one of them, but really, I am fine.

Now, I also want you to stop guessing who the murderer is. Despite your worries, Jacques seems a nice man. Beyond that, I don't know, but he certainly doesn't strike me as a cold and calculating murderer. The two widows don't strike me as the sort I would want to be friends with but that also doesn't make them murders, and the boys were all too young for the first murder. I take your point that fifteen-year-olds can be big and given that they were all rugby players, I imagine they were. So it isn't beyond the realm of possibility. But then boarding up the wall, bricking off the passageway, taking the boat out to sea and abandoning it? I've met all three of them. Hot-headed maybe, but cool and calculating? Unlikely.

It was also very kind of you to remind me that I can stay at yours. I almost did last week. I was so despondent, but the villagers seem to be utterly unfazed by the fact I have a record. Obviously, they don't know why, at least some things remain private, but I feel that I can cope with their indifference. Once the police leave, life will become very much better.

In other news, and far nicer, I have been listing some of my shoes on eBay and they are selling! I'm saving for a winter swimsuit, a pair of wellies, and a pair of walking boots. Can you imagine?! It makes me laugh every time I think about my new wardrobe.

Right, time to catch the post. I will write again later but I wanted to reassure you I am having nothing to do with the investigation.

Much love,

M

Mal picked up her bag, a pretty canvas beach bag she had bought in one of the local shop sales, and popped her letters in. Today the shop was closed, and she meant to explore more of the countryside once she had run her chores.

'Have you heard? The police have arrested Jacques.'

Mal was standing in the queue for milk, minding her own business, when her head snapped up. Ahead of her, the postmistress and another woman Mal didn't recognise were busy catching up on all the village news.

'French Jack?' asked the second woman. 'Whatever for?'

Embarrassed, Mal realised that she too was now earwigging. It was intolerable but the idea of that reserved gentleman being bothered by the police irritated her. He might be a bit stand-offish, but that was no crime in her books.

'The police were in here asking if I knew where he was, so I told them he'd been in the other day, sending mail to a prison. He was most interested in that. You should have seen him. It confirmed all his suspicions.'

'Why would he be writing to a prison?' exclaimed the other woman, in horrified glee.

'Nothing good, is my bet! But that inspector's eyes were on stalks. He thanked me and told me I had been *instrumental in providing necessary information.* And when I told him where Jacques lived, the two of them dashed out the shop ready to nab him.'

Mal wasn't the only one listening, the entire shop had now stopped any pretence of examining the shelves and were listening intently to the postmistress' words.

'I always said there was something wrong about that man, didn't I?'

'You did that.' Her acolyte nodded in sycophantic agreement.

Mal had been listening in mounting horror: Jacques was receiving a visit from the police and it was her fault. She didn't believe for a second he had been arrested, they couldn't do that without evidence. Even so, listening to him being the source of nasty gossip, and her being to blame, was making her sick.

'Why only the other day—'

'Oh, knock it off,' called Mal from the back of the shop and walked up to the counter, all eyes on her.

'He hasn't been arrested. Just because police talk to you doesn't mean they arrest you. You're simply helping with their enquiries. Like you were when you told them about his post. Have you been arrested?'

Phyllis' eyes glinted at the challenge. 'Right enough then, and I suppose you'd know all about how the police work, wouldn't you?' she said, her face twisted in a mocking sneer.

'Well, *did* they arrest you?' repeated Mal. 'They talked to you, after all.'

The postmistress looked affronted at the very idea. 'Don't be ridiculous. I'm not the one passing information to Her Majesty's Prisons.'

'And neither was Jacques!' Phyllis looked at her with clear incredulity as Mal ploughed on. 'I was. Jacques was posting a letter on my behalf as I…' She broke off for a short laugh, then carried on, 'I was busy helping police with their enquiries following developments at the shop. I couldn't make it to the post office so Jacques kindly offered to post my mail for me.'

'Well, why are you sending documents to a prison, then? Hey, tell me that?'

'None of your business. Surprised you didn't steam the envelope to have a quick gander.'

'I would never!'

Behind her, Mal could hear a quick snigger and knew that the rest of the customers were having a high old time of it. She, however, could feel her temper mounting.

'If you say so. Now if you could give me Jacques' address I'll go over there now and explain it was my mail.'

Phyllis stepped back, affronted. 'I shall do no such thing. I respect the privacy of my customers, I do.'

There was a clear snort from behind Mal this time.

'But I want to clear Jacques' name.'

'I'm sure he'll tell them soon enough if the letter was yours, as you say it was.'

'He might not. He might think it's a private matter and not tell them. He might think that's the honourable thing to do.'

'Pah,' spat Phyllis, 'and what would you know about honour? You did five years inside. Can't have been a small thing for such a long sentence. Killed someone, did you?'

The room fell silent and Mal's shoulders bunched up as her faced tightened.

'That is none of your business.'

She strode towards the front door, frustrated not to have Jacques' address, but how could she stay in there a moment longer? As she got to the door, she paused and turned back to Phyllis, giving the postmistress an evil smile.

'I have never killed anyone. But the day is young and you are on my list.'

Out on the street, she smiled shakily to herself, the look on that woman's face had been priceless, but how was she going to find Jacques?

'The Lookout.'

Mal turned around to see an older man beaming at her. He was wearing a stained fishing smock, navy canvas trousers and heavy-duty leather pull-on boots. His face was as leathered as the boots and Mal thought he could be anywhere between sixty and ninety. The grizzled beard gave no clues beyond the fact that he would look at home in the black-and-white postcards of yesteryears fishermen.

'I beg your pardon?'

'The Lookout, maid. That's where you'll find Jacky boy. He's a good'un.' He made to walk away and Mal hurried after him.

'And where is this Lookout? Please, I don't know the area yet.'

'Head up Trebarra. Turn left at the lane, there's The Lookout.'

With that, he turned and headed toward the pub. Half an hour later and out of breath, Mal finally found a driveway with The Lookout on the gate. She had taken more wrong turns than she had right, until she finally found the right lane. Golden was full of little lanes and alleys and now surely, she had explored every one of them. She had passed the fancy new builds with their glorious views but lack of evening sun, then carried along a lane heading towards the coast path.

As no one was looking, she leant on the gate and paused to recover her breath and tidy her hair. She was a sweaty mess, but there was little she could do about that, and was grateful for a light breeze blowing down from the fields beyond. She was almost on the outer edge of the village. The land here was giving way from the concerns of the fishermen to that of the farmers.

Passing through the side gate there was a battered Land Rover, but nothing that she thought the police would drive. Relieved, she walked along the drive until it reached a two-storey brick house with neatly painted wooden windows and flowerpots around the outside. The property was clearly well cared for but not modernised; Mal wondered if Jacques' wife was the gardener. Knocking on the door, she hoped he hadn't been taken in for questioning. Plus, she was now desperate for a glass of water.

A shadow appeared behind the glass of the door, and as it swung open a visibly angry Jacques stood in the doorway.

'What do you want?'

Chapter Twenty-Seven

Jacques' voice trailed off as he looked down at Mal, who had taken a step back under his furious expression. Instantly he started apologising and invited her inside.

'Did you think I was the police?'

He frowned, then shrugged. 'My God, nothing stays private in this village, does it?'

'And yet, two men were murdered, and no one knows a thing about it.'

'This is true! Mon Dieu, the nonsense I have had to put up with from that oaf of an inspector.'

Mal noted that his accent became more agitated, and she smiled. She had noticed that under duress her own accent became more clipped and more Home Counties as the situation endured. Her first few weeks in prison she spoke the Queen's English better than the Queen herself and, in fact, since she had arrived in Golden she had noticed her voice becoming tight again. *Hise* not house.

'I think I must apologise for that.'

Jacques stopped walking down the hallway and turned to look at her. 'I don't see how. Would you like a drink? Coffee?'

Jacques turned and carried on down the hall, leaving Mal no choice but to follow. The front door had opened into a hallway with two rooms immediately leading off left and right, but Jacques continued to the door at the far end of the arts and crafts wooden panelling.

As Mal followed him into the next room, her breath was taken away by the view. At some point the rooms at the back of the house had all been knocked into one and the back wall replaced with full glazing. From this position on the hill, the house looked straight out over the bay. Out on the slate patio was a table and one chair surrounded by more planters. There was a small garden, big enough for a veg patch, greenhouse on one side and some fruit trees on the other, but nothing obscured the view.

'This is incredible!'

Jacques slid open the glass wall until the entire back wall was open. The effect was spectacular, like something off *Grand Designs*, and Mal appreciated the clever way the house had been remodelled. Jacques smiled softly and invited her to step outside. The air was still and she could smell the warmth from a freshly dug bed. There was a fork in the earth, and as Jacques had opened the door a robin flew off into a flowering bush, alive with bees. As pretty as the garden was though, she couldn't take her eyes off the village below and the sea beyond.

'You can see everything.'

'Yes, this was an old coastguard lookout spot, and before that it was a naval centre. I still have the flagpole and brazier. When they sold it off during a round of cuts, I bought it. It was cheap because it was so run down, and I loved the location.'

'Hard to believe this place was ever cheap.'

'Oh yes. Squatters had been living here, and they weren't the best stewards. Eventually after a wild party, an indoor fire got out of control. The damage was severe but not beyond repair. For the first year it was like camping; if it rained, I slept on the boat. When it was dry, I slept on the floor and repaired the roof and eventually everything else. Sometimes I think this old girl misses the days when she was responsible for warning the community of danger. So once a month I make a bonfire to keep her happy. Silly, no?'

It was silly, thought Mal. Before moving to Golden, she would have laughed at the notion, but since moving into her own cottage she had a keen sense of the history and personality of the building. She shrugged her shoulders.

'Maybe a little, but I think I understand.' She turned back and looked down on the rooftops. 'I'm trying to make out if I can see mine.'

Jacques pointed out a few roofs until they worked out which one might be hers, although her little rooftop terrace remained obscured by a neighbouring property.

'Look how close I am to the sea and yet I can only see a small section. You can see everything.'

'Perspective.'

'Perceptive.' She smiled as a rejoinder, a small play on words, and was pleased to see him nod in acknowledgement of her jest.

'Come on, let me make you a coffee, then we shall sit outside and enjoy the autumn sunshine. It will be gone tomorrow.'

Jacques pottered around the kitchen grinding beans, which brought a sigh of relief to Mal's lips, then he brought out a folding chair from the shed, insisting that Mal had the cast-iron one.

'I rarely have guests.'

Mal wanted to ask about his wife; there was no evidence of one, but a man this eligible was surely in want of one. Maybe he was in want of a husband and had been born in a less kind time? She decided it was his own business and wouldn't enquire. Instead she apologised for the issue with the post.

'Ah, they were coming after me anyway. That lead detective is a fool of a man. He can only hold one idea in his head at a time, and is loath to let it go for fear nothing else will replace it.'

She sipped her coffee in delight and realised that she was going to have to buy some beans and hope that Oppy had packed her grinder. She had missed the pleasure of a well-made cup, enjoyed in good company.

'He is a policeman who does not care about the rights and wrongs of others, only his own. He is the sort responsible for miscarriages of justice.' Jacques looked across at her. 'Which you sadly are all too well aware of.'

Mal put down her cup and looked out across the water. It was quiet up here, the gulls clearly preferred to stay close to the harbour and the easy pickings. In fact, she could hear a small songbird nearby proclaiming its presence to all and sundry.

'Mine wasn't a miscarriage.'

She saw him watching her out of the corner of her eye but didn't return the look, wanting to avoid the look of disappointment.

'I was guilty. And that's how I pleaded.'

The bird continued to sing into the still air.

'Ah well, we all have histories. Any regrets?'

Mal looked across at him, he seemed curious rather than censorious.

'For my actions or my plea?'

'Either.'

'Neither.' She smiled, carefully continuing their wordplay of earlier. 'I did it, and it was obvious I did it, so there was no point in adding further lies to my situation. If you've done something wrong, accept your punishment and move on.'

Damn, her voice was getting clipped again, but she was nervous. She didn't know Jacques, but he seemed a fair sort and she didn't want to be lacking in his opinion.

'I should go.'

'Not at all. I am enjoying your company; you are a surprising woman. Now, tell me, the police seem to be under the impression that Paul Trebetherick did not commit suicide. Was this to do with the envelope I posted for you?'

Relieved that the subject had moved away from her past, she quickly explained her friendship with Veronica Wells and her subsequent observations on the post-mortem report.

'So now the police are looking at two murders, they must be very excited,' said Jacques, nodding.

'But why have they fixed on you?'

'Because I am French?' He laughed and shook his head. 'Maybe, but more likely because I lent the two men a sum of money to help them through a tough winter, with the boat as collateral.'

'If you killed them, how could they pay you back?'

'Ah, but if they defaulted on the loan, I would get the boat.'

'But why would you kill them five years apart?'

'To avoid suspicion, according to *Detective Inspector* Hemingstone.'

'That's ludicrous!'

'It is more ludicrous when I show Hemingstone that the loan was settled the month before his suicide. If I had killed him, I wouldn't get the boat.'

'He had paid it off in full?' Mal didn't think fishermen were that well paid, but maybe he'd had a good season?

'No, he had a couple more instalments but I could see how hard he and the three boys were working to make things right and I noticed that his wife had stopped drinking alcohol. I figured a little one was on the way. So

I cancelled the debt and handed him back the pledge of collateral. So really, I had no interest in him or his boat.'

Mal wanted to comment on what a generous gesture that had been, but felt it was too personal a statement. Nonetheless, it endeared this formal Frenchman to her.

'So do you think they'll leave you alone now?'

Jacques gave a small Gallic shrug and sipped his coffee. 'Who knows? They seemed pretty excited by the fact I found the tunnel, and that I was outside your shop after your break-in. By the way, have you fixed that gate yet?'

'Yes, Sean went and bought a padlock that Raffles would fail to pick or cut.'

'Sean Trask?'

Mal shrugged. 'Works for Dennis Jenkins.'

'Probably the same boy, nice family. His aunt has the hairdresser's. Dennis has a nice team working for him.'

The pair fell into an easy silence whilst Mal enjoyed her coffee and the view.

'So what else could connect the two deaths?' she asked. She had promised Oppy she wouldn't get involved, but talking with Jacques, it was hard not to speculate. 'Is it even a coincidence? They are two very different killings, after all.'

'Dead is dead, no?' asked Jacques, curiously.

'Not really. The first death is furtive. Hidden away. The second is public but disguised.'

'But that would suggest two different murderers, one is rare enough. Two seems highly unlikely.'

'If it was in the same time frame, maybe. But five years apart? What on earth would connect them?'

'Maybe the second man discovered what the first man had?'

'And then gets silenced in a completely different fashion?' Mal shook her head. 'I don't buy it.'

'So now you think there are two murderers in the village?' Jacques raised an eyebrow. 'The police will surely try to blame me for one of them then.'

He laughed easily, but Mal was worried. That inspector was just the lazy sort who would go for a quick win.

'Well then, we have to find who really killed them, don't we? I feel responsible for dragging you into this. It's up to me to pull you back out of it.'

Jacques looked at her and raised an eyebrow. 'Isn't that the job of the police?'

'It is, but look what we've been saddled with. Inspector Clouseau.'

Jacques raised his hands in protest and laughed. 'Please, that is a stereotype too far.'

Mal returned the laugh and carried on, with a quick apology. 'Sophie Taphouse is part of the case though, I'll filter all my findings through her.'

'Keith's daughter. She did well for herself. Her father was a nasty drunk. Did that family the world of good when he left them.'

'You know everyone!'

Mal was surprised that he took part in village gossip. He seemed a remote individual.

'When you've lived here long enough, it all just seeps in. No matter how much you try to stay apart.' He paused and lifted the cafetière. 'Another?'

Mal was sure she should go, but this was the first relaxed conversation she'd had in years, and she was enjoying herself.

'If I'm not interrupting?'

'Not at all. Today is my own, I'm out on my boat tomorrow so I'm enjoying today's sunshine. Tomorrow it will rain, but the fishing will be good.'

Mal looked up at the dappled clouds stretched across the large blue sky and cocked her head at Jacques.

'Mackerel skies,' clarified Jacques.

'And?' Mal shuffled on the wrought-iron chair, wishing she had a cushion.

'Clouds like that mean rain is on the way.'

Mal leant back, temporarily ignoring the cast-iron back digging into her shoulders, and sighed as she looked up at the pretty clouds.

'Is this the end of the good weather then? It will be a shame if it affects the village fête.'

Jacques leant over and pinched a deadhead from a rose, then shook his head. 'It might be good again by then, these autumn summers can be very unpredictable. The fête has taken place in gales and heatwaves, nothing ever stops it.'

'So it might be sunny? Only, I'm taking part.' She glanced across at Jacques to see his reaction and realised that she was actually nervous about being involved. She was still waiting for everyone to start jeering at her.

'That's excellent news. What are you doing?'

'Ruth Jago has me walking along with the procession, collecting money for charity.'

Jacques slapped his hands on the table and laughed. 'That Ruth. She is a hard woman to like, but there is no denying all she does for the village. Next year she'll have you baking cakes.'

'Unless she wants a visit from the Health and Safety Committee, I will suggest she passes.'

'You don't bake?'

Mal grinned as he teased her. 'I do not bake. I barely cook. Do you think I'll be run out of town when the news gets out?'

'Almost certainly! But those problems are for next year. This year you will simply have to hope for sunny weather. But not tomorrow. Tomorrow, it will definitely rain.'

Mal sighed despondently.

'You had plans?'

'I'm heading to Truro. Provisions and the like. Plus I was popping into the library for some stock ideas.'

'So what's the problem?'

Mal adjusted herself on the chair trying to make herself comfortable and picked up her cup. Jacques stood and walked over to the garden shed, returning with a cushion.

'My apologies.'

Mal looked up at him with gratitude. She had tried to be inconspicuous, but he had still noticed.

'I was looking forward to tomorrow but now it's going to be standing around in the rain, with a shopper,' her voice shuddered as she milked the melodrama, 'at a bus stop.'

'Mon Dieu! The horror. Is it the public transport or the rain?'

Mal shook her head and placed the back of her hand dramatically on her forehead. 'The shopper. I'll look like an old lady.'

'Impossible,' said Jacques gallantly, then chuckled. 'I can't help with your shopper quandary, but I can help with the bus stop.'

Chapter Twenty-Eight

The following day, Mal found herself driving cautiously into Truro in Jacques' old Land Rover. In his words, it didn't get driven enough when he was out at sea so it was at her disposal. Before she could summon up a decent argument, he had put her on the insurance and the deal was sealed. It had taken a bit of negotiating with the insurance company to insure an ex-offender, but Jacques had gallantly left the room when she had to give the details of her offence. In her eyes, his gallantry outstripped his generosity.

Now she was clattering along, it was noisy and draughty, a far cry from her old Audi, but it did the job, and soon she was navigating the traffic and parked near the library. First stop though was the market and she went off to explore.

It wasn't as big as she had been expecting, there was only one stall selling bread, one selling charcuterie, one selling veg, but each stall was bursting with the finest produce and she was pleased by the scale of it. Too much choice could result in dithering, which she disliked immensely. She hadn't meant to stop at the bakery but the loaves on display were spectacular.

'Can I get you anything?' A big man with a grin almost as broad as he was, smiled across at her. 'The Chelsea buns are particularly good this morning.'

Mal shook her head. Although he was right, they were enticing, but they were so big she'd have to invite people over to share one.

'The loaves look particularly nice but I'm afraid I'd waste it. You need to sell them by the slice.'

'Here's a tip from some of my customers. They buy a full loaf. When they get home they cut the whole thing into slices, take one out then put the rest in a freezer bag and freeze them. That way they can have a slice when it suits them.'

Mal laughed in delight. That was ingeniously simple.

'But is it only good for toasting then?'

'No, let it thaw out properly and it's fine to use in sandwiches.'

She noticed that he was using French flour in some of his loaves and Jacques had said there was a decent bakery in the market. She ordered two loaves, one for herself and one as a thank you for Jacques.

Deciding to treat herself, she also ordered a Portuguese custard tart, then moved onto the veg stall. By the end of her shop, she was laden with bacon, olives, vegetables and salami. There was a woman selling Cornish mead and some sort of hedgerow wine, Mal shuddered and wondered where she might find a decent wine merchant. Her only other disappointment was all the lovely bunches of flowers that she had spotted as she arrived had sold out. In future, she would start there.

Heading towards the library, she dropped her provisions in the car, grabbed her notepad and pen and entering the library, headed to the research department.

After her conversation with Jacques the previous evening, she had decided to look into the news reports of the disappearance of Jago and suicide of Trebetherick. Ever since she had arrived in Golden, she had been inexorably pulled into events. Now her involvement and her history was dragging innocent people into the police's investigation. The least she could do was inform herself on the history of the cases. Maybe she would spot a connection between the two of them.

Three hours later, her head was splitting from reading old newspapers on microfiche and she decided to ask for help. Nothing had jumped out at her. There had been an article about Roger Jago's disappearance with the sorry conclusion that he had drowned at sea. She did find one curious article. At first she couldn't work out why the search engine had brought up this feature on sunken treasure ships until she read on.

'Has the curse of the *White Maria* struck again?'

Two young fishermen who believed they may have located the resting place of the Elizabethan lost galleon, rumoured to have sunk carrying the treasures from the Americas, have now either died or disappeared.

The story went on to suggest that Jago and Trebetherick may have discovered the location of the *White Maria* – an Elizabethan privateer – apparently laden with treasures from the new colonies as well as treasure relieved from Spanish galleons. A storm had blown up soon after the ship had been sighted passing Falmouth. No doubt the captain was trying to outrun the weather and make it to the shelter of the River Fowey, but it was never seen again. The winds were blowing south-south-west and for months bits of wreckage drifted onto the beaches of St Austell Bay. But no survivors were ever found, nor was the treasure.

As the centuries passed, rumours grew as to the location. What was known, though, was what had been on the ship. The Spanish government lodged a complaint that the *White Maria* had attacked their vessel and made off with its jewels and golds. The sailors of the *White Maria* had taunted that the haul was minor in comparison to what they had already acquired. The money would go to the English crown to obliterate the rest of the Spanish fleet. Had the *White Maria* ever made it to London it would have been the event of the year.

Over the centuries many had lost their lives trying to find it, earning it the reputation of the Spanish Curse.

Yawning, Mal decided to head back. It had been a good day. She had found some book suggestions for her shop, discovered some local history and had lots of tasty local produce. What she hadn't managed to find was anything to clear the cloud hanging over Jacques' head. As she returned to the Land Rover, her mind was spinning with the treasure ship. Was it possible that the men had, in fact, found the *White Maria*? And if they had, where was the money now?

Chapter Twenty-Nine

Betty sat at the bus stop and shivered. High Street was a wind tunnel and faced north. With no sun and a cold wind, her bones soon knew about it. She scoured the traffic, keeping an eye out for a familiar car. She was quite tempted to stick her thumb out and hitch home, but no one did that anymore. Would today's drivers even know what she was doing?

Her prayers were answered though when she saw Jacques' Land Rover head towards her, and she stood and raised her arm in salute. She may have also stuck her thumb out for a laugh. The car overshot the parking bay and with a noisy crunch on the gears, tentatively reversed towards her, as a second car overtook and honked its horn. She'd enjoy teasing him for making such a hash of that. Leaning on her shopping trolley, she walked towards the car. As she got to the side window, she realised it wasn't Jacques. A woman was fumbling around the dashboard and, eventually giving up, leant across the passenger seat and stiffly wound down the window.

'You're from the village, aren't you? Would you like a lift?'

Betty smiled. Jacques' car shook more than the bus at the best of times. But it looked like this driver didn't even know how to drive it.

'Have you pinched Jacques' car? Shall we be Thelma and Louise?'

She watched the younger woman blink in surprise.

'Which one of us gets to be the mad impulsive one?'

'I think that's got to be you for stopping for a stranger.'

'Very well then. Jump in.'

Betty looked at her and laughed. 'Jump in, she says. Fly to the moon would be as likely. Plus, I have my shopper. Jacques normally puts it in the back for me.'

Realisation dawned on the other woman's face and she got out of the car and came around to Betty's side.

'I'm Mal by the way. Is there anything in your shopper that might break?'

'I have chrysanthemums and some homemade ready meals. What have you got?'

'Bread, wine and cheese. They'd sold out of flowers.'

Betty nodded in approval at Mal's shopping, then helped her as the two of them lifted the shopper into the back of the car. Neither woman was particularly tall and they laughed as they struggled to haul it up, eventually laying it down alongside Mal's own shopping.

'It's a nice little market, isn't it?'

'Actually,' said Mal, 'I also came into town to do Jacques a favour. Not that he asked. I'm just so mad that that ridiculous inspector thought he had anything to do with either of those murders. So I thought I'd read through the archives. See if anything leapt out at me.'

Betty watched as Mal pulled away. The woman's eyes were on the road and she wasn't breaking her concentration. Her tone of voice was outraged on Jacques' behalf and Betty felt well disposed towards her.

'You know,' said Betty, as they drove slowly out of the city, 'I thought we'd agreed on *Thelma and Louise*. Not *Driving Miss Daisy*.'

Mal quickly looked at Betty in confusion, then snapped back to the road, her eyebrows drawn together.

'Ah yes. The lack of speed is more for my benefit than yours. It's been a long time since I've driven a car, plus I don't know these roads.'

Betty winced, she hadn't meant to make her driver uncomfortable. Living alone it was easy to forget other people had worries and concerns nothing to do with you. She decided to try and change the subject.

'You seem quite determined that Jacques is innocent, despite knowing him for what, three whole weeks?'

'Let's just say I used to make a lot of money by sizing up a situation quickly. I've always been a problem solver, and I like to think I'm a good judge of character.'

'Modest, hey?'

'What's the point in self-deprecation?' She shrugged and smiled at Betty. 'We're all so quick to say we're rubbish, I look dreadful in this, I'm hopeless at that. What a negative bunch of people we are. So yes, I am rubbish at cooking, I do look dreadful in camel, I'm not great at driving; I am excellent at making decisions. See, it's easy.'

Betty laughed. 'You're driving fine enough. So, did you find any evidence that our Jacques is innocent?' She checked the wing mirror at the mounting queue of traffic behind them. As Mal slowed to take Portman's Bend, Betty considered leaning out the window and picking some blackberries from the hedgerow. However, she wasn't as good a judge of character as her driver claimed to be and wasn't sure if Mal would see the funny side or be offended. At least there was a straight section coming up where everyone could overtake. As the road straightened, car after car overtook them.

'Oh dear. Am I going terribly slowly? Maybe I should speed up a bit?'

'Fourth gear might help?' suggested Betty carefully, pleased when Mal laughed and ground the gears.

'God, I'm rubbish. I bet you wish you'd taken the bus now. Anyway, Jacques' case. No, I couldn't find anything substantial except a small speculative piece about a sunken treasure boat and a curse.'

Betty clapped her hands and hooted with laughter. 'My God, yes, it's been a while since that's been mentioned, but I dare say it's going to resurrect itself now. Every boy and girl will be claiming to know the location. They'll be out on their paddleboards and fishing boats, eyes fixed on the depths below.'

'So it's real then?'

Betty inhaled deeply, catching the scent of her flowers over the diesel of the engine. Then exhaled laughing and gave a French shrug.

'As Jacques would say, *bof*. Who knows? What I think is true is that a boat called the *White Maria* did exist, and probably sank during a storm in the 1600s somewhere off the south Cornish coast. Maybe around Golden, maybe not. And maybe she was carrying a load of treasure, or maybe that's been talked up. Then again, someone did find the treasure and sold on the quiet. And the one that keeps treasure hunters awake at night, *maybe* there is still a horde of treasure somewhere out there.'

'And the curse?' said Mal, indicating as she overtook a cyclist.

'Ah, the curse,' said Betty dramatically. 'Someone goes out looking, a week later they get hit by a car, or they lose their job. Any bit of bad luck, no matter how tenuous, is blamed on the curse. If that person was connected to the hunt, or their husband was, or the neighbour, or a friend of a friend, it's down to the *White Maria*.' She broke off, laughing. 'See, that's how curses work around here. All stuff and nonsense.'

'So, how is it connected to the disappearance of Roger Jago?' That bit had puzzled Mal. The paper hadn't explained the connection and she couldn't see it herself.

'Well, around that time a rumour started in the village that he had found the treasure and faked his own disappearance.'

'Did anyone believe that?'

'That he'd leave his wife and child behind? No. I knew that he and Ruth were having issues, but he idolised his son. There's no way he'd have abandoned him. No, it was fun to speculate, but honestly, no one really believed it and the idea of the treasure ship sank away again.' Her eyes twinkled. 'But now we know Roger was murdered and so was Paul. Maybe the two men were hiding a secret after all?'

They were approaching the village now and Betty directed Mal down a farm track, as they approached the farmyard gates, she took a smaller drive through some woods and pulled up in front of a little cottage. There were sheep in the fields beyond the cottage and a tidy little garden around the house.

'Pretty, isn't it? I have all the privacy I need and very friendly neighbours when I don't.'

Both women got out of the car and Mal helped Betty with her shopper, refusing the offer of a cup of tea.

'Then have some of my flowers, I bought more than I needed but they were just so happy. And look, I have plenty around the cottage as it is.'

Betty waved as Mal drove off, making a pig's ear of clipping the hedge and hitting every pothole. When she next saw Jacques, she would recommend he took Mal out on a few driving refresher courses. Especially if he ever planned to let her drive that beautiful Bugatti he kept tucked away in his garage.

She was grateful for the lift but needed a cup of tea to recover. Heading into the house, she said hello to the sheep in the field who all said hello back. Stooping down, she picked up the jar of honey that Mary, her neighbour, had left on her doorstep. She had a fresh loaf in her shopper; a nice piece of toast with butter and honey would be perfect. Humming the honey song, and thinking of little black rain clouds, she headed inside, switched on the kettle and pulled out one of her small golden plates with a grin. It seemed appropriate.

Chapter Thirty

'We're back!'

Sharon put her magazine down and switched off the TV. She thought the boys would be out for the afternoon, but as they came through to the kitchen, she could see the anger on Connor's face and the annoyance on Billy's.

She sighed and put the kettle on. 'Now what?'

The boys looked at her in surprise as they shrugged their coats off. 'What do you mean?'

'Don't give me that. I've known you for the past twenty-nine years. You've a face like thunder,' she said, addressing Connor, then turned to Billy, 'and since when have you ever come home early from the pub?'

She stared at them, but they simply returned her look. Two chips off the same block.

'Out with it. No one's saying that your dad killed himself now, are they? Or that he killed Roger?' Her voice was rising now and Billy rushed in to calm her down.

'No, it's nothing like that. It's just—'

'Let it go, Billy. They were being stupid. You know what this bloody village is like. God's truth and gossip.'

Her boys were now banging around the kitchen, making a cup of tea. She missed their big clumpy presence in the house. Still, she knew they were trying to avoid the subject.

'And…'

'Ah, Mum, we were in The Ship and they started to talk about the *White Maria*—'

'Are you bloody kidding me? Who was it? Was it bloody Dave? I've never heard grown men talk such bloody nonsense. First it was Roger might have run off with it, as if he'd ever leave his family. Now what are they saying?'

'Well, they were saying that before Dad died, we'd moved into this place.'

'My God. So now they think we had the treasure all along. Have they even got a brain? Did they think for those five years we were scrimping for the fun of it? Was it Dave? Was it? I'll bloody swing for him.'

Sharon slammed her mug down and grabbed her keys as Billy moved in front of the door.

'Mum, calm down. What will that achieve? Give them more gossip. For years they thought Dad had killed himself, despite you telling them otherwise. Then they find Roger's body, and the next bit of gospel is that Dad killed Roger but killed himself five years later with guilt. And now that both those theories have been proved bollocks, the village is after the next daft theory. You going down there shouting your head off will only give them something to gas about. Let it go.'

'Come on, Mum, Billy's right. Small-minded bastards, the lot of 'em. Besides which, it was the police that was asking about the *White Maria*. You don't want the police asking you questions in front of the whole pub leaning in. Sit down. I don't know why you stay here.'

The wind spilled out of her sails. Why did she stay? This was her home. She'd grown up here, her boys grew up here, and she had hoped to watch her grandchildren grow up here as well. But Connor wouldn't even bring his fiancée. Their baby was due in a few months, and Connor had said outright that she would have to travel to them. When their first baby arrived, she'd had to travel up country. Alfie was such a little dear. It broke her heart that the boys wouldn't come home, but Connor was adamant. He wouldn't bring his children to this cesspit, as he called it. Billy was the same. The boys had adored Golden until their dad had died, then they couldn't leave fast enough.

'Where else would I go, boys? This is my home. I was born here, I'll die here. Mum and Dad are up in the graveyard. So is your dad.'

'But they're dead, Mum. We're alive. Move near one of us.'

'And what about my friends?'

'You don't actually like any of your friends, Mum!'

'And what's that got to do with it?'

The boys rolled their eyes at each other, but Sharon ignored them.

'Okay, Mum, whatever, but it's time we went home.'

'So soon?'

'Ah, come on, Mum. We've been here for over a week. You know, we only came back to stand by your side. All that bloody gossip about Dad having killed Roger. Now that's laid to rest, I want to go.'

Sharon stared at them. 'Don't you want to know why your dad was killed?'

'Jesus. Mum, of course I do, but how can I stay here knowing I'm probably looking at his killer every day? It's someone in the village, Mum.'

'Oh, don't say that.'

'Who else can it be? Why did they try to hide it and make it look like a suicide? That's not an accident or a random killing. Why would a stranger go to such lengths to hide what they'd done?'

'So no one would investigate.'

'Exactly, which must have meant they thought they might be discovered.'

'Seriously, Mum,' said Connor, 'I'm with Billy. Let the police do their job.'

Billy snorted. 'If this lot had taken care of things properly first time round, we wouldn't be here. It took some bloody outsider to uncover the mess the coroner made of Dad's case.'

Sharon sighed deeply and sank back into the chair. What was the point? The village had let her boys down, the police had let their dad down. No wonder they didn't want to stay.

'Will you stay for the festival at least? That's only another two days? Maybe you could catch up with Piran?'

She felt weak with happiness when they both nodded, smiling.

'As it happens, we're off out on the boat with him tomorrow. One last haul for old times. The weather's good, so we'll have a catch for the harvest as well. Now, what do you fancy for tea? I'll cook.'

Connor laughed and turned to his mum. 'See, his Bryan is already domesticating him.' He turned back to punch Billy in the arm. 'When are you two going to settle down?'

As the tension gradually seeped out of the room, Sharon wondered how much longer she could carry on living this life. Always on edge, always ready to snap. Maybe the boys were right, maybe she should leave.

'So how is Piran doing? I don't see him much. I see enough of his mother, more's the pity.'

'He's doing fine. Fatherhood suits him. He said he was thinking of selling the boat. He doesn't want it to go on another generation.'

'Never thought the day would come when there wasn't a Trebetherick or a Jago out fishing on Golden Bay.'

'Well, tomorrow there'll be three of us.'

'Tell you what, Mum,' said Connor. 'If it makes you happy, why don't we all dress up for the carnival like we used to? Do you still have the old costumes? I bet you still fit into the mermaid one. I'll be Captain Nemo if you have Dad's outfit. And pretty boy here can be the lobster!'

Sharon scoffed at the idea of fitting into the mermaid costume, but if she got the sewing machine out, she could add a few panels. She and her boys on the floats again, showing the village what the Trebethericks were made of. Maybe if the boys enjoyed themselves, next year she could convince Connor to bring his family as well. Remind the boys of the best of Golden.

When the boys had been little, they would dress up as crabs. She probably still had the costumes. Little Alfie would be adorable as a little crab and they could dress the new baby as a starfish. His fiancée was a good-looking sort. She would make a cracking mermaid. She thought about Billy's partner. Bryan was so handsome he'd make an excellent merman.

'Penny for them?'

Sharon shook her head and laughed as the two boys were both looking at her quizzically.

'Nothing. Just thinking about costumes. Maybe next year we could all dress up?'

She watched as the two boys exchanged a glance. It was one of their long-suffering, let's humour Mum looks, but at least it wasn't an outright rejection.

'Come on then. Billy, get cooking. Connor, help me get the boxes out of the attic.'

Chapter Thirty-One

Dear Mal,

Truro sounds lovely, although I still can't picture you tucked away in deepest, darkest Cornwall. If you really are selling your shoes, can I bagsie the knee-high brown suedes? You know I always looked excellent in them. The flat pair, mind you, these days I'd probably break my neck in some of the heels you used to love. Honestly, I just can't imagine you wearing wellies. I hope they are Aigle's at the very least? I know you said you were okay for money but let me know if you're struggling.

Now onto more important matters. I know you, and I know you are probably bored out of your mind and trying to solve a crime that has nothing to do with you, but leave it to the police. Your sister and I were talking the other day and she's worried sick. It's their job. Besides which, if you still have a murderer running around, you don't want them to notice you. And don't bore me with lots of murderers are nice people actually. You were in a female prison. Female murderers are completely different, and don't argue with me.

I must say, I do enjoy writing letters. One can't be interrupted, plus one gets to say "one" a lot, which is also fun.

Have you found anyone to play bridge with down there? I have a few friends in Cornwall, would you like me to make some introductions? Do you remember Ginny and Paul? They have a place outside Rock. That's not too far from you, is it? Do you want me to see if they are staying there at the moment? Is it too soon? Am I jumping the gun? I am, aren't I? Ignore me.

That's the other problem with writing letters. No interruptions, so one witters on past the point they would have stopped sentences ago if their best mate had been standing in front of them glaring. But never fear, I can sense your glare from here. Moving on.

Jacques sounds interesting, I want to hear A LOT *more about him, and Betty sounds like the sort of person people write biographies about.*

We're seeing Oppy tonight, I'll send them your love and we'll share notes on what we think of Jacques, then tell you what you should do next.

Lots of love,

Me!

Mal laughed and sipped her wine. God, she would love to be with her best friend and her sister, but for now she wanted to be by herself and she couldn't do both. She and Caroline had been at college together and bonded over a mutual horror of the disc jockey's playlist. She was also one of the few people who stood by her side after the trial. Some said it wasn't a surprise given her involvement, but as far as Mal was concerned it could have gone either way.

Dear Caroline,

The boots, when I find them, are yours. Fingers crossed you didn't have to partner Giles, that man can't bid for toffee. I am missing bridge, maybe I'll see if anyone round here plays. It will be fun to play without the risk of the deck being confiscated for some petty infraction. Obviously, I'll never miss prison, but some of the women were very good company and excellent card players, and I do miss them.

Now, I shall write more tomorrow, but I wanted to stress that you are not to worry about me. I am fully aware that uncaptured murderers are not to be trifled with, but thank you for being a friend. Please don't mention this to Henry if you see him. The lecture would be interminable. Plus I don't want him to worry. I feel I have made all of you worry too much over the past five years.

Of course I haven't opened the champagne. Jacques and I are not romantically entangled in any way. If anything, he's a bit rude for my liking. Well, not rude, more arrogant. Well, not exactly arrogant, but you know. Not my sort, anyway.

The bookshop is proving to be a great success or at least people are coming in and buying books, which I think is the point. I'm having to brush up on my reading knowledge PDQ but I've noticed that if you ask the customers about books, they will talk at length about their favourites. There are also people who come into the shop, buy nothing, but still talk at length. They seem quite surprised when I tell them I have work to do; I seem to have broken some unwritten rule about bookshop people just sitting and listening to some tirade without interruption. I am bookselling, but not as they know it.

Someone suggested I watch Black Books, *have you seen it? Is it by David Mamet? I don't recognise the title but I think the National ran it a few years back. Am I thinking of the same thing? Ah well, I suppose Google is my friend as they say, but I have found my desire to always look things up has dwindled. It might return, but these days I don't feel so hypervigilant. The need to know everything has waned a bit.*

One thing that I didn't expect was how much the village sort of expects me to be involved in stuff. News of my incarceration got out. Don't worry, I'm okay. And honestly, the villagers didn't blink an eye. Just asked if I'd be okay walking with a charity bucket at next week's harvest festival. Apparently, it's also fancy dress. Do you remember my Pussy Galore? I wonder if that's in any of the boxes that Oppy packed. Gosh, that would be fun.

By the way, I had a letter from Miranda the other day. It seems she's going to even more parties than we did at her age. Chip off the old block!

Mal pushed back from the table and started running a few household tasks. As she pulled out a chair to hoover, she saw with embarrassment a pile of clothes that she had thrown in a corner. Her white palazzo pants and jacket. When she had come home, she'd been in such a state, she had torn them off and promptly forgot about them. It had only been a fortnight, but she already felt a different woman to the quivering wreck who had sat and sobbed into the small hours. Scared of people looking at her. Scared of facing the world again. Scared of her secrets being revealed.

Grabbing the outfit, she put it in for a presoak and hoped to God she hadn't stained the trousers beyond repair. Popping a frozen meal in the oven, she switched the TV on. As soon as the oven door closed, Mal heard a familiar thump from upstairs and moments later, Mac ran down the stairs and twisted himself around her legs until she laid a pouch of food on a small plate for him and placed it by a bowl of water.

Despite Mac not being hers, he had certainly made himself at home. She had asked around, and it seemed he was a stray. Which Mal hoped meant no one would mind if she fed him. He certainly didn't seem to object. Most of the time, she left the top door open and he came and went as he pleased, but it was getting noticeably colder now, and sometimes when she came upstairs from work the rain had soaked her carpet. It had got to the point where she would lay out towels and she realised she was going to have to stop leaving the door open. Mac would have to learn to use the front door.

He didn't always stay after he'd eaten, but tonight he wandered over to the other armchair, jumped up, stretched once and promptly fell asleep. Mal studied him in bemusement. Well, she didn't want a lap cat either. Most inconvenient.

Switching away from the news, she found a David Attenborough programme. Between him and Susan Calman, her evening could always be brightened. She'd found her taste for the high arts had softened over the years, but she drew the line at *Gogglebox* or any shows where the public were the stars, scripted or otherwise. She was just settling into an exploration of the Southern Ocean when Mac's ears pricked up and she heard a rattling sound coming from the kitchen. She'd had to turn the TV up over the sound of the washing machine, but the noise was louder than both of those. Grumbling, she pulled herself up from the sofa. It was very comfortable but hellish to get out of gracefully. Muttering to Mac that he'd better not be laughing, she headed into the kitchen to locate the source of the sound and realised it was something in the washing machine. No doubt a pen lid or a pencil sharpener, but she'd have to put up with the noise until the cycle had stopped. Until then, she'd eat her risotto and dive back into the oceans.

Mal jerked awake and saw with dismay that she had fallen asleep on the sofa and her plate had slid off her lap. Mac had eaten what was left of the prawns and salmon, but the creamy sauce had spilt across the cushion and carpet.

'Now look what's happened. Eating on my lap. Falling asleep in front of the television. You're a bad influence, Mac.'

Mac stretched, bored with the admonishment and headed off upstairs, no doubt off to harass the local rats. Heavy rain was forecast, and she was going to have to close the door again. And like last night, Mac would no doubt meow until she woke up and let him in. Between her morning swims, her midnight disturbances and shop work, Mal was constantly tired. But she knew part of it was also down to her body and mind adjusting to life outside a prison routine.

Getting up, she stripped the cushion cover and headed through to the kitchen. She was about to switch the machine over to the dryer cycle when she remembered the noise and opened the door. As she pulled out the clothes, she couldn't see the problem until the machine was empty, and sitting at the bottom of the drum was a button. She looked at it perplexed, then remembered the grubby piece of metal she had discovered in the tunnel. She had put it in her pocket then, in the subsequent panic attack, had completely forgotten about it.

Now she knelt on the kitchen lino and looked at the golden button in wonder.

Chapter Thirty-Two

Detective Inspector Hemingstone was in a good mood. He had caught Jacques out twice and was waiting for the final lie before he could arrest him on suspicion of murder. He watched as the man headed out to sea and wondered if he should have insisted he stay put. He wasn't buying his guff about finding the tunnel. He also couldn't properly account for how he bought his house, one of the finest properties in Golden. Certainly, the one with the finest view.

Peloffy had laughed when he asked him about the *White Maria*, saying he'd have more luck seeing Lord Lucan ride Shergar down Fore Street. Then, without asking permission, he stepped onto his boat and headed out to sea. These fishermen could make a run to the continent if they needed to. Hemingstone was tempted to arrest Peloffy now, but he didn't quite have enough evidence. Half the time you needed your suspect to have their hands in the blood if you had any hope of a conviction. It was madness, but he'd play along, confident that any day now he'd have the proof he needed.

He stood and inspected the harbour. They were hiding secrets here but that was fine, he'd uncover every last one of them if needs be. Other boats were heading out, including one being manned by the three lads at the heart of this investigation. Despite their attitude towards him, Hemingstone could find nothing to pin on them, and indeed they had a rock-steady alibi for their father's murder and were surely too young for Roger's.

Looking away from the water, he saw the old baggage from the bookshop and the village policewoman chatting. He was going to ignore them when he saw the policewoman, whose name he couldn't remember, hold out a small plastic bag and the older woman dropping something in it. If evidence had been found, he should be the first to know. He strode towards them, glaring at a family as he walked through their photo.

Mal watched as Jacques' boat headed out of the harbour. She had hoped to catch him in her lunch break, but the customers wouldn't leave and by the time they had gone, Mal had missed the tide. She hadn't thanked him in person for the use of the car and had been looking forward to the chance to chat. She also wanted to show him the button. Instead, she saw Sophie in full uniform walking around the front of the harbour smiling and chatting to people, and headed over.

'Just the person.'

She liked the warmth in Sophie Taphouse's smile. Maybe this young woman would restore her faith in the police force. She knew in her heart they were the good guys, and before her brush with the legal system she would have backed them to the hilt. Life inside, though, had coloured her views. Hearing the stories from the women inside of neglect and abuse over decades, her opinion had been altered.

Holding out the button, Mal explained what she had found and apologised for washing it.

'I know I've ruined any fingerprints, but in case it means something?'

Sophie whipped out a little plastic bag and got Mal to drop the button in it.

'We'll check for prints and we have yours on file. But if it's been washed, I think as you say, anyone else's prints will have gone. DI Hemingstone is in the village today. He's got a bee in his bonnet that this is connected to the *White Maria*. Every kid in Golden grows up believing there's treasure just beyond the rock pools. I suspect the tale persists each year as mothers send their kids outdoors to get out from under their feet. 'Oh God.' Sophie rolled her eyes. 'Speak of the devil.'

Mal watched as the inspector marched towards them, barging through a family photo and cutting a swathe through a coach party of old dears. No doubt they had finished milling through every shop, picking everything up, showing it to a friend, then putting it down again in the wrong place. Now they were out in the fresh air, nudging each other and pointing to boats.

She tried not to grin as a group of them told him off for bad manners and he huffed past them. A seagull glided overhead, laughing as it went, and if it hadn't been for the peevish policeman, it would have made a delightful scene. His hand was now outstretched towards Sophie.

'Give me that!'

Mal watched him snap his hand out, that easy arrogance of entitlement. He held the little plastic bag up to the sun and whistled appreciatively.

'Well, well, well. It seems my suspicions about the missing treasure were correct.' He nodded in self-appreciation, but Mal just looked at him and sighed deeply.

'It's a button.'

Shaking his head at her ignorance naivety, he smiled.. 'It's a *gold* button.' His tone dripped with condescension as he stressed the word gold.

'It's a *brass* button.' Mal's correction was polite and slightly amused.

Hemingstone's composure slipped slightly, and he glared at her. 'And now you're an expert on gold as well, are you?'

Mal choked back her first retort. There were too many children walking around with their parents. Plus, he had the power to make her life difficult as regards her parole.

'No, Inspector. I am not an expert, but if it were gold it would weigh more, and the button has a modern fixing at the back indicating it's at maximum a hundred years old, so it can't be from the fabled treasure ship, and finally, gold, due to its softness, makes for a very poor fastener.'

She paused and smiled. 'But by all means, get an expert in.'

The inspector turned the button over and looked at the back, then made a show of weighing it in his hands.

'Well, whatever it is, it will have prints on it. Where did you find it?'

Mal blew her cheeks out and looked at Sophie despondently. 'I found it in the passageway that runs down to the river in my shop.' Hemingstone's eyes lit up, but she plunged on. 'But there won't be any prints on it. I put it in the washing machine.'

'Are you bloody stupid?' Hemingstone roared at her and Mal took a step backwards. A seagull startled by the noise flew off, and several people turned their way. She could see the inspector's sidekick peel away from a group of fishermen he was talking to and come running over. A young man walking with his wife and child stopped and walked towards Mal. He took in Sophie's uniform and gave Mal a concerned look.

'Is everything okay?'

'Police business, sunshine,' snapped Hemingstone. 'Move on please.'

The man was not prepared to be waved on so quickly. 'Only this lady seems alarmed to be shouted at.'

Mal tried to intervene, thanking him for his assistance, but Hemingstone carried on. 'This *lady* is a convicted felon and is currently helping me with my enquiries.'

Sophie had been standing quietly by Mal's side. It was disappointing that the button had been washed, but she doubted it was deliberate. The inspector's attitude was out of order and constantly bringing up Mal's conviction was pretty distasteful. Williams had now arrived to stand by Hemingstone's side, to no doubt back him up, but she could see Tony and his mates heading over from their boats. Tony was her father's brother and hewn from the same lump of granite. Fists first, questions later. Arguing with the police would be right up his alley. The other fishermen weren't so hot-headed but they had no truck with a man shouting at a woman. Sophie wanted to avoid any potential confrontations so first, she needed to get this helpful passer-by to leave, then try to extricate Mal before this got out of hand.

'Thank you, sir. Everything is fine here.'

She smiled at Mal, who smiled back and nodded in agreement.

'The inspector here was disappointed that I have messed up a piece of evidence. Entirely my fault,' said Mal.

'If you're sure?'

He looked at Mal again and frowned, trying to work something out. Sophie tried to hurry him on his way. Tony was getting closer, and she wanted to contain the situation. Incidents between Tony and the police often ended in written warnings.

'Weren't you in the bookshop earlier?'

Mal patted her skirt and smiled at him brightly. 'Well, us convicts have to do something when we get out. It's bookshops or bank robberies. I chose the former.'

The man laughed loudly. 'I like your attitude. I was just saying to Chloe how nice a shop it was.' He turned to address his wife. 'The bookshop. It's lovely, isn't it?'

Chloe lifted her bag of books and smiled as their daughter waved. Chloe, wisely, didn't take one step closer to the situation.

'Alright, Sophie love?'

'Alright, Tony.'

The gallant husband, now seeing that four fishermen had joined the scene, felt happy in rejoining his wife.

'How's the new boat doing?'

Tony had recently started running tourists out into the bay on a big red RIB, pointing out seals and dolphins as well as screaming along at high speed. Not necessarily at the same time. He'd stepped on Bob Yates' toes, who had been running wildlife trips for years and had certificates and everything. Sophie knew there was some ill feeling about it, but she kept quiet on the matter. Bob was a nice sort, and her uncle was a mouthy bugger. No doubt in another year he'd be trying his luck at something else and sell his boat to Bob for a song. For now, though, Tony was pontificating about the joys of his powerboat.

'Proper job. Beats fishing.'

The other men laughed.

'That's because you're a bloody useless fisherman,' joshed one of the men; the others joined in laughing. This was good. A few more seconds and the tension would dissipate completely.

'I told you to move on. This is a police investigation and you are hampering our efforts,' ordered Hemingstone.

'Hampering your efforts, is it?' asked Tony, lightly, and the other fishermen stepped closer. Sophie shook her head at him. He cocked an eyebrow at her and carried on. 'Sounds to me like you were shouting at this lady.'

'Convicted criminal.'

'Oh aye, stabbed someone with her knitting needles, did she?'

Mal had been quiet all this time, but now grinned across at Tony. 'I'd be more likely to stab someone with my stilettos if they accuse me of knitting again.'

The fishermen roared with laughter and slapped Tony on the back. Tony joined in and shook his head.

'Ah, right you are, maid. That's me well and truly told.' He turned back to the inspector. 'So what has she done then?' He looked at the button in the evidence bag Hemingstone was still holding. 'Button theft, is it?'

The fishermen started laughing again, and Mal smiled back at him and relaxed into the banter. Only Hemingstone appeared pissed off. Williams, however, like Sophie, knew the fishermen were not yet happy with the situation, and nothing was to be gained here.

'Sir, I had an interesting lead, but I don't think I should mention it in open company.'

Well done, lad, thought Sophie, *you may be a sycophant, but you're not an idiot.* A silence fell over the group, waiting to see how the inspector would respond. Looking around, he glared at the hard faces and narrowed his eyes at Mal. Then, deciding that the mood had turned against him, he nodded curtly at Williams.

'Good, I'm glad we've got something from this village. Come on and take this.' He thrust the evidence bag at his colleague.

'A button, sir?'

'Found in the passageway, but no prints as Mrs Peck here decided to wash it clean. And now I am asking myself why she would have wanted to do that?'

He stalked off, with Williams moving quickly to catch up. Tony nodded at her once, then turned and headed back to the boats. As the other men joined him, she distinctly heard the word *stiletto* followed by more laughter and jokes about buttons. Soon it would be all across the fishing fleet.

'Alright, Mal?' asked Sophie. 'Sorry about that. If I were you, I'd keep as far away from our inspector as you can.'

Sophie was unsurprised to see Mal raise an eyebrow. This wasn't a woman to hide from a fight. She just hoped she had more common sense than some others around here. Hemingstone was whipping the village up into a frenzy and Sophie was worried how it might end.

'I'll do what I can, my dear. In the meantime, I had best go and reopen the shop.'

With that, she headed back along the harbour. As Sophie watched her go, she couldn't help but feel a deep sense of unease.

Chapter Thirty-Three

Mal stretched carefully. In the past she moved slowly after a day of vigorous exercise. Now she creaked and groaned simply because waking up had become painful. A sudden stretch and she could pull a muscle. Getting old was a bloody chore. No matter how many people wittered on about wisdom, it was a poor substitute for increasing infirmity. That said, she now stretched carefully because Mac had taken to sleeping on her bed and attacking her toes if they peeped out of the duvet.

Looking out over the rooftops from her bed, the sun had risen and the sky was blue. Mal had been keeping an eye on the forecast all week, hoping the good weather would hold for the harvest festival, and now it seemed like Golden was in luck.

Frowning, she headed downstairs carefully as Mac tried to break her neck, weaving between her feet on the steps. After placing some food in his bowl, she grabbed her swim bag and headed down to the sea. The water was getting noticeably colder now, and she was toying with the idea of buying a wetsuit, although she'd never owned one before. The money from her shoe sale was mounting up but she couldn't decide between sensibly saving it or splurging on something she might not make use of. She resolved to ask the sea swimmers next time she saw them but didn't want to get dragged into the cake and bobble hat sorority. Everybody wanted to belong to something, and not wanting to join in marked you out as stand-offish or odd. Neither of which bothered her, she'd simply had enough of having to do stuff with other people.

She nodded a greeting to the men up ladders, erecting the sails and lanterns along the harbour wall. A few shouted out to her that she was mad to be getting into the water, but it was a gentle camaraderie and she carried on. Mac came running along the pavement towards her, and Mal decided that some companionship was enjoyable after all.

The low sun shone into the gullies, offering a false offer of warmth as Mal and Mac slid into the water. Despite the sunshine and the flat water, Mal pulled herself up via the chilly metal handrail after only ten minutes. A wetsuit it was.

'Has my book arrived?'

Mal craned her neck to the polite gaze of Jacques as he held out her towel. She pretended to search her swimming costume.

'No, it's not here. Hold on.' She quickly wrapped her towelling dressing gown around her, then checked the pockets. 'Not in there either.'

She grinned cheekily at him and raised her eyebrows in challenge, smiling at his discomfort.

'I meant in the shop.' He looked about him and shoved his hands in his pocket.

'I know what you meant. But you had me at a disadvantage, you being fully clothed and me—'

'And you in a raiment of smiles and seaweed.'

Mal cocked her head in surprise.

'That's somewhat poetic.' She hurried on, noticing his embarrassment. 'But yes, your book arrived yesterday. I'll be open at ten but closing at lunch. I'm carrying a collection basket for the procession.'

She pulled the gown tightly around herself. It was getting chilly and she wanted to head home. She was about to suggest they walk back together when he cleared his throat and walked off, saying he would be in at ten thirty.

Now Mal was left with the awkward situation of following him, but a few metres behind, or waiting until a decent gap had been established. She shivered and scowled. Mac jumped down from a spot on the higher wall and came bounding over to greet Jacques. As he bobbed down to greet the cat, Mal's scowl deepened.

Men, always happy to stop and natter with no concern for those standing around shivering, waiting for them to bugger off. To hell with it. Mal grabbed her bag, but Jacques, having looked over at her and seeing her scowl, stood up abruptly and walked off.

And now I suppose he thinks I was scowling at him, not at the situation. Her parents had always warned her that her face was too expressive. She could roll her eyes so hard she could flip her entire body. Sighing, she trailed along after him. She was too old to be trying to make new friends.

Ryan Williams had spent the morning ploughing through financial reports. His hopes of a quick escalation up the police ranks had recently stalled as he had realised his new boss was an idiot. When he'd arrived with his bluff no-nonsense throwback ways, Ryan had thought he was watching a modern-day Gene Hunt. Like a wally, he had played along thinking that ingratiating himself with a rising star would ensure his own success. As the days progressed, he finally remembered that Gene Hunt, unorthodox admittedly, had a brain between his ears. Hemingstone had custard.

Now, instead of following in his boss' wake, it was up to him to steer him in the right direction, and as he looked at the screen he felt his hopes rise. There wasn't enough evidence yet, but he may be about to tie both the Golden murders and the recent drugs ring together. If he could do that, maybe his boss would stop chasing after old women. Even better, here was a name that Hemingstone already had in his sights. Printing out the records, he headed over to the office.

'Boss, I think I may have a lead on the drugs ring. A name cropped up that cross-referenced in the Golden investigation. And I think you're going to be pleased when you see who it is.'

Williams handed over the sheet of paper and pointed to the name he had already highlighted. He was relieved when Hemingstone smiled and stood up.

'I bloody knew it. Those fishermen and their swaggering attitudes. Did he really think he could make a fool out of me? Hidden wealth. Unexplained absences. Let's go down to Golden and ask a few more questions.'

Hemingstone swung his jacket around his shoulders, then untangled the sleeves and tried again.

'Just think. If we can tie him to the murders as well, we'll have proved this drug ring has been operating for decades.'

Williams was dubious. 'You think the two are linked?'

'Course I do. Bloody obvious. I was only using the treasure angle to coax people into a false sense of security.' He laughed loudly. 'Gold buttons. Who'd be fooled by that?'

'Good call, boss.' Ryan nodded along. He hadn't been convinced about the treasure, but he didn't believe Hemingstone had been that canny. That required the ability to hold two thoughts in his mind at the same time and Ryan was beginning to wonder if his boss could even hold one. Still, a lead was a lead and by tonight they might finally make an arrest.

Chapter Thirty-Four

'Just make sure no one throws their rubbish in!'

Mal looked dubiously at the woman distributing the charity buckets. Penny Trowbridge was currently organising the volunteers for the festival procession. She was dressed as a rabbit, her red hair tied up in bunches, with fake freckles painted on her face. A stalwart of the WI, Penny was involved in most of the village fundraisers, she also ran the local yoga classes. Mal had tried one, then retreated in horror. Group activities, as suspected, would not be her forte.

'But the buckets are marked "Donations" and I'll be walking alongside the floats?'

'Yes, they are, and yes, you will. And still, some bloody bleeders will try and dump their rubbish on you. Oh, and watch out for frogs. Some kids think it's funny to get a frog into a bucket. If you get any rubbish or frogs, put your arm up and one of the marshals will come over and empty your bucket of extra stuff. Same applies if the bucket gets too heavy with change. Any notes, put them in your pocket or bury them under the coins. Sometimes people like to take as well as give.'

Mal listened to all this in amazement. She had thought walking with a charity bucket would be easy. Now she had a list of dos and don'ts as long as her arm.

She was dressed as a corsair with a wide-brimmed hat and a long feather. Penny had presented the hat to her when she saw her jacket and trousers and her boots with their turned down tops.

'You look so rakish you need the hat to complete the outfit!'

She also presented her with a sweeping sword that hung at her side, and Mal was enjoying the smiles and claps as she went past.

Penny had introduced her to Ruth Jago, and the two women acknowledged each other uncomfortably. Although Mal was happy to help the cause and had a deep sympathy for the other woman's plight, she simply couldn't take to her. Ruth was currently dressed as a Georgian lady, complete with a big white wig, and was now explaining the finer details of bucket care. Repeating everything Penny had said.

'And keep an eye out for children carrying frogs!' said Ruth.

Mal thought Penny had been pulling her leg earlier, but Ruth didn't strike her as the sort to tease.

The staging field, aka the school yard, was filling with people, and the noise was building. The band kept trying to tune. Teenagers were checking their clackers and whistles were working for the umpteenth time. The local dance troop were practicing their moves to Wham!, now apparently deeply retro. Mal winced, she still thought Wham! were the next big thing. Piling out of a van in the far corner of the car park were a group of bare-chested men wearing kilts, heavy boots, and big drums. Mal wondered if ear plugs would be permissible.

As she watched, her heart sank as another car pulled in, having been waved through by the marshals. Mal watched in dismay as Hemingstone and his sidekick Williams, stepped out of the car and headed toward the main staging area. She wanted to disappear but hadn't received instructions on which float she was attached to. Penny ran this like the Iron Chancellor, and Mal was determined not to step out of line. But here came the police to pee all over the day.

She watched as he stopped to ask someone something, then headed directly towards her. She braced herself for the next round of insults.

'Mrs Jago?'

Ruth looked up in surprise, then rose to her feet. 'Good afternoon, Inspector. Can I help?'

Despite the earlier noise, people found quieter activities as they struggled to listen in. Mal imagined a good thirty people had suddenly paused what they were doing.

'We have been following a particular lead and I am happy to say we will be making an arrest presently. Someone in this village is concealing a great deal of money, and I can't help but wonder where they got it from.'

Ruth gasped dramatically and slumped down onto her chair, her blue silk gown and wig making the action even more theatrical.

'How glad I am to have a man who knows what he is doing. I am so grateful to you, Inspector. How I wish you had been here when Roger first went missing. Maybe poor Sharon could have also been spared my dreadful anguish.'

Pushing through the crowd, Piran stopped and took in the scene, kneeling down by his mother.

'What's happened? Are you okay?' He turned and glared at the inspector. 'Why is my mother crying? What have you said to her?'

He stood up now and took a step towards the officer, and Mal couldn't help noticing that these two were always the centre of attention. The village queen and prince, a king in the making. Every society had its hierarchy and as Mal watched people fuss around Ruth's dramatic display of grief, the men stepped aside to allow Piran to vent. So long without a husband or father, abandoned without explanation, how it must have hurt them. *Did the villagers also feel guilty they could not supply answers?* wondered Mal. Then when the body was found, did they feel greater shame that they had gossiped he had run away? Found the pirate's gold. Found a fancy woman. Found a sense of freedom. Turned out that all he had found was his maker.

'I was just telling your mother we are close to an arrest.'

'Took you long enough,' challenged Piran. 'Have you found the gold, then?'

'There is no gold,' scoffed Betty, who had come to stand alongside Mal. 'That story is older than I am, which is saying something.'

She got a few laughs, but the crowd was fired up by the idea that the treasure may have been found after all these years. Hemingstone looked angrily in their direction.

'What you may or may not know, madam, is irrelevant. I am not interested in village gossip but in cold hard facts, which I am about to finish gathering.'

He peered at Mal and suddenly recognised her through her outfit.

'And Mrs Peck.' He studied her bucket, then scoffed. 'A collection bucket?' He looked around the crowd, sneering at Mal then smirked at Penny, who had also arrived, clipboard in one hand, megaphone in the other, and a yellow fluorescent jacket. Everything proclaimed her as Event Organiser.

'You think you can trust her, do you? You know she's been in prison. For five years!'

The crowd looked, if anything, bored. Mal knew that word of her imprisonment was probably yesterday's news. What surprised her was how little they cared. It seemed the entire village already knew. Hemingstone was also clearly unimpressed by the lack of reaction.

'I think you'll change your minds when you discover what she was inside for.'

The crowd stirred. This was something they didn't know. Mal flinched. The bastard was about to tell them what she had tried to keep to herself, not just because she was embarrassed by the events, but also because it wasn't wholly her story to tell. In the crowd she saw Phyllis smiling a sour, vindictive smirk – preparing to look shocked and then gloat. Christ, if there was a guillotine, that woman would be front and centre knitting.

Hemingstone took a deep breath and Mal cut him off.

'I stole some money. I was guilty, I confessed, they sent me to jail.'

Her words fell into the silence. If she was going to be revealed, she would rather do it herself than give that oaf the pleasure. So far, the crowd seemed less than shocked.

'Five years seems a long time,' called out Phyllis.

'It wasn't just some money though, was it?' mocked Hemingstone, desperate to regain the upper hand. 'It was two point five million pounds, and you stole it from a bank.'

'You're a bank robber?' asked Sean, in awe.

'No,' corrected Mal, with a tight smile. 'I worked for the bank. Stole it from a client's account. Neither the bank nor the client looked on my theft kindly. I told them what I had done and I was arrested.'

'Couldn't you simply give the money back?'

Mal shook her head, smiling sadly. 'No, I'd already spent it.'

'Bloody hell, Prof! What did you spend that much money on? More shoes?'

There was no getting away from this, she was going to have to drag out the whole sorry tale. Maybe then she could properly draw a line under it.

'My god-daughter needed a series of lifesaving operations and stem cell treatments. Her parents were selling their house to raise the money. But the sale fell through. Miranda was getting sicker and time was running out.'

Mal clenched the sword by her side, her palms sweaty. She kept eye contact with Sean only. If she spoke to him, she could try to pretend that no one else was listening.

'I worked for an investment bank and one of my clients had a side-line in drugs; we handled his clean money, but everyone knew he was dirty. So I stole from him. As soon as her treatments were underway, I explained to her parents I had lied about where the money had come from and confessed to my employers.'

The reaction from the crowd was not what Mal had expected. In London she had been shunned, her colleagues had been appalled and she was ostracised almost immediately. Her memberships were cancelled, and she was thrown out of all her professional associations. Within days her social life had collapsed, workmates viewed with horror lest her level of corruption and stupidity be catching. Mal was never sure if the disgust was for the act itself or for the subsequent confession. She suspected it was the latter.

Hemingstone cleared his throat. 'Not so impressive now, is she? A thief and a convict.'

'She sounds alright to me,' said Sean, and Mal saw with surprise that a few people nodded in agreement.

'She stole two and a half million pounds!' reiterated Hemingstone, annoyed by the lack of impact Mal's revelation had caused.

'Aye, from a drug dealer to save the life of a child.'

This time there was more nodding and some smiles. Collette was actually grinning.

'She's a criminal!'

'Not much of a crime in my eyes,' called Collette.

'She stole from a bank!'

This time the crowd actually laughed at the inspector. 'I've heard worse.'

The crowd was now openly laughing, and Mal looked around in bewilderment.

'I don't understand,' she said to Betty. 'What I did was really wrong. I was vilified for what I did.'

'Well, I suppose all your banking friends would have seen it differently. Down here though we see the why of what you did. And you have to remember, Golden has a long history of not seeing customs and banks in the same way the law does. A village as steeped in smuggling as this one will always hold some crimes as less important than others.'

'But it was wrong,' stressed Mal. 'I betrayed the sacred trust between a client and their bank.'

'Some things are more sacred than money, maid.'

Mal was staring, but all she could see were smiles. She was doing her very hardest not to cry.

'Right, now this little bit of drama is done let's get on with things,' called Penny. 'The procession kicks off in half an hour. Mal remains in charge of ticket sales, unless anyone objects, and we still need marshals for the car park.'

With Penny back in control, Mal watched befuddled as the world continued to turn. Hemingstone stormed off, with Williams running to catch up with him. Collette gave her a wave from the cake stand and most people smiled at her and got on with their jobs.

'Are you alright?'

Mal turned to see that Jacques had come over to join her.

'Yes. Yes, I think so. It's… I was expecting something else.'

'Come and sit down for a minute.' Jacques walked off and came back with a cup of Pimm's punch from one of the stalls. 'Here, calm your nerves.'

'I'm fine.' But Mal saw as she took the paper cup her hand was visibly shaking and tears threatened to prick her eyes. 'It's just such an anticlimax. Did you hear everything?'

'C'est vrai. In our own minds we turn things into impossible monsters.'

He was right, the girls in prison hadn't cared either. She had been carrying her own guilt and shame for so many years that she had become her own jailer.

'And the little one. The child. Did she survive?'

Mal coughed as she laughed and tried not to sob. 'Very much so. She's at university now and writes to me of all her latest adventures. She wants to travel in her gap year and keeps asking for my advice. She thinks I've spent these last five years travelling the globe.'

'So she knows nothing about what you did?'

'No. No one could visit during her treatments, then as she recovered we said I was off travelling. I suppose at some point I will have to tell her, but I'm dreading her reaction. I don't want guilt or gratitude. But I also don't want her to think worse of me. I worry it will change the relationship between us.'

'It might. But again, you may be overthinking things?'

Mal laughed. 'That's normally considered one of my skill sets: it was what made me so good at my job.'

An air horn blasted causing Mal to flinch, still on edge from her darkest secret being revealed.

'That's the start of the procession. You had better get going.'

Mal drew herself up, then patting her hands on her lap, she stood and turned to look back at Jacques. 'Are you coming?'

'I'll be at the back of the parade carrying one of the larger paper models. Me and a few fishermen are walking a sea serpent.'

'I'll have to grab a photo. Maybe I'll see you after the parade?'

'Perhaps. But something the inspector said rang a bell. I need to check something. Now you had better run along.'

Mal pulled a face at him. 'I think my running along days are behind me.'

'Shall I order a Zimmer frame instead?'

'Oh behave, you impossible Frenchman.'

Mal laughed and strode off, swinging her bucket, towards the front of the procession. The band was beginning to slowly judder out of the car park. It would weave in and out of the lanes before stopping at the harbour for an open-air blessing from the priest, then finish at the playing fields beside the church.

Chapter Thirty-Five

Mal was having a great time. So far, she had collected the sum total of zero frogs, and lots and lots of coins and notes. People were enjoying her costume and the fact that she made a pantomime of bowing and swinging her hat in a wide swoop. She was laughing hard and couldn't remember when she had last had so much fun. She was enjoying a friendly rivalry with Clemmie, one of the village teenagers who had dressed up as Elsa. She got the coins from the children, whilst Mal was getting the notes from their grandparents.

When Mal had first taken her station, Clemmie had laughed and shaken her head.

'Competition, I see.' The white curls from her long wig bounced on her shoulder. 'Bloody hell. I hope I look as good as you at your age!' She shook her bucket at Mal. 'Pirate or princess. Let the best babe win.'

Mal grinned back. Babe indeed. But the gauntlet had been dropped, and she and Clemmie began playing to the crowd as the procession headed off.

They had paused now at the front of the harbour, the priest was blessing the fleet and mercifully the band had fallen silent. Mal was flagging. Her arm was sore from holding out the bucket, her feet were sore from walking on cobbles in heeled boots, and she had a thumping headache from all the whistles and the brass band. The noise echoed through the lanes, bouncing back at you in painful harmonics. Still, there was a brief respite and Mal shared a can of coke with Clemmie. The drink tasted vile, but the camaraderie made up for it.

'Which of us is ahead do you think?' asked Mal.

'I reckon you are. I don't care, I just want to beat Rhi.'

Mal looked blank.

'The slutty mouse with her boobs shoved up under her chins.'

'Not a fan?'

'Are you having a laugh? After she stole Robbie from me. Then ditched him saying I had made him too boring. As if! He was boring all by himself.'

Oh God, thought Mal, *teenage love. Was there anything more painful?*

'I'm sure this float is going to win the largest collection. We do have a bit of an unfair advantage.'

Whilst Mal and Clemmie were well dressed and playing wonderfully to the crowd, there was no taking away from the fact that their float comprised the toddlers' group. All the little ones had dressed up as fish, and one Buzz Lightyear. Their mums and dads were having a great time calling out to the crowd, and Mal was certain that they would raise enough money this year for some new equipment in the children's allotment.

Peter Hoxley was walking towards Mal with a replacement bucket, although Mal's bucket was only half full. Peter was the landlord of the Harbour Lights, one of the six pubs in the village, and was always the first in line helping in village events and fundraising. A born and bred Golden man, he had told Mal that he'd visited London once but couldn't see the point of it. His comment had blown her away. Imagine dismissing London so casually, but he was simply a man that loved his own home more. And that was fair enough. Now he gave her a wincing smile.

'Mal, I need you on the front float. Young Billy twisted his ankle and has had to go home.'

'Ah fair play, Mr Hoxley,' shouted Clemmie, 'Mal and I are killing it back here. Don't take my bae.'

'That's as maybe, but I think you've got the prize in the bag. This float has taken double what anyone else has collected.'

'Even the Young Farmers' float?' asked Clemmie gleefully.

'Even them.' Turning his attention back to Mal, he swapped her buckets over.

'Do you mind? It's noisy up there behind the band but the procession is nearly done.'

Mal swept her hat off her head and swung it in a slow graceful bow. 'As my lord requests.'

'That's the spirit,' Peter said, and continued back along the procession, squeezing through the crowds making sure everyone was ready for the off.

Mal turned and pulled a face at Clemmie. 'I shall be deaf at the end of this!'

'First round's on me,' said the teenager. 'We all gather in The Barley Sheaf afterwards. I'll see you there.'

Mal headed forward; she hadn't been to The Barley Sheaf yet. It was the first pub in the village and therefore the furthest from the sea. For that reason, it was less popular with visitors, although as the only pub with a beer garden it could sometimes get rammed in summer. That said, Mal didn't think she'd be making it to any pub. She was dying on her feet and convinced she had more blisters on them than a new chef had on his hands.

Taking her position at the front of the float, she looked up to see what the theme was. Nearly everyone was dressed as a mermaid, even the men, and Mal wondered if there were any coconuts left. The men not dressed as mermaids were naval captains or Neptune – big, heavy navy wool coats or tridents.

As she looked at the faces, she saw the Trebetherick family and friends. Sharon was dressed as a mermaid and was in her element waving at some of the older men in her low-cut bustier. Billy was sitting beside her waving a trident and trying to make her behave.

Despite his censure it seemed in good spirit and the pair of them were laughing. As Mal watched, Connor walked around from the other side of the float to join them. He was wearing a heavy navy peacoat, and as Mal looked at him, she realised the buttons on his coat were familiar. Seven buttons featured a dolphin and trident on the shiny gilt face. An eighth was missing and had been replaced with a brass button embossed with an anchor.

Mal pulled her phone out of her pocket and took a photo, zooming in on the jacket, then took a few more pictures to try and hide what she was doing.

'Are you okay?'

Mal turned to the voice and muttered. Because she was so short and her hat brim so wide, she had to remove it to see who was speaking if they stood too close. And in these crowds there was no other option. Removing her hat, she looked up at Piran Jago. The one person she really didn't want to see. How could she tell him she had just discovered a clue to his father's murder?

'All good here. What are you doing with that bucket?'

She pointed to the bucket full of blue and green paper confetti in his hand.

'It's to bless the little opes and alleys that those processions don't go through. Me and a few other volunteers from the church walk every step of the village and throw confetti on the floor. It's largely symbolic, but it shows that God is taking care of the whole village.'

'That's a lovely tradition.'

'It is. We've had do-gooders in the past who complained that we was littering, but we soon put them right.' He huffed in disbelief. 'We only use paper, and in the morning each street sweeps up its own section.'

He spoke defensively and Mal nodded in approval.

'Sometimes people don't understand tradition and stability.'

A slow smile of relief spread across Piran's face and Mal thought he might be a more pleasing young man if he wasn't always frowning. But then he had had a dreadful time as a teenager, and these past few weeks had been awful.

A trombone slid into action and a bang on the drums made her jump.

'You keep staring at Connor? Is everything alright?'

Mal shook her head and pointed to her ears. 'It's fine, I was taking pictures for my Instagram.'

Until she knew for certain that the coat was connected to the button, she didn't want to raise the lad's hopes. He was looking down at her phone and she swiped the screen away from the zoomed-in image of the coat.

'It's a hobby of mine. They look happy, don't they?'

Mal was shouting over the noise, but now Piran was staring at the family group as they waved out to the crowd. Connor spotted Piran and waved at him. The young man waved back and indicated a drink later, then turned and pushed his way through the crowd.

She watched in concern as he made it to his mother, currently standing on the podium on the jetty. From where she was watching, they appeared to be arguing and Mal hoped she hadn't made the situation worse. There was no reason for Piran to work out what was special about the coat but he didn't seem happy. Ruth's holierthan-thou attitude stuck in Mal's throat but she wouldn't wish her further grief. Hopefully, this would soon be resolved. Mal didn't think for a second that the two Trebetherick boys were involved, but that coat was one hell of an issue. She needed to find Sophie and tell her what she had discovered.

The band walked away from the harbour. The on-foot processions headed off to the left-hand side of the village, whilst the floats moved slowly along the main road up to the church fields. She saw Jacques in the distance carrying the tail of a sea serpent, and he looked her way and waved. Waving back, she saw Piran had gone, no doubt to spread more confetti through the tiny footways, and hoped she hadn't upset him about the button. As soon as she stopped she would tell Sophie about the coat and suggest that she investigate further, but for now, she needed to shake her bucket.

An hour later, Mal hobbled away from the playground and down to the harbour and a deep bath. She had just enough charge left on her phone and dialled Sophie's number.

'Mal is everything okay? I'm a bit busy right now.'

Sophie sounded tense, but Mal knew it was important that she told her about the button. As she explained, she could hear Sophie swear at the other end of the line.

'Damn it, Mal, that's lousy timing. We're about to arrest my bloody uncle Tony for smuggling. Seems he's been involved in the local drugs operation. I'm praying it's just bloody fags.'

'How did they find out?'

'They've been running pretty much everyone's financials that had anything to do with Paul and Roger. Seemed that Tony's new shiny speedboat was paid for in cash that he can't account for. I swear to God, if it's drugs, I'll swing for him.'

Mal felt so sorry for Sophie, the fury in her voice was clear.

'Would you like me to call Hemingstone directly and tell him about the button?'

Sophie snorted. 'He won't answer. He's leading the raid. It's like Hollywood down here. He's ordered in tactical as well as dogs.'

Mal looked around at the harbour. People were out on the streets laughing and drinking, music and light was spilling out of the pubs, and the boats rocked to and fro on their moorings. There was no evidence of a raid taking place.

'Where are you?'

'Falmouth. Look. I'll make sure Hemingstone knows about the button. I'll tell Williams as well, he seems bright enough. Someone will be round in the morning to take a statement, okay? And don't tell anyone what you found. Bollocks. Got to go.'

In the background, Mal heard barking, then Sophie hung up. Mal limped on home and hoped that the case would soon be solved. She had a sense that things were speeding up but she couldn't say why. Deciding that she had simply been disturbed by the sounds at the other end of Sophie's call, she dismissed her worries and headed past the merrymakers as the crowds continued to dance and sing into the night.

Chapter Thirty-Six

Mal opened her eyes in the darkness. Something had woken her. The sky outside was dark, but the moon lent shadows to the rooftops. Even the harbour lights were off so it had to be the small hours, and everything was silent. Even the gulls were asleep. Mal lay in bed wide awake, her heart pounding. She could hear nothing now, no matter how much she strained to listen, but something out of place had woken her. Was it inside or outside?

A gull screamed out and flew up into the night. Under the noise of the bird, Mal heard it. The hollow echo of metal. Someone was creeping up the fire escape that led to her patio.

Did she have time to slide out of her bed and tip-toe downstairs without drawing attention to herself? Could she jump up and lock the doors before whoever it was could run across the roof and slam into her? Neither option seemed viable, and as much as she didn't like the idea of Plan C, it was the one she was going to try. Very slowly, she moved in her bed and dropped her hand over the side until she felt what she was after.

When her brother had heard of her sleeping arrangements, he had insisted that she place various items by her bedside. Right now she'd give anything for a rifle, but, as she had pointed out to Henry, guns and parolees were a total no-no. Instead, she grabbed the cannister and crept towards the open doors. A pale hand emerged on the top handrail and Mal knew she had the element of surprise. Stepping onto the patio, her heart racing, she squeezed the lever and the ferocious siren of a foghorn tore through the silence of the night. In her other hand, she turned on the torch and shone it down onto the ladder.

A voice shouted in alarm, and in the darkness Mal could only make out a shadowy figure as it fell from the steps and landed on the roof below. Keeping to the edges, they ran away across the slates and down the next roof ladder. All the gulls were now awake, screaming in defiance that their slumber had been shattered. For a brief moment Mal grinned to herself, *see how you like it.*

And then she was back inside. Locking the patio doors, she grabbed her dressing gown and hurried downstairs and outside. She had ditched the foghorn but still had the torch and now swung it up and down the street, hoping to get a glimpse of her intruder's face. The street was empty and she jogged down to the harbour in her slippers, adrenaline fuelling her pursuit.

The visibility was better away from the narrow alleyways and the large moon hung overhead, but there were still too many shadows. He could be hiding anywhere.

'Malachite?' A voice called out in surprise and the beam of light from Mal's torch shook as she tried to hold it steady.

'Who's there?' Damn it, her voice was as shaky as her hand as a tall man walked out of the dark towards her.

'Malachite. It's me, Jacques. Are you okay? What's happened?'

Mal sagged in relief as Jacques guided her towards a bench and she explained what had happened.

'And like a mad woman, you ran out into the night to give chase?'

Mal shrugged and laughed nervously. 'Well, yes. But dammit, Jacques, that's my space they tried to break into. I'm not some little mouse.'

'In my eyes, you are a lioness. But stay here, let me see if I can see anyone.'

As he walked off into the shadows, Mal caught her breath, her whole body aching from the pain of adrenaline thumping through her body. She had choked once and remembered the same painful sensation then, her fingers stinging painfully as she tried to calm her heartbeat. What had she been thinking? She knew the right thing was to try to catch her intruder and demand an explanation, no matter how stupid that sounded. She thought ruefully about what she had said to Jacques. She might not be a mouse but she had been behaving like one. Before she had gone to jail, she had never once thought of herself as old. Sixty-five was no age but being one of the oldest women in prison had played with her mind. And here in Golden, people seemed old before their time. She had fallen into the pull of other people's expectations and like a rudderless fool had gone along with their interpretation. It was about time she reclaimed her narrative. For now, though, she was just going to sit and shake.

As she sat on the bench, she listened to the gentle sounds of the water softly rocking the boats back and forth. Nothing dramatic, like the closing motions of a baby falling asleep. A rat ran along the harbour front and she watched its progress. Out here, the rat bothered her less; this was where it belonged, and it probably loved this time of day, unbothered by brooms, shovels and people screaming. Poor thing. Still, if it came any closer, she would shine the torch at it, and if that didn't work she'd throw the bloody torch instead.

'Malachite.'

Mal jumped in alarm. How had he got so close? Jacques took a step back.

'It's me, Jacques.'

Now she laughed, utterly embarrassed at her foolishness.

'Yes, I know. I'm sorry. I was watching a rat and wondering if he could talk what he would say.'

'He'd say, *good evening*, then be on his way.'

Jacques sat down at the other end of the bench. 'Are you sure you're okay? I couldn't see anyone.'

'Oh, he'll be long gone. Back into his own house no doubt.'

The idea that her would-be burglar lived so close filled her with a deep sense of unease. In London, the threat of danger always came from *away*. Lockdowns were placed to stop people escaping, neighbours would all cling together in shared alarm. Someone from outside had threatened the peace of the area. Travelled by tube, caught a bus, some of Mal's more challenged neighbours would also mutter about refugees in boats, but Mal had always wondered why people thought like that. Had her neighbour ever been in a small boat? Maybe they thought these refugees were all coming across in super-yachts, knocking back champagne, pearls wrapped around their necks.

Here in Golden, though, the person had simply to run a few streets and jump back into bed, or maybe out onto a boat?

'What were you doing out here in the middle of the night?' Mal tried not to sound suspicious.

'After the festival, the youngsters can get boisterous, so I usually sleep on the boat to make sure no one does anything silly.'

'But you weren't asleep?'

'No, a noise woke me.'

'Probably my air horn.'

He chuckled to himself. 'I imagine that was it. Look it's cold and you are shivering in your dressing gown. Would you mind if I came back to yours and checked the patio doors are properly locked?'

Mal was certain she had locked them. But what if the man hadn't snuck back into his house, but had instead snuck back into hers? What was he after? This was twice now that someone had tried to break in.

'Are you sure it was a man?' asked Jacques, interrupting her thoughts.

'I thought it was a man, but I suppose it could have been a big woman. I'm being sexist, aren't I? Lord knows, I spent enough time with female criminals; I should know better.'

As they walked back into the shop, Jacques went ahead, switching all the lights on and refusing to let Mal enter a room until he had checked every area big enough for a person to hide. Mal hadn't expressed her worries out loud, but clearly Jacques had been thinking the same thing. Now, fifteen minutes later, the kettle was coming to the boil and Jacques was shuffling a deck of cards.

'And you leave the patio door open all night?'

'Well, otherwise Mac scratches at the glass and I hate getting up when I'm fast asleep.'

'You could ignore him?'

'He's terribly persistent. Plus sometimes it's raining.'

'And you leave your doors open in the rain?' Jacques looked at Mal as though she was insane and began to deal.

'It is a nuisance, I know. But I can't think of a solution. I swear, in winter I shall freeze to death, then Mac will have to find some other fool to annoy.'

'What about a cat flap?'

Mal picked up her cards and placed them in order. She had a winning hand, she just needed to outsmart Jacques.

'But the doors are fully glazed.'

'Not a problem. I could fit one for you if you'd like. I can also repair the loose tread on the fire escape.'

'No, leave that, it's what alerted me to the break-in. I heard it creak. But a cat flap sounds excellent. How much do you think it would cost?'

'Nothing.'

'Rubbish,' chided Mal, 'I'm not accepting charity.'

Jacques gave a small shrug and looked at his cards. 'Okay, let's play for it. I win, you accept this gift. You win, I will let you pay me.'

Mal grinned. She'd been playing cards all her life, there wasn't a game she didn't know, or one she couldn't pick up after a few rounds. In prison she had even started up a bridge club and was delighted to read it was still going strong after she left.

'Okay, you're on.'

As morning dawned, the coffee cups piled up and Mal finally conceded defeat. She had underestimated Jacques, and laughing, threw up her hands in disgust.

'I should never have gone easy on you in those early hands. You, sir, are a monster.'

He yawned and stretched, a lazy smile on his face. 'A tired monster. I tell you what, I do the cat flap and you cook lunch. Does that sound a fair swap?'

Mal nodded and walked him downstairs. It was six a.m., and the village was stirring. As she watched Jacques walk away, she knew she had two problems: the first was that she didn't know who had tried to break in, or what they were after. Her heart sank as she realised she would have to tell the police.

Her second problem was that she only had the morning to learn how to cook and impress a Frenchman.

Chapter Thirty-Seven

Yawning, Mal headed towards the post office for some second class stamps. All she really wanted to do was sleep, but she had bills to post. It was now eight o'clock and she was surprised to see so many people out and about, standing in little groups talking anxiously and looking around them. She smiled and nodded at those she recognised. She was surprised when no one smiled back. She had expected more of a buzz following a successful festival.

The roads were still covered in litter and graffiti. The village looked like it was suffering from a massive hangover. With her total lack of sleep, she sympathised, it was like walking through treacle.

At the post office counter, another group were talking in low, sombre voices. She stood quietly, her brain barely awake as she tried to think how she was supposed to function today. Maybe she'd put the closed sign on the shop door. But the village was so busy for half-term, and lots of other shopkeepers had warned her this was her last chance to make money before Christmas. If she closed at four, she could go straight to bed, and she was closed on Mondays, anyway. However—

'Miss Peck! I said can I help you?'

Mal jerked out of her thoughts and yawned, apologising. 'I'm so sorry, I had a break-in last night and haven't slept. I'm rather bleary this morning.'

She immediately regretted her words. The little group of women all turned their heads like owls, beady eyes fixed on her, and all started talking at once.

'What time?'

'Did you get a look at them?'

'Do you think it's connected?'

'What do the police say?'

Mal shook her head, trying to gather all the questions together. None of them seemed sympathetic that she'd had an intruder, they seemed more excited by the event itself. Not concerned by how terrified she might have been. Their claws were ready to scratch over any morsel of gossip, ready to spear the juiciest bit to pass on to the next group they met. Mal decided to be brazen.

'Actually, I ran him off.'

Phyllis scoffed. 'How did you do that, then?'

Mal explained the foghorn and how he had run off across the roofs.

'So, you didn't see him at all?' asked the woman with the forty-a-day face.

'No, I bumped into Jacques and he went looking as well, but he had disappeared.'

'Jacques was out on the harbour?' asked Phyllis slowly, and the women all looked at each other significantly. The postmistress continued, 'And what time was this?'

Mal shrugged. 'Around three-ish.'

'Have you told the police yet?'

Mal shook her head wearily. She was unnerved by the way the women were responding to her story. There was something almost feverish in their attention and she wanted to leave them to it, have a large coffee and open up.

'I'll ring them soon. The burglar didn't get anything.'

'You don't need to call them. They're down on the harbour, out by Bell Rocks,' said Phyllis, her voice full of drama.

Mal looked at her blankly. One of the women gripped her friend's arm, weeping.

'Where they found Connor Trebetherick.'

Mal was tired and trying to work out what was being said and continued to stare at the women.

'He's dead. Found this morning, face down in the water!'

As she stared at the women, their faces merged into a tableau of caricatures and Mal sprinted out of the shop towards the harbour. Connor had been so full of life the previous afternoon, waving and smiling at the crowd. He had a pregnant fiancée upcountry waiting for him. A little boy playing with his toys, ready to show his daddy what he had achieved. How could he be dead?

Mal had suspected it had been him on the roof, he was the right sort of shape and size, and he'd been wearing the coat she was sure had been worn when Roger Jago had died. But now he was dead himself.

She turned the corner towards the working end of the harbour. It was taped off and groups of men were standing around uncomfortably. Mal walked up to the cordon, relieved to see Sophie.

'Was he wearing his jacket?' Her voice was breathless, and she knew how blunt she sounded, but she was certain that the coat was the key to this.

Sophie cocked her head, deciding how best to deal with the question.

'Miss Peck. Mal, I'm afraid this is an active investigation. I can't discuss anything with you.'

Mal persisted. 'It's important. There was a button missing. What I told you last night.'

She knew the men were listening and was aware she might be saying too much.

'Someone tried to break into my place last night.'

Sophie looked around and glared at a few of the fishermen, who instantly turned away, some even took a step back. Pressing the receiver on her radio, Sophie called for backup and a few minutes later a young officer, also in uniform, came around the corner and nodded at Sophie. Frowning, she turned back to Mal.

'Right, let's go back to your place and you can tell me all about it. Jamie,' she turned to the constable, 'no one is to get past the corner. I don't care if their boat is sinking. Anyone who tries gets arrested.'

The last bit was said loud enough so that all the groups of men were in no doubt that Taphouse's youngest was fully in charge of the situation.

Back at Mal's place, Sophie had looked at the patio, then called for a crime scene officer to come and dust for prints.

'If you saw the whites of his hand, then we'll have the bastard's prints.'

'My house is going to be covered in powder at this rate.'

Sophie followed Mal back downstairs to the kitchen and sat on a stool.

'What first alerted you?'

Mal tried to recall and heard a creaking sound. 'I think one of the treads on the ladder must be loose.'

As she said it, she remembered Jacques had already offered to fix that for her. How did he know, had she already told him? She was so tired she could barely think straight.

'Now, why did you want to know about the coat?'

As Mal explained the significance of it, the coffee kicked in and woke her up. As it did, she noticed that Sophie's eyes were red, and in a moment of self-disgust Mal remembered that Sophie and Connor had been friends. The poor girl must be struggling right now. Despite her pain, she was still asking questions. On top of that, last night there had been a raid on her uncle's boat. Mal didn't think this was the right time to ask, but the poor girl, what she must be going through.

'And you didn't mention the button to anyone?'

'Lots of people know about the button after the inspector was waving it around on the harbour. But I didn't tell anyone about the coat. Although Connor would have seen me taking photos of him. Oh, and Piran was standing beside me asking what I was doing. I didn't tell him. I didn't want to upset him, but I wonder if he guessed. I saw him talking to his mother shortly after and they were both looking at the float, so I think he told her. And of course Connor and his family saw me taking photos of them.'

Sophie rubbed her eyes with the palms of her hands, and Mal got up and offered her one of her fancy chocolates. Sean had nearly finished them off when he'd been working. He'd developed a taste for the marzipans and would have one with his morning brew, but there were a few dark chocolates left.

Sophie murmured a bit about her diet, but then swore and popped it in her mouth.

'You have a photo of the coat? Let's see.'

Mal showed her the images. Including the ones where she had zoomed in on the button.

'What do you think? It's the same design, isn't it?' asked Mal, keen to distract the young woman from her grief. 'Look, here's a photo I took of the button after I cleaned it.'

Mal drummed her fingers as she waited for Sophie to swallow her sweet. As she flicked back and forth between the photos, her face grew pinched and Mal could see she was trying not to cry.

'Mal, I grew up with Connor. We went to school together, he was full of fun and mischief and never hurt a hair on anyone's head. Seeing him lying like that on the ground...'

She broke off, and Mal stood and poured away her cold cup of coffee and poured a fresh brew. It was no good. Sophie's grief could not be tidied away. The poor child could not be distracted from her pain by chocolates and puzzles.

'I'm sorry, my dear. This must be dreadful for you.'

She squeezed Sophie's hand. She knew the girl would have to go back to work in a minute and put her professional face back on, but if Mal could provide a few minutes of privacy and grief that was what she would do.

'Would you like me to get some doughnuts from Jennie?'

Sophie laughed weakly. 'No one will be open today.' She wiped her face with the palms of her hands and tilted her head, sniffing loudly. 'Mark of respect. There won't be anything else they can do but they'll be able to do that.' Now, she picked up her pen. 'But I can. I can do more than that. I can find his bloody killer.'

'It was murder then?'

'At the moment, they think he drowned. But, Mal, he wasn't wearing a coat, and there was nothing on the side of the harbour.'

Mal leant back on the chair, relieved that her instinct was correct.

'Give me a minute. I'm going to call this in and action a hunt for the coat.'

She stood up and walked away from the table. Adrenaline was coursing through Mal's veins and she felt guilty for her excitement. She also felt guilty by how relieved she was that she wouldn't have to open today. Had her time in jail desensitised her to massive acts of violence? The stories she had listened to had made her cry herself to sleep each night until she had worked out how to live with them. She yawned. Then again, maybe she was just human.

Now she sat up as Sophie returned to the table, her face worried.

'Have they found the coat?'

'No, DS Williams has said they will keep an eye out for it, but they aren't that interested. They have arrested Jacques Peloffy.'

Chapter Thirty-Eight

'Sit down, you need to stay here for the SOCO team.'

Mal was still pacing, she wanted to shout at the inspector, to roar at Phyllis; she felt so stupid and guilty that she had opened her big mouth and now Jacques had been arrested.

'This is intolerable. Why didn't the inspector come and speak to me? The man on my roof was not Jacques. Plus, for what it's worth, since no one seems to have noticed, Jacques is not a murderer.'

'Mal, please, sit down.'

Mal continued to pace. The room was too small, the things on the shelves weren't hers. Decisions were being made that she had no control over, and now the first person who had been truly friendly to her had been arrested. And it was her fault. Sophie stood up and put the kettle on again. Having done that, she headed over to the table and, helping herself to a sheet of paper and a pencil, she put them out, then looked at Mal expectantly.

'What? You want me to write a statement? Like the horse that has already bolted.'

'No, you bad-tempered moose. I want you to tell me why you don't think Jacques is a murderer, and then we are going to sit down and try and work out who is.' She paused and smiled softly. 'Now, please sit down.' She pulled the chair out and waved theatrically. 'I want Connor's murderer found as much as you want your friend's name cleared. It seems like the inspector only wants a quick result.'

She headed back into the kitchen and poured a cup of coffee, looking over her shoulder back at Mal.

'Any more sweets?'

'Those were the last. I have Ryvitas?' said Mal, and smiled as Sophie recoiled in horror, then started laughing weakly.

'Very well. Just coffee. Now then, why isn't Jacques Peloffy a murderer?'

She sat at the table and cocked her head. Mal sighed and came and sat down.

'Because I don't think he is. No, don't laugh.' She looked across at the younger woman, and was relieved to see her face was enquiring rather than dismissive. Mal plunged on.

'I've always been an excellent judge of character. It's one of the skills that made me good at my job. I could read the room, the situation, the market. My second skill was to rely on my gut instinct and act accordingly. Sometimes I was flying in the face of all the received wisdom, but I still prevailed.'

'Were you some ball-busting businesswoman?'

Mal laughed in reflection. 'No, some of my contemporaries were, and very good at it, they were. But I like being nice too much. Still, in the early days I got the reputation for maybe being a little stubborn. A recalcitrant donkey was a phrase I once heard. But slowly I wore people down and eventually my track record spoke for itself.'

'Did it bother you?'

'It did, initially. I would listen, as a man with no more evidence than I had, would be lauded as someone with instinct, thrust, uncanny abilities. When I made similar pronouncements, they said I had followed a whim, plucked it out of thin air, had a funny feeling.'

'So how did you deal with it?'

'Lack of insecurity helped. My folks never viewed women as second-class citizens, neither did my school. All-girls education. Highly recommend it, although I seem to be out of step with society on that one.'

Sophie looked at Mal in surprise. 'You believe in single sex education?'

Mal scoffed, then had a quick drink of coffee, savouring the warmth as it woke her up.

'Essential, until expectations and treatments are equal. Otherwise, girls are hobbled from the outset. They need to hit the adult world knowing they are equal, not wondering. Because God knows, the workplace still has an opinion on their worth, as does politics and government.'

She sighed, then continued, 'Anyway. The point is, I don't think Jacques had anything to do with this.'

'There is a lot of evidence pointing his way. He discovered the tunnel. He was out in the lane when the footprints were discovered. He was on the harbour front around the time Connor was murdered. And it turns out that he has a very expensive car in his garage, attached to his very expensive house, and a very healthy bank balance. I mean, Jacques is loaded. Where did all the money come from?'

Mal paused and thought about it. She couldn't explain the money but being wealthy wasn't actually a crime, nor was it evidence of wrongdoing. Still, she didn't think fishing was known for its rates of pay. Setting that aside for a second, she focused on the other circumstantial evidence.

'Okay, why draw attention to the passageway? SOCO hadn't found it. He could have kept that quiet. Being on the lane when the footprints were discovered was bad timing. And as for being out on the harbour last night, well, he has a boat there and was sleeping on it in case any festival revellers got feisty.'

Sophie nodded. 'Aye, right enough. One year a group of teenagers got on to the boats and made a hell of a mess.'

'Were they ever caught?'

'Course we were. There was bloody hell up!' She grinned. 'Carry on.'

'And as to why he was walking about, he said he heard a noise. Well, it was either poor Connor being murdered or my foghorn.'

'We've started doing a door to door and it seems like a lot of people heard your foghorn, so that's a possibility.'

'Except I think whoever tried to break into my place had already killed Connor.'

'Same person?'

'Yes. Too big a coincidence otherwise.'

'Coincidences happen all the time. You'd be amazed in this game how often they occur.'

Mal paused and listened to what Sophie was saying. She hadn't known her long, but she respected the younger woman's opinion, plus she was part of this community. Her take on the situation would be incredibly valuable.

'What's your gut feeling?'

'Not a coincidence,' said Sophie, with certainty. 'If not the same man, then definitely connected.'

Mal thought about the final piece of evidence against Jacques.

'Jacques has a Land Rover that's not worth more than tuppence. What car are they talking about?'

'He has a Bugatti in his garage.'

Mal nodded appreciatively. 'Now that is a fine car. No wonder he didn't lend me that one. But so what? He has money. Do you really think if he had a load of sunken treasure, he'd still be going out in a fishing boat every week?'

Sophie shook her head. 'Honestly? No. I think this treasure is a red herring. I also don't think he's a drug smuggler. Unlike my dope of an uncle.'

Mal looked across questioningly.

'Fags and booze, thank God.' Sophie sighed despondently. 'Not great, I know, but not the county lines they all thought it was last night.'

'Right. The investigation seems to be losing sight of the proper questions. Why was Roger Jago killed? If we have the why, we'll know the who.'

'Agreed. So, let's start at the beginning. Roger was killed by a blow to the back of the head. He was wrapped in a carpet and hidden in the wall.'

'And we don't know who the builders were?'

'No.' Sophie sighed. 'All we know is that the Wallises – the couple that owned the shop before the Cramptons – went away every winter for a few months to Spain. There's a few in the village that do that. Make their money in summer, spend winter overseas.'

'And have the Wallises been interviewed?'

'He's dead, she has dementia. She had little to say that was helpful. Some years, they would have work done while they were away, they'd use local men, often fishermen. They would leave a key at the pub next door in case of fire or flood. So it was entirely possible that Roger was working in there doing repairs, or he simply borrowed the keys.'

She looked across at Mal. 'We also interviewed Gary Crampton. Did he say anything to you of interest?'

Mal stopped scribbling on her pad. 'No. He bought the place a few years after Roger had gone missing. Never noticed anything untoward.'

She put her pen down.

'Here's the way I see it. Interrupt me if I'm barking up the wrong tree. The murder happened on the shop floor. I don't think it was premeditated, as the killer had no control over the environment. I think either the killer or the victim were working on the property. Probably the killer. How else do you explain that you've built a wall in someone else's shop? Plus, they would also have a set of keys. For whatever reason, Roger was killed, and I'm leaning towards accident.'

'Why?' Sophie frowned and shook her head, baffled.

'Because the cover-up was so difficult. Why not just explain the accident? Unless the reason they had been arguing in the middle of the night also needed to be kept hidden?'

'Why the middle of the night?'

'Because whoever killed him, slipped out of the tunnel and took Roger's boat out to sea, set it adrift, then rowed back himself via the dingy. He'd need the cover of night to do all that.'

'Himself?'

'True. Could be a she.' She laughed in bitter reflection of some of the ladies she had got to know over the years. 'Could easily be a woman.'

'Okay. So far, I think you're right. But we are sorely lacking in any evidence. We have one washed button.'

Mal grimaced for the hundredth time. 'But we do now have a match for the coat.'

'Except the coat is now missing.'

'Right, let's not jump ahead.'

Mal looked across at Sophie, things were falling into a narrative. Starting at the beginning was making sense.

'Paul Trebetherick's suicide. Was there any evidence there?'

'The only thing of excitement was some hairs. But they turned out to be a filial match for the victim himself.'

'Billy and Connor?' Mal said. It seemed obvious, if disappointing.

'Exactly.'

'How old were they at the time?'

'Twenty, but they were both away at a rugby tournament in Bath. Besides which, their hair was probably already on their father's body from the normal course of his life. And at the time, no one thought it was murder. So no one investigated it too closely.'

Mal tapped her pencil on her tooth, a habit her old colleagues had got used to, despite their annoyance at the sound.

'The police think this is the same murderer, five years apart, don't they?'

Sophie paused. Mal watched as she wrestled with her conscience, then continued.

'They do. Hemingstone seems to think this is linked to the missing *White Maria*. Or the drug ring. Honestly, with that man I think his opinion changes with the wind.'

Mal continued to tap her teeth. 'Makes no sense though, does it? What are they suggesting? Roger was killed to cut him out of a share of the treasure? To reveal the source of the treasure? If either of those are the case, then why wait five years to kill Paul? Unless Paul was the murderer and was then in turn killed five years later for the same reasons. Like some dreadful game of pass the parcel.'

'But Paul did start to get wealthier after Roger's death.'

'Sunken treasure wealthy? Or drug smuggling wealthy?'

'Either, but that's the theory they are going with. The men died over money. And it does have some merit, Mal.'

'The only merit it has is that it explains the two different types of murder. One appears to be a heat of the moment job and carefully hidden. The other had to have been premediated and publicly staged.'

'Two murderers, though, is also very unlikely, Mal.'

'Five years apart.'

'Agreed. Which brings us on to this murder. Ten years after Paul's staged suicide.'

'Why him? Why now? Are they going to charge Jacques with the murders of Paul and Roger as well?'

The two women looked at each other and sighed.

'All I know is that last night Connor was wearing a coat that is missing a button which is a match for the button I found in the passageway. The following morning, he is dead and the coat is missing.'

The women continued to thrash out the problem as the SOCO arrived and dusted the ladder for prints.

'Right, leave it with me,' said Sophie. 'I'll call and let you know when Jacques is released.'

'Do you think he will be?'

'If he's as innocent as you think he is.'

Mal snorted, causing Sophie to pause.

'We aren't all corrupt in the police force, you know.'

Mal paused, she didn't want to upset Sophie. She liked the girl, and she was clearly a credit to the force. But in Mal's experience not all her colleagues were. In the silence, Sophie continued, 'You confessed to your crimes. It wasn't a miscarriage or anything.'

'I do know that,' said Mal sharply. 'I believe I was present. That said, I met lots of women inside who protested their innocence daily. Or who should never have been convicted or imprisoned.'

'Are you judge and jury now as well?'

The two women glared at each other and a wave of tiredness washed over Mal. She hadn't meant to be spiky, but she had barely had any sleep, she'd had the fright of her life last night: she was responsible for Jacques being arrested, and she was deeply saddened that a young man had died. She stood up.

'SOCO are finished, so why don't you leave as well? I don't need a babysitter.'

Mal knew she sounded petty, but she was upset with herself and felt it was better to have Sophie out of the flat before she said something even meaner. Sophie looked at her and was about to say something but thought better of it, then followed her colleagues back downstairs. Mal traipsed after them, ensuring the front door was properly locked.

Back in the flat, Mal sat down and placed her head in her hands. She had handled that badly. Her head was spinning. Nothing made any sense. She hadn't told Sophie that Jacques had mentioned a squeaky ladder in case that was the evidence Hemingstone needed to charge him. She was just so tired and so scared that she simply couldn't remember when she had first told him.

Could it be Dennis Jenkins? He had been a builder for decades. Had he done the renovations all those years ago? Had he known what was about to be revealed?

Was Sophie trying to point the finger at the Wallises, rather than blame someone in the village?

A gull landed on the kitchen sill and tapped on the window causing Mal to jump in alarm. Spooked and cross with herself for overreacting, Mal grabbed her hairbrush, slapped on some war paint, then added a necklace and her favourite rings. She'd had enough of this village and the way it made her suspicious of everyone. She was ready for battle and headed out to have a word with Phyllis.

Chapter Thirty-Nine

A group of villagers were standing around the counter of the post office when Mal strode in. There was no pretence of anyone actually making a purchase. A man she didn't recognise was currently holding court, jabbing his finger at another man in an alarmingly hostile manner.

'Course it wasn't an accident. Why arrest a man if it was an accident?'

'Because Phyllis Cooper is a gossipy witch and falsely accused a good man of murder.'

All faces swung around to stare at Mal as she marched up to the counter.

Phyllis began to speak, her face flushed, but Mal was on a roll and not prepared to let her have another second of breath.

'Spare me your justifications. I've only been here a few weeks and even I know Jacques is a decent, kind, and hard-working man.'

'Well, there's no smoke without fire.'

'Course there bloody is, the prisons are full of people falsely accused. The streets are full of people who lose their jobs and their homes through idle gossip, from people so bereft of kindness or intellect that they will ruin a person's life with no more thought than what makes them look clever or informed.' She took a deep breath. 'You are a snitch of the first order.'

Having said her piece and feeling overwhelmingly satisfied, she swung around and headed out of the shop.

'Malachite, wait up.'

Mal turned to see that Betty had followed her out. She stopped. As much as she wanted to walk off her anger, her respect for the older lady stayed her feet and she turned to wait for her. Her eyebrow upraised.

'Oh, don't get high and mighty with me. You made my year. I shall go to sleep warmed by the angry flush on Phyllis' face. Now, walk with me down to the bakers. I want to get there before they sell out of almond slices. They don't make so many now the tourists have gone.'

'Couldn't you ask one to be put aside for you?' asked Mal, pleased to have a momentary respite from her worries about Jacques' arrest, and her part in it.

'I could but then I'd be obligated to come down, and I care little for obligations. Besides which, I enjoy the gamble.' She grinned at Mal. 'Such as it is.'

The two women headed along the road. There were no pavements in the old village, which caused a squeeze in summer as tourists tried to navigate their big heavy cars through tiny lanes. All desperate to not scratch their bodywork whilst also trying to avoid pedestrians. Now as the village quietened, it was lovely to walk along the roads without fear of having your toes run over. Mal was still quiet, the joy of having taken Phyllis to task had been ephemeral; Jacques was still at the police station, Connor was still dead, and a killer was still on the loose.

'Don't worry about Phyllis. She's still bitter about Jacques. She set her cap at him when he first arrived. He was by far the best-looking man in the village. Jet-black wavy hair. Bright blue eyes, a tanned complexion. Walking around with that mysterious French air.' Betty chuckled to herself. 'However, Jacques was having none of it.'

'Was this before she was married?'

'Nope!' Betty smiled mischievously. 'Not that I care about that sort of thing. But Jacques did. He took it very personally. Most affronted he was. But Phyllis kept trying, I think she thought a Frenchman would have looser morals. Anyway, she became so irritating, showing up at the pub, meeting him off the boat, that it became almost laughable. Eventually Jacques had enough.'

'What did he do?' Mal couldn't imagine how Jacques would deal with such an unsubtle and unwelcome pursuit. What little she knew of him, he was reserved and restrained. He mixed well and helped out, but wasn't what you would call the life and soul of the party. How would a quiet newcomer have dealt with such a harpy?

'He went and spoke to her husband.'

Mal blinked in astonishment and burst out laughing. 'He did not!'

'He absolutely did. And that was that. She stopped running after Jacques and swapped lust for loathing.'

'What did her husband do?'

'Nothing. It wasn't like it was the first time his wife had played away. If anything, Jacques gained a mark of respect for doing the "decent thing".'

'Not sleeping with his wife?'

'No, coming and telling the husband. Old-fashioned bunch around here and at the time there was a spate of loose morals going round. Lots of affairs and infidelities.'

'Really?' Mal couldn't picture it. Golden seemed locked in some historic aspic; cobbled streets, fishermen mending nets, children playing out on the roads and alleyways. That it was also a hotbed of promiscuity seemed wrong. But then what did she know? They were just people, and the winter months probably lasted a long time here.

Betty tutted in glee. 'You wouldn't believe it. I imagine it still goes on today and like as not, always did, but back then it seemed particularly rampant. Probably because the then vicar was very riled up about it and every week's sermon was about lust and betrayal. I tell you what, even I attended those sermons; it was great fun to watch a congregation squirm. Even Ruth Jago.'

'What!?' Mal stopped and looked at Betty as she walked on, then turned round, grinning at Mal's shock.

'Oh, before she became this old high and mighty pillar of the community, she had a dreadful reputation. When Roger disappeared there were plenty said he'd had enough of her ways.'

'Why didn't he just divorce her?'

'Like Phyllis' husband did?'

'Was that because of Jacques?'

'No, it was years later, but you can be sure Phyllis blamed Jacques for that as well.' Betty shook her head. 'But no, Roger wouldn't have divorced Ruth. Like I said, traditional bunch around here. Takes a while for what seems commonplace to catch on here. Might not be a bad thing either. Not that I've anything against divorce. If you've hitched your wagon to a wrong'un, then jump. But honestly, sometimes it feels like no one is prepared to work at a thing.'

They had arrived at the bakery and Betty patted Mal's arm. 'Listen to me. Maybe I'm getting old.' She turned and smiled as she saw a slice in the bakery window. 'Coming in?'

'No, I think I'm going to keep on walking.'

Smiling, she said goodbye and headed along the road away from the harbour. Something Betty had said was echoing in Mal's head. She didn't know what it was, but she knew a thought was building. A way of seeing things that hadn't been seen before; a potential solution was rolling around in her brain, firing up synapses and connections. Normally she would go to the spa and swim until the idea emerged, but she felt too restless to go back to the house. Plus the winds were picking up. This was no time to head out into unfamiliar waters.

Pausing for breath, Mal stopped and took in her surroundings. She had been walking uphill and was now on the edge of the village nicknamed Saints. The houses were all set in extensive grounds overlooking the sea, with none of the smell of the harbour. The church was up here, as was the graveyard. Few cars came up here as the one lane that threaded through the houses continued across open countryside and down to an even less occupied area of Cornwall. No buses or tourists bothered these residents. Mal could imagine the dinner parties here, the latest art acquisitions, drinks on the terrace.

Saints was a world away from her little ancient property down on the harbour. There were no benches up here, people weren't invited to linger, and as she leant against a cobbled wall, the smell of a nearby bonfire filled her senses. A large beech tree overhead was on the turn from green to red, and the light dappled through. She paused as she looked across the road and saw a red wooden door in the wall. The slate nameplate read Parson's Rest. Presumably, the driveway was further up the road and this was the lower entrance into the house and garden. The smell of the bonfire had become stronger, and Mal became aware of another scent under the burning leaves.

She had once had a bet with a friend that the rug she bought wouldn't burn. They had all been rather merry. It was a trick she had learnt from a rug seller in Marrakesh and could be quite dramatic. The game had been a disaster, the rug hadn't burnt, but the smell was horrendous. And that's what Mal could smell now – someone was trying to burn wool.

Mal got her phone out. Sophie didn't reply, so she sent a text.

'Meet me at Parson's End now. I think I've found the coat.'

Hitting send, she crossed the lane and opened the gate, peering cautiously around. The garden gate opened into the lower end of a large lawned garden. The house sat higher up the hill and appeared to be surrounded by more formal gardens. Across the lawn, Mal saw a large smouldering bonfire with smoke rising out of it but no clear flames. Leaving the gravel path, she walked across the grass towards the bonfire.

From the house, she heard a woman shout at her, and Mal hurried towards the fire. Beside the smouldering heap stood a fork, its prongs stabbing the earth. With an effort, Mal loosened it and quickly glanced over her shoulder to see the woman now running down towards her.

Mal plunged the fork into the leaves and almost immediately hit an obstruction. Twisting the fork, she pulled at the item. She slipped on the grass as the fork flew backwards depositing a smouldering navy woollen jacket at the feet of Ruth Jago.

Chapter Forty

Half an hour later, Mal, Sophie and Ruth were sitting in Ruth's garden room waiting for Detective Inspector Hemingstone. Sophie had suggested a nice cup of tea but Ruth had told her she wouldn't offer her the water from her pond. After that they sat in silence until the doorbell rang.

Ruth had been savage when Mal yanked the coat out of the bonfire and had been all for throwing it back in. Mal pointed out that it was wool and wouldn't burn, but her neighbours would all come knocking about the smell. She had then threatened Mal with the police, which was when Sophie turned up and Ruth's face went puce as she stormed back to the house with Mal and Sophie trailing after her. Sophie carrying the coat by its sleeves, its singed hem trailing across the grass.

Now, Ruth jumped up to let the detectives in. Mal and Sophie looked at each other as they listened to the reassuring murmurs of the inspector and Williams out in the corridor.

'I'm sorry about earlier,' said Mal, clearing her throat. 'I haven't had much sleep. I know most police are hardworking and caring. It's just—'

'It's just you come to Golden and instantly fall foul of one who isn't. For what it's worth, I don't think he's corrupt, but I do think he might be a little bit stupid.' She whispered this last section as the door swung open and

Ruth waltzed in, preening under the deferential attention of the two policemen.

'I want this woman arrested for trespass and property damage.'

'Sir.' Sophie was on her feet. Mal remained sitting. Today would be the death of her if she didn't get some sleep soon.

'Miss Peck contacted me and said she was concerned that evidence was being destroyed. I said I would be with her as soon as I could.'

'Did you give her permission to enter the property?'

'I did that on my own,' interrupted Mal. 'I was worried the coat would be destroyed. I know it's pretty hard to burn a coat, but I wasn't sure if a hot enough bonfire would work.'

'This is a load of silly nonsense,' said Ruth dismissively. She gave the detectives a winning smile. 'Who cares if I get rid of some old clothes? I suppose I should have given it to the village jumble, but it's hardly a crime, is it?'

She laughed and smiled again at the inspector. 'Where are my manners? Can I get you a cup of tea? What about you, sergeant? Something to warm you against the wind?'

Ruth was heading towards the kitchen but Williams coughed awkwardly.

'Shall we address the issue of the coat first, boss?'

Hemingstone looked at his two junior officers and nodded. 'Come on then.'

All five trooped out onto the patio with Ruth remonstrating loudly that it was moth-eaten. That she was clearing the attic. That she had every right to dispose of her clothes how she saw fit.

'Look, sir.' Sophie opened her phone and showed him the photos that Mal had forwarded to her. 'That's the victim last night on his float. If you look closely,' she touched the screen and zoomed in, 'those buttons match the one found in the passageway leading from the site of Roger Jago's murder.'

'For heaven's sake. Every other man in Golden has a coat like that.'

Ignoring Hemingstone, Sophie carried on. 'But the button design is quite distinctive and if you look at the photo, it's clear one of the buttons is a replacement.'

Now Sophie leant down, asking Williams for help as the pair of them turned the jacket over. The bonfire had almost gone out when the coat had been shoved into it, and it was too poor a fuel to set the fire off again. Instead, it had simply smouldered and become lightly singed.

Williams studied the coat, the photos, and Sophie's face, then cleared his throat.

'Boss. It looks pretty clear to me. This is the same coat our victim was wearing last night. I reckon you may have just found our murderer. Pretty smart of you arresting Jacques this morning. You gave the actual murderer a false sense of safety.'

Hemingstone paused, momentarily baffled, then hooked his thumbs into his waistband.

'Can't get one past you, can I, sergeant?' Turning to Ruth, he drew himself. 'Mrs Jago, can you explain why you were burning the coat last worn by Connor Trebetherick?'

Ruth protested, then came to a sudden halt. The enormity of the evidence overwhelmed her and she stumbled. Williams lunged forward and Mal saw her for a fifty-year-old woman held up by no more than years of malice.

'I did it. So what?' she spat. 'Connor found out I'd killed his dad and my husband and he was threatening to tell the police. I couldn't have that. That stupid bitch had worked out the significance of the coat and the button.' Mal knew Ruth was referring to her but decided not to comment. The woman was on a roll. Give her enough rope and maybe she'd hang for all time.

'Piran mentioned it to me in passing and I knew the game was up. Poor Piran didn't understand. But I did. That's why I had to confront Connor. Get that coat off him.'

'And then you tried to break into Mrs Peck's house and steal her phone,' said the inspector, eager to bring the case to a close. For a moment, Ruth looked confused but nodded quickly.

'Just trying to tidy up loose ends.'

Sophie had been staring at Ruth in horror as the woman spat out her bile.

'But how could you? Connor was Piran's friend. He has a little boy and his fiancée is pregnant. Think about them. And what about Sharon?'

Ruth gave an ugly laugh. 'What about Sharon? Fat old cow has another son. It's not like they even bother to visit her.'

Mal stared at her. She hadn't caught sight of her intruder, she knew it was a tall person, but she'd had felt certain it was a young man. For a while she had thought it was Connor himself. As she watched, Hemingstone took a deep breath and stepped forward, chest puffed out.

'Ruth Jago, I am arresting you for the murder of Connor Trebetherick, Roger Jago and Paul Trebetherick. Williams, read her her rights.'

Silently, Ruth regained her strength and followed the inspector and Williams to the car. Sophie was instructed to safeguard the house for the SOCO team, then they left.

'Bloody hell. I'm always on SOCO duty.'

'What now? Will Jacques be released?'

'Well, you heard her. She confessed.'

'I know. It all seems weirdly anticlimactic. She just kept staring at the fireplace, then just gave up.'

Mal wandered over to the mantlepiece and looked at all the family photos gathered along the slate shelf. Piran as a little boy on the swing, his father pushing him into the air. Piran in his school uniform with that cheesy grin beloved by school photographers. *He was lucky he didn't have any siblings,* thought Mal. She still winced remembering her own sister's hand on one shoulder. Christmas portraits where her brother was roped in, all wearing the same daft grin as their mother admonished them, laughing from the sidelines. At least in Piran's photo, he didn't have to fight with siblings for attention.

In other photos, Piran was standing in a team shot for rugby. All the teenagers with their chests puffed out, a trophy in Piran's arms. A picture of him in a school uniform and his father standing on the doorstep. This was when the photos stopped. Mal sighed. Poor Piran, to lose your father so young. Why had Ruth done it? As far as Mal could see, there was no obvious motive. And why then kill Paul? Presumably he had discovered her murder.

Leaving Sophie to wait for the SOCOs, Mal walked down to the lower village. The walk downhill was easier on her tired limbs and Mal thought she could sleep for a thousand years.

The mood on the harbour was subdued. News of Ruth's confession clearly hadn't made it down here, and Mal would not mention it. The far end of the harbour was still cordoned off, but there was access to the boats and men were quietly moving around loading and unloading. A few bundles of flowers had been put by the cordon and Mal looked at them with none of the annoyance she'd felt watching them pile up around her shop, only a sense of overwhelming sadness at such a vibrant young life lost.

Not for the first time, Mal wondered how on earth Ruth had managed to strangle and hang Paul? She might be tall, but was she really strong enough? How had she managed?

'Mrs Peck, are you okay?'

Mal was surprised to discover that she must have drifted off and now Piran's wife was standing in front of her. Her eyes were red with tears as she held Sam's hand. The toddler was crouched down and playing with a bit of seaweed on the road.

'It's so horrible, isn't it? I've just laid flowers. Piran is so upset he's taken the boat out. Wants to be by himself. They were so close as boys. I reckon if he hadn't left after his dad's suicide, he'd have been our best man. Him or Billy.'

She started sobbing. 'I saw him earlier supporting poor Mrs Trebetherick. To lose a husband and a son.'

Mal handed her a tissue, uncertain of how to speak to this poor girl. Any moment she was about to discover her mother-in-law had confessed to the murder. Life was about to become even worse for this nice quiet girl.

Little Sam, having examined the seaweed from all angles, stood up and proudly offered it to Mal, who received the wet smelly strand with apparent delight. He was a pretty child, and blessed with long lashes that framed his green eyes.

'Did you know he had a little boy? Same age as Sam here.' Her face crumpled again and Mal felt this was the source of her grief. Imagining telling her child that his daddy was never coming home. 'Look, don't they look lovely?'

She held out her phone and flipped through some photos on Facebook, where Connor was sitting with Sam and presumably his wife.

'Did you go up and visit them a lot?'

Eden shook her head. 'No, I never met them. I was looking at his Facebook page. Do you think that makes me ghoulish?'

Mal thought it probably made her human, but she was surprised by Sam's presence in the photo and said so. Eden gave a sad little laugh.

'No, that's Alfie, Connor's boy. They look alike though, don't they? Kids often do. Apparently Piran and the Trebetherick twins also looked really similar when they were little. I think it's the green eyes. It's quite rare.' She sobbed again. 'I can't believe she's a widow. Billy was telling me she's pregnant as well.' As she spoke, Mal felt as though a bucket of icy water had been poured down her spine and she jerked back in alarm.

'Bloody hell. There's another explanation!'

Startling Eden out of her tears, she made her apologies and headed over to the boats as quickly as she could. Had she been a young girl she'd have been sprinting, but the outfit she had worn to challenge Phyllis was not designed for the racetrack, and neither was her body. Instead, she stepped smartly along the boat sheds until she saw a face she recognised.

‘Bob! I need your help. Where’s Piran Jago?’

‘Headed out not five minutes ago. If you swim quick, you might catch him.’ Bob laughed at his own joke, then stopped short as Mal glared at him.

‘We need to catch him. Is your boat ready?’

Bob blinked and began to shake his head. ‘I’m not sure—’

‘His mother has confessed to murdering her husband as well as Paul and Connor Trebetherick.’

‘Are you—’

Mal flapped her hand at him. ‘No time to waste. I’ll explain on the boat but we have to stop him. We can’t let him get away with it.’

Chapter Forty-One

Bob's boat was the bright-yellow RIB that took people out for wildlife cruises and occasional speed fests. Each seat was a collection of metal rollbars and secure harnesses to strap passengers in as the boat flashed across the waves, crashing through the surf and turning on a hairpin, spinning out plumes of showy white water. For now, mercifully, the boat was heading in a straight line out to sea.

Mal was standing next to Bob at the helm. She was wearing a heavy blue woollen sweater with the sleeves rolled up, and a red knitted hat. Both swamped her but as Bob had pointed out, she wasn't properly dressed and would freeze out at sea. With nothing to stop the cold autumn winds as they slammed across the tops of the waves, the drop in temperature caught many unawares. On top of the sweater, she was wearing a heavy-duty life preserver and felt like the Michelin man.

'There he is!' Bob pointed to a boat out on the horizon.

'Call the coastguard. He's the killer. Don't let him escape.'

Bob looked unconvinced and Mal groaned.

'Please. When they realise Ruth was lying, they'll try to pin it back on Jacques. That policeman's an idiot and wants an easy arrest.'

'Yeah. I know his sort,' said Bob, as they picked up speed. 'But are you sure about Piran killing Connor? I'm sorry, maid, but that's hard to swallow. He was proper upset before he left.'

'Not upset, Bob, guilty. I think his mum tipped him off and he's making a run for it. Tell the coastguard to check with DS Williams and PC Taphouse.'

Mal had known from their expressions that neither had been happy with Ruth's confession. Hopefully, that doubt would be enough for them to support her request.

'Sophie Taphouse thinks Piran is the killer?' asked Bob, preparing to listen.

'Well, she sure as hell doesn't think Ruth or Jacques are. Look, ask him yourself in a minute.' Mal knew she was stretching things but, in her gut, she knew Piran was responsible for Connor's murder. She just didn't know why, or if he was involved in the murder of the two other men. One thing she was certain of was that little Sam and Alfie were the key to the mystery.

The boat bounced through the last few waves as it came up towards the fishing boat.

'Bloody fool, why doesn't he stop?'

Piran was standing in his cabin, ignoring the power RIB as it pulled alongside.

'Hang on, lass, best sit down. Get your seatbelt on. Shoulder straps as well.'

The boat accelerated and Bob zoomed in front of the trawler, then swerved and cut across its bow. The boat blared its horn, with Piran gesticulating wildly from inside his cabin, but Bob wouldn't stop zipping back and forth. Mal wondered how much a chiropractor was going to cost her. She also thought she was going to throw up. Who thought this was fun?

Eventually, in fury, Piran switched his engine off and came out to the side of his boat. He started swearing at Bob.

'Leave off,' shouted Bob. 'The maid here wants a word with you.'

Mal struggled to her feet and came to the side of the boat. The floor lurched under her feet as the sea rocked back and forth. She wasn't sure how to go about things and either wanted him to confess in front of Bob, or stall him until the coastguard arrived.

A wave splashed between the two boats rocking back and forth and a slap of sea spray caught Mal off guard.

Spluttering, she tried to take control.

'Your mum's confessed, Piran. She'll go to prison.'

He looked across at Mal, a cold hard look on his face. Looking at the brown curling hair and the broad forehead, she wondered how she'd missed the resemblance before. Now he sneered across at Mal.

'Good. That's what she deserves for killing Connor.'

'She didn't kill him though, did she?' called Mal. 'Plus, she's confessed to killing Paul Trebetherick and Roger Jago.'

Piran grabbed the side of one of his large plastic ice crates. 'The stupid cow. What did she do that for?'

'Enough of that,' shouted Bob, 'she's your mother and she deserves more respect than that.'

'Oh sod off, Bob. What would you know? What do any of you old-timers know? Waffling on about the good old days and respect.'

'That's what they teach us in church and its good enough for me, boy. I thought it was good enough for you as well. You're in there enough.'

'Ruth's boy is a blessing, isn't he? A pillar of the community.' Piran mimicked the praise of the villagers before his voice turned ugly. 'Well, the community can eat its own arse for all I care.'

'Come on, lad,' shouted Bob, trying to calm things down. 'I know this news about your mum has upset you.'

'Too bloody right. Why did she confess to the other two murders?'

'It's a shock, lad, I know.' Bob tried to cajole him into calm but Mal wanted him unsettled. The cocky little bastard was so close to escape.

'Messed up your plans, hasn't it? You were happy to let your mother take the blame for Connor's murder, but once the police investigate Paul and Roger's deaths, they'll discover she had nothing to do with either of them.'

'They won't convict her, lad. Not if she's innocent,' said Bob, reassuringly.

'Well that won't do, will it, Piran?' jeered Mal. 'You couldn't care less if she goes to prison. You don't care who goes to prison so long as it isn't you.'

Mal was trying to see if he knew the full truth of the situation but she didn't think he did.

'Shut up, you old crow. I didn't kill anyone. Do you think anyone would believe I killed my old man?'

Mal laughed bitterly. He didn't know.

'Ah, you didn't kill Roger Jago, but you did kill your father.'

Piran scrunched up his face and looked at her, then laughed, shaking his head. 'You're bloody mental. Bob, have you got a licence to drive nuthouse patients around the place?'

'Roger wasn't your dad, Piran,' shouted Mal across the water. Several gulls had now landed on the boat, hoping for some scraps. 'I think that's what Roger and Paul were fighting about. I think Roger discovered Paul had been sleeping with your mum. I don't know how long the affair had been going on, but look at the resemblance between your Sam and Connor's boy. Look at the three of you. You have the same bloody father. You're brothers. I think Paul found out and fought with Roger. I also think it was an accident that Roger died, and Paul panicked and covered it up.'

'Bloody hell, Mal,' said Bob. He shook his head in disbelief as he continued to steer the RIB.

'You're a bloody liar,' screamed Piran 'He wasn't my dad. He'd have said so.'

'When? When you were killing him?'

Bob's head was flicking back and forth listening to the two of them shouting.

'Ah, lad. Tell me you didn't kill Paul. Why would you do that?'

'It was an accident. I didn't mean it. He wouldn't tell me where the gold was.'

'What gold?' shouted Bob. 'Wasn't that just a rumour?'

'Paul kept going on about it, so I figured I should have some. If he found it with Dad then half of it should have been mine. So I challenged him about it in the net lofts. Then he started banging on that he'd only said that to cover up Roger's disappearance. That was when he started shouting at me that he'd done everything to take care of me. I didn't know what he was going on about.' Piran was almost sobbing in rage now. 'He'd have said if I was his son. I didn't know what he was going on about.'

Piran was pacing back and forth, unaware he was confessing in front of Mal and Bob. Or maybe he simply didn't care.

'I don't think he knew either,' called Mal. 'Maybe he guessed.'

'He didn't. I know he didn't. He had so much money that I thought the rumours about the gold must be true. But he kept crying and telling me how sorry he was,' screamed Piran. 'He kept snivelling and saying sorry, and I realised he was telling me he had killed my dad. I lost it. I started choking him. He fought me but there was nothing to grab onto, I was in my weatherproofs. His fingers slid off.' His face contorted as he remembered. 'Then he stopped moving and I knew what I had to do.'

'You strung him up and let everyone think he had killed himself.'

'He murdered my dad. He got what he deserved!'

Mal wanted to remind him that he wasn't his dad. But he had begun pacing along the side of the boat, getting increasingly agitated.

'So, did Connor discover what you had done?'

'No, that was you. You and your stupid bloody fussing about the button.'

'I don't understand?'

'No, neither did I until yesterday when I saw you staring at the float. There was Connor standing for all to see in his father's old coat with that bloody missing button. Soon as I saw the replacement button, I knew the police would cotton on. Especially with you running around taking photos of it.'

A heavy swell passed under both boats making them rock. It caused Mal to fall back on her seat but both men remained standing. Piran looked at her and scoffed.

'You can't even stay upright on a bloody boat. You've been here less than a month and think you can destroy everything.'

'I didn't ask to find a body in the wall,' shouted Mal, trying to regain her feet as she held on to the metal poles of the seat frame.

'No. But you couldn't let it lie either, could you? You had to poke your bloody nose in.'

'But I still don't understand the button.'

'For Christ's sake. The police were happily looking for one killer who had discovered the missing gold. They'd even arrested old frog face.'

'But he's innocent!' shouted Bob.

'So what? What, do you think I was just going to walk up to the Old Bill and say it was me? Behave!' Piran roared, throwing his arms wide. He was getting increasingly agitated, pacing back and forth. 'That button proved Paul had been in the tunnels when Dad was murdered. And if Paul murdered my dad, then who murdered Paul? I knew they'd investigate further. I needed everyone to believe they were both killed by the same person. Don't you see? Then I'd be in the clear. I was too young when Dad died. I needed to get rid of the coat.'

'So it was you on my ladder? Not your mum.'

'Stone me, why did she confess to that? She's ruining everything.'

'She's trying to protect your miserable arse, you little shit.'

'What's that, Mal?' said Bob, trying to stop the boat from hitting the other boat and listening to the story ravel out. Mal explained the attempted break-in the previous night and Bob looked aghast.

'You tried to break in to a woman's house?'

Bob was appalled and Mal smiled to herself. 'I think he was going to do more than break in, Bob, I think he was planning on killing me.'

On the other boat, Piran started laughing. 'It seemed the only way to shut you up. I'd already got rid of Connor, you were a loose end.'

'How did you get the coat from him?' asked Mal.

'Told him I was cold. Stupid sod was so drunk he handed it over. Just like that. He was always like that. Any of the lads on the bus had a broken lace or a headache he always had a spare or some pills. We used to call him Mum.' Piran was smiling now, remembering good times. 'There was this one time up at Exeter when—'

'He's dead, Piran,' yelled Bob, harshly. 'You killed him. You don't get to reminisce about the good old days. He's got a little boy at home. His wife is pregnant. You've stolen his dad from him.'

'Well, his dad stole mine!' roared Piran, spittle flecking around his mouth.

'*You* killed your father, you bloody fool,' screamed Mal, 'and you killed your half-brother as well!'

Chapter Forty-Two

Piran began to shake as Mal spelled out what he had done. Shouting incoherently, he ran to the end of the lockers on the boat and undid the latches on a small box. As he pulled out the flare gun, Bob swung sharply away from the fishing boat. Mal stumbled as she snatched at the seat frame, her feet slipped, and for a second she thought she was falling overboard. Bob threw the boat in the opposite direction, flinging her onto the floor of the RIB rather than into the icy water beyond. A plume of red smoke hung across the top of the boat; he had actually fired the flare at them but missed. The air was full of smoke and feathers as the gulls wheeled around in alarm, screaming in fury.

'Mal!' shouted Bob. 'Get up and belt into the seat. We're going after him.'

Sore and bruised, Mal pulled herself up off the floor and belted in. The palms of her hands were grazed and her tights and skirt were soaked through. She wanted to stand up beside Bob but agreed this was safer. Piran was now speeding his boat away from them, and although Bob had the advantage of speed and manoeuvrability, Piran had more shots in his flare gun.

'If he hits the boat with a flare, will it puncture?'

'It shouldn't but I don't plan on testing that. I'm more worried if he hits one of us.'

Bob chased Piran's wake. They were close enough that Mal could see Piran standing at the helm, his body taut as he stared ahead. She watched in despair and realised they had no way to stop him. She hoped she had done enough to clear Jacques' name completely, but now she wanted Piran arrested and brought to justice. Another noise filled the air and Mal wondered if the boat had been hit as she listened to the rhythmical whomping.

'Thank God, it's the cavalry,' shouted Bob. 'Hang on, girl. It's nearly over.'

Mal didn't know if he was talking to her or his boat, but she looked up as he pointed to the horizon. A helicopter was racing towards them low across the water. As it got closer, a loudspeaker broke the airways.

'Boat number FY989. This is the *RNAS Brightstar*. Switch off your engines and prepare to be boarded.'

Mal gazed in awe at the Royal Navy helicopter as it hovered overhead. The noise of its engines now audible over the sound of its rotators. A strange downwards breeze was catching at her hair around her shoulders and the sea danced and rippled around the boats.

'How can they board his boat from the helicopter? He'll drive off!'

Bob simply pointed back to shore where a large police vessel was now heading towards them.

Piran ran out from his cockpit and, bracing himself against the upright of the cabin, he aimed the flare and fired it up at the Sea King.

The helicopter rapidly banked away. The down draught of air knocked Piran off his feet and both boats rocked dangerously in the water. Mal grabbed at Bob as he also fell over, and was relieved as his harnesses snapped taut and held him to the helm. Swearing, he climbed back up on his feet.

'The boy's lost his head.'

'What's he doing?'

Mal watched in astonishment as he ran back into the helm and turned the boat back toward them, throttling on a collision course.

'He's going to ram us. Make the police stop pursuing him to come rescue us.' Bob checked his harness, then looking over at Mal, gave her a wild smile.

'Hold tight. The day hasn't come when a fishing boat can touch a performance RIB.' Laughing manically, Bob shouted out a *yee-hah* and pushed the throttle forward. Mal had enough time to see the savage grin on Piran's face as he bore down on them, then they were gone. Mal's head snapped back against the reinforced headrest as her body was crushed against the acceleration of the g-force.

The helicopter had now come back at a higher altitude and was warning Piran to cease immediately or he would be fired upon.

Bob turned and looked at Mal in alarm. 'Time to get out of here.'

'But what if he's trying to get to international waters?' said Mal, in concern. 'Doesn't that mean no one can touch him?'

'International waters means anyone with a vested interest can make a claim against him. Maybe he's hoping for that confusion. But I don't reckon the Navy's going to let him get that far.'

Bob's radio squawked and the police vessel established who they were, then told him to fall back.

'Don't need to tell me twice.'

He was about to turn when, ahead of them, they watched in horror as Piran leant out of the window of his cockpit and shot a flare directly at the helicopter. A red plume of smoke shot up and skimmed past the lower carriage of the red and grey metal sides.

'Hang on,' yelled Bob, as he punched the throttle forward.

Mal was aware of a massive explosion as she and Bob were flung forward. The boat continued to race away and suddenly she was pitching up and down as an enormous wave ran underneath them, followed by several aftershocks. The surrounding water was boiling and she shook in fear as freezing water drenched the pleasure boat. Bob was still upright, his arm thrust forward trying to outrun the explosion. The floor of the boat was covered in seaweed and Mal looked in amazement at a fish, flapping wildly on the floor of the boat. For a moment, it was as though there wasn't a sound in the world. Just her and the silver fish flapping hopelessly in front of her. There was a roaring sound in her ears and her skin felt prickly – she was about to faint.

'Mal. Professor. Are you okay?' Bob was staring into her face. He was too close and Mal panicked. She was going to throw up and didn't want to hit him.

Struggling to the side, she twisted away from the fish and threw up over a neighbouring chair. Wiping her mouth along the sodden sleeve of her blue jumper, she looked in revulsion at the bits of vomit smeared across the navy woollen fibres.

'Sorry about that,' she muttered, weakly.

Bob laughed. 'Not the first, won't be the last. And I reckon you had more cause than most.' He smiled at her reassuringly, then leant down and threw the fish back overboard.

'What happened?'

'Look for yourself.'

The RIB had now swung around and Mal could see with relief the helicopter hovering in the sky. The last thing she had seen was Piran firing at it and she'd had visions of it plunging into the sea below. Across the water, the police boat was now floating alongside a pile of burning wreckage. The trawler was no more.

'Did they fire on him?' shouted Mal. She could barely hear her own voice over the ringing in her ears.

'He hit a Sea King. They blew him out of the water.'

'Do you reckon he survived?'

'If he jumped maybe. I think that's what the police are doing, looking for the body. Dead or alive.'

'I thought the helicopter had come down.'

'So did I!'

Bob's radio crackled again.

'*Wild Rides*, do you require any assistance?'

'All good here. Did Piran survive?'

'We're retrieving a body. Are you aware of anyone else on board?'

Bob looked over at Mal, who shook her head.

'Okay,' the voice came across again. 'Return to Golden. You will be met and interviewed.'

'We need to get dry. We're both wet and I think my passenger may be suffering a bit of shock.'

'Like hell I am! It's the fish that's got concussion.' Mal started laughing and coughing.

As they returned to shore, the police had told them they would be offered first aid and that statements could be taken after. Bob switched the engine off for a second and undid the front locker and retrieved a flask and a tuck box. Pausing, they feasted on stale cheese sarnies and rum. Mal threw up again and grimaced as she felt every bone in her neck clatter against each other.

Splashing some sea water over her face and wringing out the sleeve of a jumper, she grinned weakly back at Bob.

'Okay. Let's go.'

He smiled back at her. 'That's the spirit. Jacques is going to be so proud of you. The whole bloody village is. Come on then.'

Chapter Forty-Three

The next few hours went in a blur. Mal had insisted on being allowed to go home and change, and had almost fallen asleep, but was disturbed by Jacques throwing pebbles at the window like a schoolboy. He had escorted her to the police station and sat by her side as she recounted her story. Bob had already told his tale and gone home to a hero's supper. Jacques permitted no less for Mal. He had wanted her to stay at his but she refused. He only relented when she said he could cook for her at her house. Following a quick bath, she fell asleep over her soup.

The following morning, she woke to discover Mac asleep beside her and, as she headed downstairs, Jacques had cleared away everything and left a note saying the rest of dinner was in the fridge and that he'd call around later. She crept around the kitchen and realised that she probably had whiplash. The pain in her neck was severe and her back felt like elephants had been tap dancing on it.

Groaning, she picked up her coat and headed out towards the local doctor's surgery. The air of excitement in the waiting room was obvious.

'Oh my God, Mal, you look dreadful.' Collette sprang up from a chair and told Mal to sit down. Calling over to the receptionist, she told her to give Mal her spot.

'I'm okay. Just sore.'

'Mal, what happened? We all saw the helicopter, the flare and the explosion. First Jacques was arrested, then Ruth, then Piran was blown to kingdom come. You have to fill us in.'

By now the other patients had given up any pretence of reading the magazines and were watching Mal avidly.

'The police are saying Paul Trebetherick was Piran's dad. That Ruth had been sleeping with Paul for years,' said a small mouthy-looking woman who looked far too gleeful for Mal's comfort.

'Is it true?'

Mal sighed. 'Apparently.'

'And he killed Roger.'

'No.'

'Told you he didn't,' said Collette. 'He was only a kid. So, Paul killed Roger, when Roger found out about the affair. And when Piran found out, he killed Paul and made it look like a suicide? Is that right, Mal?'

Mal twisted to look at Collette, and winced as her neck jarred in pain.

'I guess.' She really didn't want to get dragged into the gossip. It was all so horrible.

'So why kill Connor? Did Connor find out what Piran had done?'

'I don't know.' She studied the faces watching her and wanted to escape. 'I know Piran wanted to get rid of the coat Connor was wearing. Paul had worn it the night he killed Roger. I guess Piran realised that once the coat and the button were put together, the detectives would make the connection between the first two murders.'

At that moment, a doctor walked into reception and looked towards Mal.

'Mrs Peck.'

'Professor Peck,' called out Collette. 'She's only gone and solved the murders of Roger Jago, and Paul and Connor Trebetherick.'

Half an hour later, Mal left the doctor's office with a physio appointment and a prescription for pain killers. Avoiding eye contact, she shuffled out of the surgery and headed back to the shop. Some people recognised her and smiled in her direction, others ignored her. Mal wondered when she would know who was local and who was on holiday just by looking at them. And as she headed along the cobbles back towards the harbour, she surprised herself by smiling. Despite everything that had happened, she felt relieved.

'You alright, pet?'

Mal blinked and stared at a woman dripping in make-up and jewellery. She had a dog in a handbag, and was holding a little girl's hand who was dressed in pink ruffles.

'I said are you okay, pet?' The woman was speaking loudly and slowly. 'Do you need help?'

'No.' Mal smiled. A slow sense of revelation flooded her thoughts. 'I'm fine. I was heading back to my place.'

She thanked the holidaymaker and headed off towards the bookshop, something unfurling inside of her. Locking the door behind her, Mal pulled herself up the banister and felt the hands of her predecessors helping her along. As she walked into the living room, she looked at all the little trinkets on the shelves and the pictures on the wall. There had been a note in the doctor's surgery asking for donations to a tombola and Mal realised it was time to mark her own stamp on the property. Gary Crampton had already told her she could ditch the lot. The idea of them possibly raising some money for the surgery felt good to her.

Smiling as the painkillers finally took effect, Mal made a coffee and picked up her pen and paper.

Dear Oppy,

I have been having an adventure. You may have seen it on the news and no doubt you'll be on the phone soon, but I wanted to tell you about it on paper.

Mal continued scribbling and wondered when she could book a chiropractor. Gingerly rolling her shoulders, she looked around at all her cardboard boxes. It was time to properly unpack. When she had spoken to the tourist just now, it had struck her that the woman had viewed her as a local. She picked up the pen again.

And so finally, I wondered if you would like to visit? I've made some lovely new friends whom I should love you to meet and I'd love to show you where I now call home.

All my love,
M

Smiling, Mal finished the letter. This was indeed her home and she looked forward to settling into Golden and all the adventures that awaited her. Hopefully, though, there'd be no more bodies.

Author's Note

Dear Reader,

Thank you so much for accompanying Malachite as she arrived in Cornwall. This book has been wonderful to write and I have had so much fun with it that I can't wait to write the next one.

Some readers may recognise the village of Golden as that of Mevagissey and, although there is a lot of Meva in it, there are little fabrications all around. The people are also complete inventions; don't go looking for them, they don't exist. What does exist, though, in Mevagissey, as in Golden, is an excellent independent bookshop and a range of fabulous pubs and shops.

In writing this book I am hugely grateful to the assistance of my early readers: Helen Sullivan, Kate Fairbairn, Angela Nurse, Anna Mullarkey, Amanda Graham, Zan Paige and my editors, Aimee Walker and Andy Hodge. All mistakes are, of course, my own.

Yours sincerely,

Anna Penrose

P.S. You can pre-order book two now.

P.P.S Or to stay in touch visit **www.annapenrose.co.uk** and sign up to my newsletter.

BV - #0204 - 270423 - C0 - 198/129/20 - PB - 9781913628093 - Matt Lamination